Extraordinary Praise for
Bang Bang

"Theo Gangi portrays the people of the criminal world not only in a way that brings them to vivid life, but life felt at the extreme, out where suffering, pity, even tenderness and love have their own stark reality."
    —David Plante, author of *Age of Terror*

"Theo Gangi's first novel *Bang Bang* is a classic extreme thriller, with some surprising literary subtleties, and a level of Escherian interlocking that would make Tarantino's head spin."
    —Madison Smartt Bell, of *All Souls Rising*,
        a National Book Award finalist

"Gritty and gripping, full of tense moments and sharp prose, *Bang Bang* is a debut worthy of attention. With the ear of a poet, the insight of a psychologist, and the attitude of a true New Yorker, Theo Gangi brings empathy and pathos to every gangsterfied page."
    —Adam Mansbach, author of *Angry Black White Boy*

"Theo Gangi is a superb craftsman. His work displays diverse characters and wonderful dialogue that would make Elmore Leonard stand up and applaud. He is a new talent that has finally arrived."
    —Eric Jerome Dickey, *New York Times* bestselling
        author

BANg
bAnG

THEO GANGI

KENSINGTON BOOKS
www.kensingtonbooks.com

KENSINGTON BOOKS are published by

Kensington Publishing Corp.
850 Third Avenue
New York, NY 10022

All Kensington titles, imprints, and distributed lines are available at special quantity discounts for bulk purchases for sales promotion, premiums, fundraising, educational, or institutional use.

Special book excerpts or customized printings can also be created to fit specific needs. For details, write or phone the office of the Kensington Special Sales Manager: Attn. Special Sales Department. Kensington Publishing Corp., 850 Third Avenue, New York, NY 10022. Phone: 1-800-221-2647.

Kensington and the K logo Reg. U.S. Pat. & TM Off.

ISBN-13: 978-0-7582-2054-7
ISBN-10: 0-7582-2054-5

First Printing: November 2007
10 9 8 7 6 5 4 3 2 1

Printed in the United States of America

Acknowledgments

I wish to thank the following people for providing support, criticism and inspiration in more ways than they can know:

Letizia Valentin, Ma and Pop Gangi, Jess Gangi, the Great Gatsby, the Real Turtle, Madison Smartt Bell, Jud Laghi, Rakia Clark, Stacey Barney, Karen Thomas, David Plante, Alan Ziegler, Binnie Kirshenbaum, Kathy McCormick, Reggie Cash, Tony Rukaj, Arben Selimaj, Cindy Aquan, Adam Mansbach, Maggie Griffin, Sifat Azad, and the Crucial Minutiae Crew.

BANg
bAnG

Chapter 1

Izzy wondered what you called a stickup kid who was thirty-eight.

Leaning against a cement rooftop banister, a high wind smacking his ears, he scanned the modest Queens skyline, Manhattan looming behind like a graveyard. The street below was a residential wash of redbrick, from brownstones to small housing complexes with grassy courtyards. Through the misting rain an ethnic jumble of blue-collar and professional city commuters were gridlocked in their rush to unwind. Izzy intermittently glanced at a window through a pair of opera binoculars he had picked up in the West Village. He breathed in the moist evening. The dim gray sun waned as factory smoke became visible against the dark. These were familiar, tedious hours, a deep breath before the push.

"Ben doesn't show up quick and I'ma cut his ass," hissed Mal.

"No hurry. Their man's not there yet," said Izzy, in his easiest voice. *No stress, don't sweat Benny, relax,* Izzy thought to himself. Izzy could always tell Mal to relax, even before they were about to rob somebody.

Izzy had never heard of a stickup man. His people never said it. Cops never said it. An eighty-year-old could rob a drug spot, and they'd call him a stickup kid. Maybe stickup boy. Spot rusher. Jack boy. But again, he'd never heard of a jack *man*. Cops might say holdup man. But that was for when legitimate spots, like a bank or a convenience store, got held up. Izzy never robbed a legitimate spot before. They didn't really have cash anyway. Seemed wrong that robbing someone legit made you a man, while Izzy was stuck being called "kid." He liked "Banger" better, like Mal had said after their first bang. "We the Bangers." That way he didn't sound like he was sixteen.

"You ever heard of a stickup man?" asked Izzy.

Mal shook his head. "Maybe someplace. Like in an old seventies cop show or some shit. But people always seem to say stickup kid."

"You a kid?" asked Izzy.

"I'm whatever."

Do-rag and hoody over his XXL ironed white tee, Mal would forever dress like he was sixteen.

"How 'bout 'Banger'?"

"Why you care? You printing business cards or something?" asked Mal.

Izzy shrugged, turning back to face the street and checking his black rubber watch. "The first pitch . . ." he said to himself, annoyed he was missing the game. He immediately regretted saying it, knowing Mal couldn't stand to watch a moment of baseball.

"The national pas-*time* is victimless *crime*," chanted Mal from behind, drawing out the rhyme. Maybe he heard Izzy, maybe not.

Izzy picked up on the song in Mal's head, saying the next line to himself. *Repeat it to yourself. This is a victimless crime.*

The redbrick facade of the brownstone stood shoulder to shoulder with others just like it, nothing to indicate that twelve uniforms had once broken down the door and scaled the fire escape. Only the neighbors could know about the current of characters that Izzy and Mal had seen streaming through—short blacks in Big and Tall white tees; flashy Dominicans with gold sunglasses and cowboy boots; chickenheads with their hair and clothes in ribbons, popping gum in six-inch heels, pistols in their purses.

Izzy checked on the crew through his brass-rimmed binoculars. Within the oversized living room window Charlie Brown and his dumb hip-hop boys argued while playing video games—another in a series of middlemen who could afford to sell weight, not have to step on it and push vials. Izzy recognized their malaise of hustle and gratification, one second barking orders and making deals on a cell, the next blazing up and playing video games, watching TV, or getting ass; whatever happened to be in front of them. Izzy could see the electronic football play in Charlie Brown's eyes, his mouth hanging open in focus like a nine-year-old's. Half a mil in cash was on its way through, and *this* guy was running the show.

A while ago, Izzy had tried to be a hustler, but the relentless scheming and uncertainty were too much for him. He had known some who were good at it—too good at it. Men like Shea Mason, who kept so many transactions and facades in motion at once it seemed inevitable that gravity would catch up; well-connected men with a deal in every borough and a girl for every deal. That kept Izzy away—doing business meant deals, and deals meant trusting people, which Izzy didn't do. Yet here he was, partnered up with a man he couldn't call trustworthy. Not that Mal would snake him on the take; he just liked the violence too much, got reckless. But Izzy could trust him to get reckless, trust him to muscle up when he got scared, the way you could always trust a man to be himself.

The shorter, darker Mal paced the roof with the abruptness of an angry chef, curses announced by his posture. His small eyes restlessly shifted in his elongated head, bottom lip set just to the left of his upper, crooked face too big for his thin frame. Over his hoody, Mal wore a long, black overcoat to conceal his baby, a short-nosed shotgun with a pistol grip and a laser scope. Izzy would tell him it was ridiculous to have a laser scope on a sawed-off, but Mal got off on it, shining it in faces like a traffic cop with a flashlight. Stuck in his belt was a nickel-plated baby .22, with an expensive silencer. Even the shell casings they used were from robberies and wouldn't help the police any. Izzy had two .22s on him just like Mal's, wore a shoulder strap with a holster on either side for his pistols, and a pair of all black Gary Sheffield batting gloves.

Izzy bore the weight of the heavy steel naturally. It wasn't that he loved guns. He figured one would kill him one day, but he was most comfortable with his enemy close by.

One rule was known between Izzy and Mal—you kill one; we kill them all. The only time they had to worry about the cops was if they killed somebody. Somehow, taking drugs, money, and guns off drug dealers never seemed to bother the NYPD. The bodies were the problem.

The only time they had to lay anybody out was on account of a woman. It was in a row house basement deep in East New York. Izzy could still smell that moldy draft, the sweat of panicking hustlers. All was well until the young one pissed himself. Izzy was tying the other's wrist when Mal caught the scent.

"You call yourself a man? Fucking pussy," Mal yelled, and cracked the kid in the head with his shotgun.

"You leave him alone!" A crazy lady with a pigeon neck and heavy arms started swinging on Mal. It was like she came from nowhere. Mal ducked and dodged until she caught up to him. Izzy couldn't get a good shot, and the lady seemed even more fearless when she saw the guns, like she had a death wish. Mal granted it. She shook his head in heavy, ashy hands, repeating, "Leave him alone," as Mal's mask began to slide off his face. He freed his hand and popped her with the .22, blood misting on the wall as she fell. Izzy was relieved that Mal had used the .22. That shotgun would have been real messy. He fought away the image of what the shotgun would have done. Mal did the wet guy execution style, then looked at his partner. Izzy could still hear the sinister hiss and pop of the gun. He had heard a silencer before but never the sound of a head opening up. The bullet had forced a hole that was never intended, and the echoing pop crawled down Izzy's spine.

The last thug was in a wild panic. His name was Won. That's what he called himself. Like "I won." Like "Won time." "Won love." His watery eyes swelled beneath the slanted imprint of a fitted cap brim. His face was fat and round, his nose and mouth flat like a pug's.

"Do the last one," Mal had said.

"You going just fine," said Izzy.

Mal raised the .22 and pointed it at his partner. "You ain't leaving here a witness, man, that's the point, no witnesses. You either a killer or a goddamn victim."

Izzy considered this. Won struggled and cried on the old, filthy cement—a fish caught in a dry bucket, awaiting the cleaver. The room smelled like sweat and piss. Mal's logic made sense. Izzy didn't want to do it, but it was too late for all that. He squatted down and held up a gloved hand to block the spray. With his other hand, he pulled.

In the car afterward, their masks off, Izzy told Mal, "Next time you put your gun on me will be the last time."

It wasn't the first time.

After the 82nd Airborne, before Izzy's first fall, he had tried hustling. After he saw how to cook crack, thinking he could sell some, Izzy hit the streets. He was a lookout, a runner, and for a while, he handled vials. He hustled enough to afford a gun, an old Detective Special. Then he figured he didn't have to work for anyone on the arm anymore, so he set up a meeting with Mal to cop, and when Mal asked him for the money, he showed Mal the Detective Special instead.

"Give me the blow," he told Mal.

Then he realized he was looking at a barrel himself.

"I'll blow a hole in your fucking head," said Mal.

Standoff: *Shit.* "How 'bout this? You hand over the product, I'll let you live," said Izzy.

"Fuck that, give me the cash right now."

"Ain't no cash."

"Well, there ain't no motherfucking blow!"

They stared at each other, in competition to see whose expression could show less. The weight of the Detective Special was heavy, but Izzy felt he could hold it for hours. The temptation to pull the trigger was immense. Desperation put him there, but logic told him to shoot. There was something counterintuitive about showing a gun and not firing it, like putting your hand on a light switch and not flicking it. He wanted to shoot. The warning that both guns would go off kept his finger still. He just wasn't sure, even then, how much that would have bothered him.

Nobody moved. Then Mal smiled. "I been looking for somebody like you."

Izzy had to admit. He liked Mal's style, standing there with two live guns, recruiting a partner.

There was still something about Mal that invited attack, an impulse Izzy often had to resist. The entitled cock of his skinny neck, the way he would cross people's boundaries within minutes, made Izzy feel like a father who was about to beat his son. On that Queens rooftop, Mal bit his lip with sharp teeth like a restless child. Izzy always thought of Mal as a child, as children were capable of anything.

"This bitch-ass fucking failure," muttered Mal.

Izzy rolled his eyes, well accustomed to Mal's temperamental fixations. He shrugged, and repeated his message. "Chill. Their connect still didn't show up."

"But when he do, we got to be in there. How hard is it to steal a van, anyway?"

Izzy stepped aside and put his finger to his throat, taking his pulse. The soft, fluttering rhythm was all that resembled peace when Mal was around.

"How's the count?" interrupted Mal.

Izzy maintained concentration. Not hearing Mal, the patter of rain, the hum of cars streaming through the wet pavement below, only that faint beat, pulsing from neck to finger.

"Doctor!" said Mal, abruptly, unleashing his hyena cackle.

Izzy exhaled. "Good. Seventy-seven. Usual."

"Feeling accurate?"

Izzy took the binoculars from Mal. "Deadeye."

Izzy could dot the *i* of a Pepsi can with a handgun from fifteen yards consistently. A racing pulse never helped him. He knew how to breathe, knew how to control his heart rate and focus when necessary. Pulse at eighty, maybe he'd put a hole in the P. Ninety, stand clear. You couldn't be a professional anything at ninety.

A professional stickup kid. Stickup man. A professional jack boy. Jack man. Banger. He did need a business card.

Why was he trying to label himself? He was older, sure, but that's why bangs were getting bigger and less frequent. He had done two jobs in the last three years and lived well. Why did he care if he was a stickup kid or a stickup man?

Oh, right. The girl, from earlier. Eva. Great name.

"Jack," said Eva, and got a warm, fuzzy feeling anticipating the drink, deciding to make him her new boyfriend.

"You want some water with that?" asked the bartender, pouring her the Tennessee whiskey.

"Water? Never touch the stuff," she said, and leaned in a

bit closer, her tone conspiratorial. "You know fish have sex in it?"

The bartender didn't get it. Someone did, laughing a few seats down. Nice-looking, café au lait with green eyes. The bartender slid the glass to her. The rust-colored liquor splashed and settled at the bottom.

After the burn distracted her from the feeling, and the feeling distracted her from her thoughts, she remembered why she came to this bar, drinking by herself in front of a ball game like an escaped husband. Her fucking cousin.

Not just her cousin. First, her day. Eva was a social worker who ran a Catholic Charities program providing housing services to former offenders, drug abusers, and the mentally incompetent. On that day, the police called her because someone complained about a smell coming from one of her apartments. Eva was the one with the keys who had to let the police in. She gagged on the smell, a monstrous, overwhelming decay stronger than industrial bleach. She had been to that small apartment many times, picked out the secondhand table and chairs that were now upside down and splintered. Her client was on the bed. Her name was Elma, and her arms were strewn across the unmade sheets like she was reaching for a hug. Her skin, once a healthy chestnut, was now a pale bluish green, with crusty white lips and a thick bruise tracked around her neck like a choker. Her eyes were open, staring up into an abyss. Eva stared back with the irresistible conviction that Elma deserved what she got.

Eva left the room and threw up in the toilet. Then she got as far away from the apartment as she could before the police detained her, and the detectives showed up to question her. They were big, gruff assholes, obeying some code of matter-of-fact suspicion that made little sense to her. They were so apathetic to another addict dying that Eva wanted to cry. How could she react the same as them?

She went home and did cry. It was after three. She set her purse down in the kitchen and the dam broke. She hurried into her bedroom the same way she had hurried into the bathroom to puke, and let out all the tears and sniffles. She couldn't be seen crying in the kitchen. Eva knew what Theresa would think. As the tears dried, even Eva began to think herself a fraud.

She put Hendrix on, with his energetic and mournful guitar playing blues riffs in ways still unimaginable. His smirking voice eulogized;

> *And some castles made of sand*
> *Fall in the sea*
> *Eventually.*

Eva fell into a deep sleep dreaming of sand castles. When she awoke she brushed and gargled the taste from her mouth, feeling hungry again. She treated herself to her favorite Italian spot, with a view of the river, lights reflected in the dark evening water, trying to get the stink and sight of death from her mind. When she went to pay for her Seafood Fra Diavlo, she noticed her cash was gone. Fucking Theresa.

Freeloading Theresa, supposed-to-be-in-rehab Theresa, robbing her of money, time, space, and that day, her spirit. She knew what to say to family members of drug abusers; rehab isn't necessarily a fix; it takes time; they can't control themselves. But when it came to her own family, fuck that. Theresa could control herself.

"Would you rather I trick for it?" her cousin said when confronted by Eva. Like it was Eva's fault. The drugs didn't make Theresa nasty. Theresa was just nasty.

Before she went and ripped out the bitch's weave, Eva went to see her man.

Jack. Ever reliable. Sure, he got around, but at least this

was known. No tricks. Once he was in her glass, he was all hers.

Eva looked at the men around her. All blue collar, stinking of dry plaster, stagnant family lives, and domestic beer. There was the one who had laughed. Dreamy, calm face, nice hair. Looking hard now. He thought he was cute. He wasn't wrong.

The light eyes moved, and Eva forgot them for a moment. Then they were right next to her.

"Hi. Buy you a drink?"

Original. Wearing a white T-shirt with the Exxon logo that said "Ex-Con" instead. He thought he was really cute.

"I've got one," she said, holding up Jack. "And he's the jealous type."

"What's his name?"

"Jack."

The guy held up his own glass, looking similar. "Johnny. But I'm Iz."

"That your street name, or government?"

"Iz, not I-s or anything. Short for Izzy. And you are?"

His eyes, a shade of green lighter than his skin, seemed disembodied, amused by some far-off comedy.

She considered going no further, because of his T-shirt. But she said, "Eva," and shook his hand, because of his eyes. Then she looked demonstratively at his shirt. "So, what do you do?"

I'm a stickup kid. A grown-up stickup kid. Not a grown-up, really, but not a kid—grown. All the same, I rob drug dealers. And I'm thirty-eight.

Izzy didn't want to answer that question. So he didn't.

"You seem distracted by my shirt."

She shrugged. She had smooth Indian skin, could be Indian hair, long, black, and straight, maybe straightened. She could be Indian, but also could have some black in her, so Izzy guessed Caribbean, West Indian. Almond eyes, long, white teeth that seemed to bite her lower lip when she smiled. It was different from how Mal would bite his lip. She was less sinister—playful, even if she didn't mean to be.

"You seem proud of it," she said, looking at her Jack.

Izzy grinned. "You a ball buster?" he said carefully, not to seem hostile.

"Hey, you came to me."

"So I gotta take whatever you dish out?"

"Pretty much."

Izzy nodded. "Fair enough."

She smiled a long, white smile. The lines left her face. She looked younger. "So, are you proud of it?"

"I'm not ashamed."

"You shouldn't be," she said.

Izzy sensed he was being toyed with. He was unsure if this was a good or a bad thing. "So, what's the problem?"

"Who said there was a problem?"

Now he smiled, maybe nervous. Izzy didn't know—he had trouble recognizing nervousness. He was something; unsure, making him call it a problem. Still smiling sheepishly, he glanced around at the bar. Dark, with colorful gambling machines and a jukebox, weak wooden booths, and a patchy pool table, like an unkempt lawn. What was this woman doing here?

"Where'd you do time?" she asked.

Was she making conversation? Or did she like cons? "Clinton, Green Haven. Also Baltimore, actually."

"You from there?"

"No, just passing through. Stayed a bit longer than expected. In Steelside Corrections Facility, on Eager Street." She was nodding. "In New York, they send you away, and most times, they send you *away*—upstate somewhere. In Baltimore, they send you to Baltimore. A jail, right in the heart of the city, on a street called 'Eager.' Tell me, who puts a jail on a street called 'Eager'?"

She laughed.

He considered going on, but figured he would lose her once it wasn't a joke, it was his life. He had always told Mal, take the work seriously, not yourself.

"And what do you do?" he asked her about herself instead.

"I'm a social worker," she said.

"Oh. So you have some experience—"

"I know a lot of people who pump their gas there," she said, pointing to his shirt. Izzy looked down. Exxon. Ex-con. "But they come to me once they've repented. That you?"

Izzy paused. He had a general rule about lying to women. Why make himself something else, when there was always someone who liked what he was? Still, he couldn't answer. Today, he wanted this one.

"Your hesitation says it all," she said, finishing the last of her Jack.

"Let me get the next one," he said.

"Not necessary."

"I'd like to."

She looked in his eyes, and nodded. It was a good, honest look; a look that appreciated a drink offered out of honest friendship.

Or maybe she was out of cash.

He leaned forward and stood to get some money from his pocket. His silver "Hand of Miriam" slipped from under his shirt. His mother was a Jewish lady who had Izzy in Harlem at the tail end of a fatal heroin binge. He still wore a Hebrew symbol for his mom, a *hamsa*, or "Hand of Miriam," which was his mother's name. It was a silver hand half an inch long, with the thumb and pinky spread out like wings and an eye in the center of the palm. The hand gave him connection to an abstract notion of Judaism he knew virtually nothing about.

"Are you Jewish?" she asked.

He nodded, and ordered another round.

"I love Jewish people," she said, as if to herself.

Izzy shrugged. "I love us too. Where you from?"

"I was born in Trinidad," she told him.

He knew it. "Accent?"

"Ya hear it, soldja, when she want ya to."

"A Caribbean gal drinking Tennessee whiskey?"

"Sitting at a bar with a black Jew. Or do you prefer Jewbian?"

Izzy laughed.

"I think the stereotype game has gone far enough," she said smugly.

Izzy leaned back to look at her, getting a wider perspective. Eva shifted on her stool, seemingly unsure if she was more amused or annoyed. Her ambivalence was making things fun, but Izzy sensed that it went further than him and Jack.

"You had a bad day," he deduced.

"The worst."

"Want to talk about it?"

No response.

"So all social workers can do is listen?"

When he thought he had lost her, staring off into her whiskey, twisting and bending the feeble red straw, she smirked.

"I saw a dead body," she told him, maybe hoping the seriousness would back him off. Instead, she cracked a door for Izzy to squeeze through.

"That's unsettling," said Izzy.

"You ever seen a dead body? I mean, aside from touched-up ones at wakes."

Izzy could remember the first body he saw, within those scraps of childhood that survived the fog of high-grade weed, numbing violence, and televised baseball. It was when Izzy's mother was still alive. Izzy went by himself to a corner just off MLK for some Skittles. Or a Baby Ruth. He heard these booming cracks, like distant fireworks. He smelled an invisible smoke. He drifted into the store as the smoke drifted out.

Izzy would come to think he'd been drawn into the whirlpool of frantic, violent commotion inside, and a more sensible boy would have run. He never remembered walking in, only being well inside the entrance before a ski-masked face. The mask was pointless, because anyone could have recognized him again by the unmistakable blistering insanity in his eyes. That must have been why he was murdering bystanders as he waited for the stalling cashier. Without hesitation, the man put the heavy, hot steel against the boy's head. The gun kicked and the man's shaking hand jumped back. Izzy held his brow. He remembered seeing that pile of bodies just to his right. Three, maybe four bodies, all fallen together, blood and limbs intermingled like one hideous starfish. The man was first to realize that this mixed little shit-head kid should not have been seeing anything, ever again. The man's crazed eyes became confused as he took the bag of money from the cashier and shot her, as though to see if he were still able. It ripped her neck open and she fell straight down as if there were never any legs under her to begin with. The man brushed past Izzy, maybe assuming he was a ghost, and was gone.

Izzy never knew how long he stayed there, only that he didn't cry or move until he was forced to, and that blood was on him, which he didn't remember happening. His mother said it was weeks before he spoke, but his disposition was fine. He wasn't depressed and he ate plenty. When he was able, Izzy remembered a mild feeling of disappointment, a child whose new toy didn't work. He rarely ever recalled the terror that held his thoughts and actions in a timeless standstill. It was a dream, his dreams often resembled the experience anyway, the details always changing—the color of the mask, the face and ethnicity of the cashier. But when he could remember that it was real, it made sense why he was happy to see the sun every morning, and why he always expected to die that day.

From the first body to the last one. The last, Won—the bounded man with silver duck tape bracelets and a red bandana in his mouth, struggling. *You either a killer or a goddamn victim,* Mal had said. A gun in his hand, Izzy didn't feel like a victim. A man was at his feet, contorting in his binds, who seemed more like a victim. As if complying with some natural order, Izzy solidified who was who with a squeeze of a trigger. All he had wanted was the man's drugs and money. He wound up taking everything.

"What, you can't remember?" asked Eva.

That was part of the problem. Izzy didn't remember, the same way he could never recall how many women he had been with. Won was the one. Won was right there in the front of his mind: Izzy wasn't even sure if he had bothered to look at the dead man after it was done, yet the image was pristine in his mind: a clay face, glass eyes, a juicy mouth half submerged in a shiny red puddle. The more time passed, the bigger the puddle grew, until it was a crimson lake and the face had drowned.

"I do. I did, I saw a body one time," fumbled Izzy. Won time.

"For me, it was heavy, but maybe I'm just sensitive. The woman was a client of mine. Her boyfriend was found a few hours after the body. He had smoked too much PCP and didn't remember a thing, so he said. Couldn't recollect how his fingerprints got on her neck. Makes me sick."

"One of the few things someone can do and can't undo."

The jukebox played an old song, brought back by a Tarantino movie. Steel guitar strings announced the morbid melody. A breathy, somber woman sang.

Bang-Bang.
I shot you down.
Izzy always liked the song. He would guess this Trini liked him. He still thought the song fit his fate tonight.

Her neck turned, her straight hair all falling over one shoulder. "Who does this song?" she asked.

"Nancy Sinatra," said Charlie Brown. "It's a Nancy Sinatra song." He was cold, playing Xbox and wearing his black leather jacket, with a huge image of Charlie Brown swinging a baseball bat and missing the ball embroidered on the back.

"Who?" asked Re-Up, the bandana tied around his head covering one of his stoned, bloodshot eyes.

Charlie Brown, Re-Up, and Shells all waited anxiously in their Jackson Heights town house, hoping casual conversation would help them feel casual. There were ten kilos of uncut Peruvian Gold in the refrigerator. A Dominican was coming with $430,000 in cash. There were two Beretta nines on the coffee table, next to the hydro. A .45 with hollow tips was under the coffee table. There was a sick, possibly OD-ing, blow-for-blow-job whore in the bathroom. Young Buck's version of "Bang, Bang" played, the heavy drawled Tennessee rapper baring himself over the gangster rhythm and Sinatra vocals.

"Nancy Sinatra," repeated Charlie Brown. "Frank Sinatra's daughter."

"Damn," said Re-Up. "She was gangsta like that?"

"Nah, dawg. Bitch was talking 'bout her man, or some shit."

"Oh," said Re-Up, with a deep nod.

Shells came into the room, wearing his Ron Artest jersey, which rarely missed a week on his back since the basketball player had started throwing punches at fans in Detroit.

"Yo, this bitch looks real, real bad right now."

"Take her to the hospital, then," said Re-Up.

"Nigga, you take her. Like you ain't the one called her up," said Shells.

"I ain't taking her. Then they go start asking questions like where she got that shit made her sick like that?"

"You don't take her in. You drop bitch in the street outside the hospital, and drive off."

"Ya'll remember my cousin, Maurice?" asked Re-Up. "He doing life right now behind some shit just like that. Bitch OD'd, an' Mo had nothing to do with but it was his junk. I aint going to jail behind that shit, hell no, son." Re-Up sounded scared. "Maurice aint even have no priors."

"How they gunn know it was our shit?" asked Shells.

"You forget the train already? DNA, nigga. The girl in that bathroom right there got something from all of us in her," said Re-Up.

"Fuck," said Shells. "I ain't going out like that."

Charlie Brown had heard enough. Eyes held on Madden on the thirty-six-inch plasma TV, he exclaimed, "Ain't none of you dumb, panicky niggas going anywhere. Our custie be here any minute, and we all gonna be right here when that happens. Re-Up, you gonna call somebody knows the bitch to come get her. What's her name?"

Re-Up paused. "Theresa."

THERESA flashed bold on the green LCD screen of Eva's cell phone. Eva rolled her eyes, rage overcoming the Jack and Izzy buzz.

"Yes?"

It wasn't her cousin. Sounded like a moron. "You Theresa's cousin?"

"Who wants to know?"

"Answer the fucking question," he said. Then someone

scolded him, and he composed himself. "I'm a friend of Theresa's. She real sick and ain't nobody can take her to the hospital right now."

Fuck. Eva's threshold broke. She'd had it with the girl. She actually said, "So?"

"You her cousin?"

Eva took a moment and calmed down. "Yes. Okay, where are you?"

The man gave her the info in a garbled drawl, and then hung up. Jack was getting soupy, with ice like small, floating jewels. Izzy was waiting, eyebrows raised to the high TV set.

"That your cue?" asked Izzy.

"After I finish this drink," she said, resisting agitation.

Izzy checked his watch. "Looks like it's about that time for me. Any chance you want to see me again?"

"Sorry, I don't date clients," was her knee-jerk response.

"Ouch," said Izzy.

He was right, it was mean. Thinking about Theresa made her mean. He laughed it off, though. He held his kidney as though he'd been stabbed.

Eva laughed. "What would we do?"

"Maybe a movie. No, wait the Aquarium, that's more your speed. Go get some seafood after. Randazzo's Clam Bar, Bay Ridge."

"So we're going to go see fish, then eat them?"

"Sure. There's something about the Aquarium smell that puts me in the mood for seafood."

She laughed. "That's just dead wrong."

"Why don't you give me your number?"

She shook her head. "I don't do that. I just met you. How about . . . you give me your number?" she offered, like he was a very lucky man.

"Sorry, I can't do that."

"Excuse me?" she said, surprised.

"I can't. I would." He was serious. "But really, give me your number."

She was perplexed. "How about here, in two days, same time?"

He nodded. It was an honest offer.

"I'll be here," he said, smiled, and turned to leave.

So why didn't she believe him?

Chapter 2

"Impossible," said Huna. "You don't need no more cocksuckin' silver."

Bruno, the manager at Benny's Steakhouse, in a thin mustache and suspenders, stuttered. Huna was at the bar in a track suit and Jordans, hunched over his *New York Post* like a white buffalo at a watering hole. The bar was large but he was still too big for it, even when it was empty. His interchangeable sweats perpetually clashed with the woodgrain-and-brass-trimmed old-world décor. His staff privately wondered if he owned any formal clothing at all. Huna deliberately avoided the dinner rush, hanging around during the day to deal with operational problems like this one.

"C'mon, get outta my face," said Huna with his face still in his newspaper, reading about the girl from John Jay College who got raped and killed by a club bouncer.

Finally, Bruno got out a sentence. "I—I'm sorry to say, I—I cannot even set the dining room."

Huna leveled his gaze from his paper to his employee, trying to remember whose idea it was to hire this pencil-dick *peder*.

"You ordered silver two fuckin' months ago," said Huna.

"It was four months ago, at least."

"You correcting me?"

"No, sir."

Huna's hard brows arched like the point of a dagger and burrowed into Bruno. "Then what the fuck are you doing?"

"T-trying, sir," he said, eyeing his toes, "trying to get some more silver."

Huna's gaze followed to Bruno's black Pradas, slowly rising up the perfect crease in his pants, to his G for Gucci belt buckle, to his metrosexual purple-and-pink-striped button-down. It was Zoron who wanted to hire this cocksucker. Zoron the moron.

Huna dropped his hand down on the bar, rattling the glasses, the plastic stirrers, and the display bottles. He stood up, his face close to Bruno.

Huna could not believe this faggot was Albanian. Zoron said he knew how to run a fine dining restaurant, knew about French service and etiquette. Fuck French service. This was a fuckin' steak house anyway; the guineas didn't give a shit if you served them bread with a fork and a spoon. Zoron was a corny motherfucker, putting all that energy into the front, while the Russians and eye-talians were linking up with big stock scams, thinking outside the box, making real money. So what if the steak house nets eight hundred or nine hundred thousand, when they should be stacking mils in a pump-and-dump? Not that Huna understood the stock scams. Fuck if any nine-to-five piece-of-meat in a suit could tell him how to make money. Just as bad as listening to this fake Frenchman Albanian tell him how to spend it. Huna raised his meaty hand and stuck a finger in Bruno's face, waving it back toward him.

"Come," he said, walking back to the kitchen with Bruno in tow.

Huna stopped at the dish station, by the garbage can beneath the metallic counter. He looked for a moment, feeling Bruno rolling his eyes behind him.

"There," said Huna, pointing into the trash.

Bruno came up behind him and looked. At the bottom of the can, between half a chewed steak and some chicken bones, was a shiny piece of silver.

"Get it," said Huna.

"Paco!" called Bruno.

"No," said Huna. "No Paco, no Javier, no Gustavo." Huna pushed his fingertip into Bruno's thin bird chest. "Bruno."

"But . . ."

The Mexicans in the kitchen continued to work, their spirits uplifted, resisting smiles.

"You told me you were trying to get silver. So. Try."

Bruno caved. He removed a cuff link and rolled up his sleeve, reaching into the discarded lunchtime food and pulling out the lone fork.

"We would not lose so much cocksuckin' silver if you would tell the busboys to be more careful when they throw out the cocksuckin' food."

"Yes, sir. But still, one fork," said Bruno, rolling his sleeve back down.

"No," said Huna, grabbing Bruno's biceps on the sleeve, pulling him down the back stairs, to the storeroom, where piles of full trash bags waited. He flung Bruno so he lost his balance and almost fell in the pile.

"It's a big dining room. Get busy, nigga."

Huna turned to the stairs, annoyed. *There it goes. That fuckin' nigger shit again. Saying nigga like a nigger. It's Benny and them, all talking like the* zezaks. They got it stuck in his head and that shit just pops out. Huna was using Izzy and Mal to take care of the Queens problem, but he didn't get why Benny had to go with them. Yeah, it was a nice take, and Benny didn't like regular work, but also dangerous. And fuck treating those *zezaks* like partners. Benny the other day coming to the restaurant with those two stickup kids like they're a crew.

"Huna, son, where're the crills?" said Benny, arms around the shoulders of the two stickup kids, the light-skinned one tall, the darker one short. Benny wore tinted glasses, his perpetual smirk, an army fatigue jacket with the collar popped, and low-top Pumas. Huna could never decide if Benny looked like a hipster or a bum, or what the difference was, anyway.

Huna embraced Benny.

"What up, cuz? Break out the raws, cuzzie-cuz," said Benny.

"Listen to you," said Huna, putting two fingertips to Benny's broad head and pushing. "Talkin' like a fucking fiend in my restaurant."

"Yo," said Benny, not missing a beat, dropping his knees, twitching his shoulder and tapping his arm like an addict, "you got those raw crills?"

Huna laughed, and headed down to the basement.

The stickup kids weren't introduced until they were downstairs and four healthy lines of Peruvian Gold were on the table. Everyone knew everyone anyway, but Benny made it official. Huna and Mal and Izzy shook hands and everyone looked everyone in the eye. Huna was impressed. Either they knew to look an Albanian in the eye, or Benny told them to, or they were stand-up men. Benny began to roll up a twenty into a straw, until Huna stopped him and peeled a fifty off his wad.

"The bigger the bill the better the blow," said Huna, and they laughed.

Everyone snorted a line except Izzy, and Huna happily inhaled his. He caught a good buzz, his head numb and invincible. He wanted to talk with Ben, tell stories about Montenegro and tough men. He always did when he got high, but he didn't want to talk around the *zezaks*. They were here for business.

"You heard about my situation?" he asked, checking Mal's eyes, his raging large pupils.

"Benny mentioned you got a problem."

Huna shrugged. "Problem, I dunno, that's a strong word. I'm irritated."

"Sucks to be irritated," said Izzy.

"Sucks for sure," said Mal.

"Yeah, these niggas are trying to play games with me, you know?" Huna knew he said niggas to a couple of niggers but he didn't care. That was the only time it was okay to say it. "They think I don't know what they're doing and I do. Cocksucker used to work for me on the arm, right? Never paid on time, always short. Over the years, he makes me money but owes me more. So I cut off his credit, cash only now. Then he comes to me with a big number, bigger 'n anything he ever asks me for. Says he's gonna flip it, and pay his debt. Only these are some Baltimore cocksucker niggas, and soon as I fill his order, come to find out, cocksuckers bought train tickets."

Izzy and Mal waited, making sure Huna was finished. Izzy spoke.

"And you want . . ."

"Twenty percent."

"Ten," said Mal.

"Ten, fuck ten. This is a gift. Fifteen."

Izzy and Mal exchanged glances.

"Deal."

Now Huna stood in the basement, remembering that session, how he doubled up on both nostrils thanks to Izzy. He fished in his pocket for his little green gram baggie, snapped the seal, tapped a bit out onto his knuckle, and ripped a quick skizzie for his nizzie. He turned to the rummaging behind him, Bruno elbow deep in filth with a small pile of dirty silverware at his feet. Huna was surprised; he thought

Bruno would have quit for sure. He tapped a little more blow onto his knuckle and held it out to Bruno, who stopped digging and leaned over with the back of his hand closing one nostril, and inhaled.

Huna went up the metal stairs, opening the sidewalk door to the street, his giant chrome Benz G550 sparkling silver in the fading sun, everything bulletproof on that motherfucker. The Mercedes G-class was boxy, resembling a slimmer Hummer, with the vanity plate ARMD LXRY. Huna had bulletproofed the windshield, windows, doors, even the rims. He swiped a bright orange ticket from a wiper and dropped it to the curb, heading out to JFK.

Izzy had gone to the bar to catch the pregame. New York was a baseball city. No matter the crisis—Tsunami, Hurricane Katrina—baseball claimed equal, dedicated headline page coverage from the blue-collar newspapers. Only 9/11 managed to override the baseball soap opera addiction. For a handful of days anyway.

Izzy was a real baseball fan. He would buy the *Daily News*, *Newsday*, the dumb *Post,* and the *Times* just to read about a game he had already seen. The few who knew him well knew that when it was warm, after 7:00 PM he was in front of a TV set, although no one knew which set. He had nine favorite spots spread throughout the city he systematically visited, from Meat Packing to Park Slope to Washington Heights. Which one he went to was often a matter of impulse, though he never went to one more than once a week, figuring that was the best way to avoid predictability. From hours of stakeouts, Izzy had learned just how unwittingly predicable people were, and what that could cost. His cash was spread out in different safe deposit boxes across the city. He would take out a grand at a time and keep his expenses low. He would maybe smoke a little Sour Diesel or Humble County, or drink a little Stella, Corona, or Johnny

Black, and sit in front of the television and watch the Mets and Yankees play, sometimes at the same time. Izzy was the only New York baseball fan he knew without prejudice. He was equally diligent about watching both teams. He just didn't know which to root for, the lovable losers or the dedicated winners.

Izzy did have a favorite player. Mariano Rivera, the Panamanian Yankee reliever who shared more with Izzy than skin color. Rivera was the closer, the pitcher the Yankees would bring in at the end of the game to get the three most important outs. Nobody who ever played was as good at getting those outs as Mariano, or Mo. Izzy identified with him. He would patiently sit around all game, until the ninth inning, when the Yankees would have a narrow lead. Then Mariano came to life. His unvarying motion casual and easy, he would fling vicious, precise cutters that would handcuff hitters and buzz-saw their bats. That was Izzy. Patience. Effortless accuracy. Get it done.

Izzy found himself comfortably in the middle of New York's deadly cross fire. Witness to countless, venomous bar arguments, when forced to draw an opinion, Izzy would just shrug. "I'll leave the losing to you."

That night was a big game. It was the third of a subway series between the two New York teams. They had split the first two games. Izzy saw every pitch. Tonight was Al Leiter, the former Met ace turned old, ailing but potentially brilliant Yankee, versus Pedro Martinez, the unofficial ambassador of the Dominican Republic, and one of the great all-time pitchers. Once, after a horrible beating when he was with the Red Sox, Pedro, with his loose but appropriate grasp of English, crowned the Yankees "My daddy," offering New York fans the irresistible taunt "Who's your daddy?" Leiter and Pedro were perpetual tricksters, evened out by Pedro, the better of the two, throwing against a high-priced Yankee lineup, and Leiter pitching to the mediocre

Mets. Izzy had been looking forward to it all day. Though he didn't root for any team, from inning to inning he would find himself pulling for one side or the other, never really sure why.

So he had gone to the bar. He had seen the pregame. He had seen the players politely deny that the game had any extra significance, just because it was New York versus New York, lying through their necks. No extra significance because Leiter was pitching against his team of the year before. No extra significance that Pedro would continue his rivalry against the Yankees, now from across town. No significance that the former Yankee player and coach, Willie Randolph, was now the Mets manager. Just another ball game. No significance at all.

He saw the girl, Eva. He forgot about the game.

Back up on the chilly Queens roof, the rain remained a mild mist. Izzy wished he could have given her his number. But local thugs would be looking for him soon, and a cast of uninterested bystanders did see him speak with the girl. Izzy would rather those thugs didn't call him, or break anything of Eva's. He might try and meet her in two days, stake it out all day, make sure it wasn't a setup, maybe take her for a ride. Risky. Very risky. But he was still thinking about her, wanting to see her again, thinking of cracks she might appreciate.

"This girl was off the meter," he told Mal, his steady breath like smoke rising in the cool, wet air.

"You met a girl?" Mal spat with disdain. "What, you got a date?"

Izzy shrugged. "Thought maybe I'd come stake the place out all day, make sure it's not a setup," he said, bouncing on the balls of his feet, staying loose, and considering his words. "It's risky."

"Real risky. I wasn't planning on coming to Queens until I absolutely had to. You forget Sandi already?"

"Sandi! Moved out and the girl called the damn cops. Baltimore PD at that, before I got there. Like, pop the trunk, he's got dope and guns."

Mal doubled over in laughter. His laugh was aggressive, white teeth showing, mouth open wide like a bear trap, rapid fire "Ha's" aimed at Izzy. "When you left, it must have *killed* her, dude! How is that? How you get a girl to need you that bad?"

"All I know is, I did two years behind that shit. No dope, no paper, just a handgun with the serial scratched off. Who gets their ex locked up?"

"I don't know. You the one wants to go meet a girl in a bar next to somebody we just banged. Who lets a female do him in twice? Women are like cats, bro. They'll kill anything smaller than them."

"Better than your ugly, homicidal ass."

"Shut up, you dirty fucking Jew," shot Mal.

"Fuck you, you filthy savage."

"Why don't you just evict me, then, dirty Jew?"

"Why don't you go sell drugs to schoolchildren, you filthy savage?" replied Izzy.

"'Cause you keep raising the rent."

"'Cause you drive down the property value."

They laughed off their routine.

Mal raised the small binoculars, observing the quiet street below. Charlie Brown's customer pulled up in a tricked-out Denali.

"That's definitely not a van. That's a Denali," said Izzy.

"Fuck!"

A man with bright white sneakers, and shades glimmering silver in the rain, entered the town house with a red gym bag and came back out a few minutes later with a green gym bag.

Subtle, thought Izzy.

"Custie's gone."

Mal took the binoculars back and looked out. "There's nothing to see."

"Wait," said Mal. "It's a woman."

Mal passed the binoculars back to Izzy, who looked through and saw a figure at Charlie Brown's door, huddled under a long coat against the rain. Okay, no problem, except for that one time, a woman usually just cried and scared everybody even better. Izzy knew Mal liked it better with women there.

The rain was pissing Eva off more. She was done putting up with Theresa. She should cut her off like her stepmother had. Eva had come from Trinidad to New York to live with Theresa's mother and stepfather when she was twelve, to help around the house and with the already out-of-control Theresa. Eva thought of her own father with a shudder, and of her aunt's husband with a smile. He was tall, goofy, wealthy, and Jewish, running a golf store in Darien, Connecticut. Gentle and generous, he refused to lose his cool, a necessity in a house with three combustible Caribbean women. He single-handedly rescued Eva from condemnation to ·man-hater-dom. All the men in her life owed her uncle thanks. When he died of cancer at fifty-five, Eva and her aunt were devastated. After his days of walking and going to the bathroom by himself were done, he took his last breath neatly tucked into a white hospital bed. The man was still warm, and Theresa walked into the room.

"I'm getting the Porsche," she announced. And she did. She got the Porsche, and her mother hadn't spoken to her since. She smoked the Porsche, if that was possible, and Eva was jealous, not of Theresa, but of her aunt. If Theresa's mother still spoke to Theresa, Eva wouldn't have to.

Eva had been working this out with Ms. Gail Glaser for years now. Actually, not Ms.—Dr. Gail Glaser. Eva's shrink had earned a PhD four years after Eva began seeing her, and she couldn't get used to calling her "Doctor." It was strange enough revealing intimate secrets to someone she called "Miss." That was how it worked with shrinks, though, and Eva desperately wanted a private practice, so she could leave the addicts and felons alone. "Ms. Glaser," she'd said the other day, when referring to a charge for a missed session. Gail shot a chilled look back at her.

Eva actually liked that about Gail, as she called her shrink in her mind only. Gail was a haughty Jewish woman who didn't take shit from anybody. Some left-leaning Jews were susceptible to race rage, and all Eva had to do was talk aggrieved patois to get her way. Gail Glaser, with her glazed, insightful smile and pensive eyes, was an authentic professional. That was why Eva had been seeing her for eight years, and they had exchanged Christmas (or Hanukkah) gifts for the last four.

Eva thought back to yesterday's session. She had been zoning out in the white on cream-patterned walls, which were pink when Eva first began there. The office was big, the living room of Gail's home, with two blue couches, two leather love seats, and Gail's swivel chair, her counseling throne, a light reddish brown leather with regal whittled armrests. Gail gave her that inquisitive smile that seemed genuine but was surely well practiced.

"Where are you going?" she asked. Smooth.

I'm going nowhere. I'm sitting right here. Won't be going anywhere for another forty minutes, Eva thought, but held it back. "My job."

"What about it?" Gail turned sideways now.

"I love my clients, I do."

"Okay . . ." said Gail, dubious.

"But maybe I'm ready to love them from afar." Silence. "I was interviewing people for a new unit that just opened up. After I was done hearing the same thing, over and over, I felt like I had a CD on repeat. I crossed every candidate off my list, looked up, and there was no one left to interview. I just don't believe them."

"Why is that?"

"Common sense. I get used to their cycles and it's boring. I'm basically supposed to pretend they're not full of shit, pick one, go get lunch and a manicure."

"Do you really think they're all . . . full of it?"

Come on, Gail, say shit, just once.

"I guess not necessarily. Theresa, she's the model that's ruined me. These candidates sit in front of me, and talk about how they lost their lovers, destroyed their families, stole from their own kids, and I think, why? Why do they even get another chance? You sold out your family to get high. There's no taking that back."

Gail squinted, turned her head, blinked, and looked up, then back at Eva. "Okay, I've seen some turn it around. Theresa makes them all look bad. I come home and there she is, random men, dealers, the air saturated in weed, back there getting fucked every which way for shit."

Long silence now. Gail took it all in, but Eva felt she had said something improper, smeared this pastel bubble with her personal sewage. That was the work; Gail had to know that you can't pick your clients' lives. Still, Eva wanted to belong, like she too could practice on the Upper West Side and treat clients making $150K-plus. Hear about dating scenes, corporate backstabbing, liberal guilt, and who they had to fire. Too bad the only West Indian advice white people wanted to hear was from tarot cards.

"I'm sorry," said Eva, "maybe I should talk about my love life. Remember that banker? I was supposed to meet him at Starbucks, and left after waiting for five minutes. Saw him come in another door on the way out, but five minutes late seemed like an insult from a guy who works for a Swiss bank."

"Wait, now. I think you were on to something there. I mean, that is an extraordinary, volatile living situation, and of course you can't focus on work or men. Isn't there any way out of it?" asked Gail with that inquiring look.

Eva thought of the four or five times she had thrown Theresa out, all with the same futile result. Her cousin was her one weakness, and Eva barely comprehended her own involuntary deference. When Eva was home and she heard the door close and those wobbly, careless heels tumble in, her heart would speed up, afraid of running into Theresa on her way to the bathroom or in the kitchen. They would mutter averted and swallowed greetings, Eva feeling the sneers and snickering, the silent leverage game that ended with Eva awake in bed, sick with impotence. Gail knew it well; she wanted Eva to talk about it but she didn't get it. No one got it and that's all there was to it.

"If I wanted out, I'd have to kill her."

Eva thought about breaking up with Gail again, but it would have been redundant and masturbatory as every other time. Gail would stand up, thank Eva for working with her, sincerely wish her the best, tell her that she would succeed and prosper because of the quality of her integrity, shake her hand, and Eva would typically be back within two weeks. So Eva rode out the rest of the session avoiding eye contact with quiet glances, thinking if she wanted to break up with someone, she should date. When the clock's second hand made the revolution moving the minute hand to the 9, Gail smiled peacefully and nodded with a long blink, saying, "We have to stop."

Eva got herself together and nodded good-bye, as she never said it. Gail's son waited for the elevator with her, a tall young man noticeably darker than Gail, smiling at Eva. She liked that Gail, at least in one regard, knew some black folk. The young Glaser let her go through the lobby first with

melancholy eyes, and as Eva held the door for him, she wondered if her Theresa issue wasn't the reason she had so far
failed at becoming a therapist.

Now to see some drug dealers and spend the rest of her
unending day at the hospital. Being around the low-life,
scumbag shit peddlers was bad enough. She could barely
deal with them when their attitude was cut with concilia-
tion, and she was getting paid. This was neither.

It wasn't so chilly now but it was wet, the spray misting
in Eva's eyes. She pulled her hood down over her nose,
tilted her head back, and knocked. The Jack had been
strong in her but was fading, and she didn't want it to. Agitation was creeping in. She imagined what waited inside
and imitated it. Yo-yo, what up, bitch, ya nah mean? If they
kept her waiting any longer she would give them flashbacks
of their mothers, take off her shoe, and bang on the door
with it.

It opened and an averted, menacing, pocked black man
turned and went inside without a word. She was surprised
by how quiet they were. One was in a leather jacket, playing video games, looked like football. Anther leaned against
a wall with a bandana over his brow. The walls were covered with loud hip-hop posters and graffiti, as though they
only moved to this town house so they could mess up something that was once nice. An open glass jar full of weed was
on the coffee table, like candy at Grandma's, but nothing
else illegal was in sight. They probably removed the contra-
band for her, forgetting that weed was illegal. A plasma TV
was on mute, the TV too big for the room, the hue of the
room changing with the images: yellow, purple, blue, green.

There were two ways to deal with them. She could quietly get in and get out, or jab them, loosen them up, and
maybe get some help with the car service and docile Theresa
transportation. Be foulmouthed for no reason—these macho
scumbags loved that.

Strange was groggily waiting in a dirty lab coat, in old, thick-rimmed glasses with magnifying lenses. He raised his hands from a table with crude surgical equipment, and held them high in the air. Mal sidestepped in, aiming behind the doc.

"Nice to see you too," said Doc Strange, through his wrinkled, buzzard neck.

Mal grabbed the old man by his shirt, pulled him closer, and put the gun behind him. Nothing there.

"Seen Izzy?" asked Mal.

"Why? He hurt too?"

"Nah, man." Mal let go of his shirt. "Me and Izzy? Not cool no more. I see him? And that's his ass."

Doc Strange looked at Mal's shoulder. Strange was a local Harlemite who had lost his suspiciously earned license due to Medicaid fraud. According to records, at one time he saw over three hundred patients per day. After the government seized his license, and the near millions his fraudulent practice earned, Doc Strange got locked up and became acquainted with people like Mal, who needed his dubious though reliable services.

"Got cash?" he asked Mal.

"Yeah."

Strange shrugged. "Izzy and you are none of my business."

Mal grabbed Strange's flabby, wrinkled neck this time, and stiffly held him at arm's length, using the gun for hand gestures as he talked. "Nah, it is your business. You with me. This concerns anyone that's with me. Somebody gets the drop on me while I'm here? You better hope they finish the job. If not, you a dead fucking doctor." Mal let go of Strange's neck, but his glare was just as stiff. "Now give me some drugs, man. And you better have something stronger than Vicodin."

"So, where is this bitch?"

They all laughed, breaking the tension.

The one in his leather jacket asked her, "Want a drink?"

"Whiskey?" she asked, relieved.

He shook his head. "Champagne or beer."

She grunted. "Pussies." They laughed again.

Charlie Brown came back in with a paper cup full of champagne. Eva took a big sip. "Swear, this girl gets me so mad I could kill her." The three buffoons laughed even harder. Eva didn't think it was that funny. She took another big sip. "Where is she?"

"In the bathroom," said Charlie Brown, smiling like he knew something. No one else seemed permitted to speak, their laughter quickly sucked back in, leaving a creepy silence. Eva felt exposed, as though she wore a hospital gown in a lab full of quietly snickering doctors.

She grew dizzy. She took a few steps into the bathroom, losing her balance. There was a green hunting knife on the sink. Why was there a knife on the sink? There was Theresa, snuggling the porcelain pillow. Theresa getting up. Theresa back down. Theresa rolling. Theresa coming. Something shiny. Something metal. Something fell.

Chapter 3

Benny finally pulled up in a van that said IN LINE CON-TRACTORS. Izzy could make out the large shape of his head from the roof. "I know that cranium," he said, but Mal had already started downstairs.

Izzy saw Mal when he reached the marble-walled lobby, charging through the glass doors. A little something extra for the security camera, thought Izzy. They had knocked out the roof camera, but not the lobby one. So Izzy went down one more flight to the warm, humming laundry room, and then through a humid hallway to the service exit, stinking of garbage.

On his way to the van Izzy noticed a pigeon on the sidewalk, resting against the base of the building. He had seen it there the other day, walking weakly and pressing its chest up to the brick, its beak downcast. At a glance he realized today it was dead, and that its last strength was used to position itself right where it was. Izzy felt a momentary pang of jealousy. It was a dignified animal that could choose where it died.

Mal gave Izzy a nasty glare through the rolled-down passenger-side window. Izzy crouched in through the sliding door.

"What? You forget the lobby camera?" he asked.

"Who, Izzy? Who's going to watch that shit? The cops? These niggas is going to call up the cops, and say, 'Officer, they took my dope money.'"

"Yo, it's cool, Iz," said Arben.

"And you," continued Mal, to Arben now, "don't even agree with me. You're late, you burnt motherfucker."

"Sorry, bro, there was cops all over the fucking place."

Izzy looked around the van. Drywall dust covered the walls and floor, already on his boots. The van was used for demolition. Izzy was pissed.

"Beautiful, that's a fucking beautiful trail. Better than bread crumbs. See this?" Mal half glanced from up front. "Take a look now, 'cause next time you see it will be in a courtroom, in an evidence bag. Mal, fuck this. Not now. In a residential neighborhood? Cops hear guns, and they're here. This ain't some ghetto, hundred-dollar-a-month crib. Now we got a white fucking dust trail? As long as we waited already? Fuck it. Dead it."

Mal shook his head emphatically. "Look, we here," he said, using his throat through gritted teeth. "We know the money's still in the spot, 'cause nobody left yet. We got silencers. Let's just do it, man, bang, bang. Like always, you talkin' that bitch shit. C'mon, Z. Where your heart at?"

Good question. Mal meant it at as a challenge, but Izzy heard a question. Struck by ambivalence, Izzy did what came natural to him.

He shrugged.

Mal nodded rapidly and turned to Arben, good to go, and Izzy steamed. He had been raising questions with Mal for a while, who systematically ignored him. Izzy wanted to pick up some fake badges, get his whole operation to go smoother, not rely on guns so much. It could be like back in the day, when they jacked those two rookie housing police for their shields. Got all their standard-issue gear, even used the radios, until it got hot. Shaking them down at gunpoint was crazy, but running into a dope spot flashing an NYPD badge was low risk. Mal shot it down. "Talkin' bitch shit. Where your heart at?"

Izzy didn't know the answer to the question that wasn't even asked. Where was his heart? He had made his choices a long time ago, accustomed himself to doing whatever was necessary. If a man was in his way, that man had to go, and his heart had accepted it. He never worried about consequences much, figuring he'd be dead before anything caught up to him. The heart of a stickup kid, guy, jack boy, rude boy, bad man, thug was a simple, vicious thing. But a man, just a man, with no precursor, no tag, no alias, was different. A man had options.

The ride moved, and Izzy had already been strapped in. Arben drove about fifteen feet across the street. Izzy and his partners pulled handkerchiefs over their faces, jumped out of the van, and stomped toward the door, white dust trailing as they moved, like Old West bandits in different colors.

Mal picked the lock with his tension tool and rake, holding a long wire between his teeth like a toothpick as he tinkered. The door was open in about thirty seconds. Inside, instinct took over. Izzy drew the weighted handles, and unlike in the van, he could stop thinking. An odd peace took hold, Izzy knowing now the action was live and all his ambivalence was irrelevant. With the frenzied smell and the rush of hands to metal came a promise of conclusion. It didn't matter anymore if he was a kid or a man. He was a soldier again, with objectives and order. He always felt good when in the shit. His arms extended with two silenced .22s, shooting all the hands and feet he saw. Two men, a big one with a bandana over one eye, and another in a Ron Artest jersey, rolled on the floor. He had shot them before he had seen them.

Was this it? Was there another one? Where was the girl?

* * *

Eva had a monster headache, up against something fleshy. Her knees hurt, pressed on cold, hard tiles. Something was rank, something she had smelled before. Her eyes opened and saw red. It was Theresa. A glaze of blood pasted her cheek to her cousin's stomach. Theresa's mouth and eyes were wide open, tiny pupils staring at nothing, dried puke on her cheek. Eva was about to say her name, until she saw the knife plunged in Theresa's chest, in her heart.

Eva's hand held the grip.

Eva didn't scream. She wanted to. The shock stole her breath. She let go, like the handle of the knife scorched her. She would scream if she could breathe.

The body looked so natural; Theresa's head rested in the nook between the toilet and the tub, the knife sticking up from her heart like it had sprouted and grown there. She was clearly dead—so much so that she didn't look like she was ever alive; rather she was some life-sized voodoo doll of Eva's imagination, complete with a pin. She shook Theresa, not hoping she would spring to life, but hoping she was a fake, hoping her touch would reveal movie prosthetics, a plastic cosmetic that only looked real from one angle. What she felt instead was as unreal. A human body, bones, blood, flesh, muscle, with no reaction; no autonomy, no pulse. It was human, and a doll.

Now her only hope was that she was dreaming, and was due to wake up once it was intolerable. Only it seemed like that point had already passed.

She stood, shaking, took one breath before she couldn't again, and then staggered toward the closed bathroom door, obeying an impulse to *run*. From outside, she heard footsteps. Four sharp hisses. Two loud thuds. Moans. She opened the door, smearing blood on the knob.

She saw three men, in black overcoats. A pair of light eyes that she knew. The eyes froze to see her.

* * *

Izzy knew before anyone else did; he couldn't move. He'd froze. It was the girl from before. She held her bloody hands out by her side like talons. Her mouth stretched open in a gaping, breathless scream. Izzy had no idea where his pulse was. He didn't even know where the guns in his hands were. The seconds were going by around Izzy, but inside him, the clock had stopped.

Mal was saying, "Yo!"

He was thinking, *What . . . the . . . fuck . . .*

The rest happened in slow motion, like he was watching it on TV. Charlie Brown, in a leather jacket, came in with what looked like an automatic .45. Izzy had time to take him out.

Izzy didn't. The man let his gun loose. Sounded like a .45. It tore three holes through Arben. A red laser appeared on Charlie Brown's chest and a *boom* sent the man clear out of the room, shaking the foundation.

A disaster. Izzy blew it. He was the point man, him and his .22s. He let them all down. His guns were at his side. He fucked up bad.

"Dumb, sloppy motherfucker!" said Mal, all business. He dropped the shotgun, drew his .22, and popped the kid in the Artest jersey in the back of the head, muttering curses. He popped the other one and looked up at Izzy. "Take care of her," he said and went to the kitchen.

Izzy looked Eva up and down, tears streaming down her face. He looked inside the bathroom, where a girl lay faceup with a knife in her chest. Eva offered no explanation. He was on his own.

Izzy held his gun up to her.

Mal came back in with a red duffel bag over his shoulder, like a hunter back from a kill.

"They was about to bounce with this," he said, and stopped walking. He looked at Eva as if at a poster on a wall. He scanned her up and down, glanced at Izzy, then went to her, and with a serious expression, put his fingers up to her throat, attempting to check her pulse. She swiped him away like a startled cat.

"Why is she still breathing, dog?" Mal asked, still watching Eva, who stared back. "You going to do her or what?"

Izzy lowered his gun. "I know her," he said, finding his voice.

Mal's eye went crooked. "I don't think I heard you."

"Let's go."

Mal processed Izzy's words by glancing from the floor, to Arben, to the girl, to Izzy, to his gun. Then, all frown and baffled eyebrows, he said, "Son, you let these niggas shoot up Arben! Now 'let's go'? You got a lot of fucking nerve. We 'bout to have a whole clan of Albanians *on us*."

Izzy shook his head. "I know her," he repeated, as if to himself.

Mal chuckled. "Yeah, that's it, hey, how are ya? Good to see you, we're getting outta here, come with? After what she just saw me do? Nigga, is you out your goddamn mind? Do her, or we got a problem."

"You want it done, you do it," Izzy told him.

"Then we got a problem."

Time was running out. This crazy fucker had to take it there, no matter what. "A problem? Mal, you think I'm gonna roll on you? With all the shit you got on me?"

"Problem is, I'm the only one here who dropped bodies. Which I had to do on account of you. Problem is, she saw me do three men. I'm dirty and you're pure as the driven snow."

Izzy knew he was right. By their rules, by the soldier's creed, Izzy had agreed to shoot her before they entered the town house, before he met her at that bar, when he had first partnered up with Mal. Izzy felt for his gun and it was already in his hand. He slowly raised it again, her breaths be-

coming heaves as the barrel leveled with her eyes. Izzy became aware of her heartbeat, as though he could feel her
pulse as his finger pressed the stiff trigger. Then he realized
it was the racing of his own pulse beating against the remorseless metal.

Desperation and anger swirled in her eyes, while her
mouth was a quiet, quivering frown. Her hands reached for
her wrists, fingers stroking her veins. Izzy had noticed how
when people were scared they would touch their wrists or
neck. But Eva didn't beg or negotiate, she silently pleaded
with a dignity that seemed so fixed to her character she was
incapable of losing it, even neck deep in shit, facing an
abyss. Fear couldn't take everything.

Izzy closed his eyes and felt like he was in a free fall, careening down an endless elevator shaft. He thought of Won
and how desperately he cried, that same desperation he
lived and hustled by. Won had played a game and lost, and
Izzy happened to be the scoreboard that told him so. Won
didn't plead to live, he pleaded to get back in the game, for
a chance to win. Eva had nothing to do with any of it. She
should die like that pigeon, naturally, in a place of her
choosing. Izzy realized that an ounce more of pressure on
that trigger, and he would cross a line he'd never crossed. A
line even Mal had yet to cross—the murder of a thoroughly
innocent bystander.

He watched her, the seconds ebbing by, her gasping chest
and despondent expression, and most shocking, the blood
on her hands as her gaze resigned itself past Izzy. His forearms firmly framing his .22, he glanced behind her, and
thought of something, wishing he might be so resolute
when he faced the object of her stare.

"I can't," he said.

"What?"

"I can't do it."

Izzy lowered his gun and locked eyes with Mal. He re

membered their history, all past confrontations, and he
knew Mal did too. Mal had already threatened to kill him if
he didn't kill a witness. Izzy had already promised the same
if Mal's barrel so much as angled at him. There was nothing
idle about these speculations. They knew that about each
other better than anyone.

Mal took a step closer, the shorter man's breath hitting
Izzy's face. "This is about the rules. No witnesses."

"She's not a witness. Look in the bathroom. Girl's a goddamn killer."

Mal glanced into the room at the girl with the knife in
her chest, the handprints crawling along the subway tiles
like those of a child with watercolors. Mal started to laugh;
Eva choked, bending down; Izzy stared at the bathroom,
the motionless body with a green hunting knife sticking
straight up like a bare flagpole. Mal's laugh was everywhere. So were bodies. Izzy felt filthy, as if newsprint covered his skin. He couldn't walk three steps without kicking
a corpse. He was supposed to murder this sweetheart of a
woman. And everywhere else was Mal's cackle, escalating
with lethal life.

If the rules of good soldiering demanded that he kill her,
then it was time for new rules.

"Damn, bitch, what did she do," Mal mustered between
laughs, "insult your cooking? Borrow some heels without
asking?" He calmed down. "You right, Iz, you right. She
don't got to go. *She* don't."

Mal's arm went stiff. When he spun back around, Izzy's
gun was already raised. A very loud *bang* echoed around
the room, drowning the hiss of the silencer. Eva hit the wall.
Izzy checked himself. He was okay. Mal was on the floor.
Eva, back against the wall, was holding a .45.

Her face had found expression—she was pissed, with a
contorted sneer, and crazed, haywire eyes. She fired again,
unaware that Mal was down. The plasma screen shattered.

Sparks flew as it jumped back, hit the wall, then fell face-down, just missing a dead dealer. Mal moaned. Izzy looked up again, and saw his bullet, buried deep in the drywall directly in front of him. Mal, bleeding from his shoulder, was moving; his good hand grabbed the shotgun he had dropped earlier.

Izzy took the motionless Eva by her arms and threw her behind the couch.

Her hand smacked the blood-soaked carpet. Maybe she screamed, maybe it was still inside. She didn't know what was in or out anymore. She was face-to-face with one of the young men, looking into the bullet's crater, down the ravaged throat of tunneled bone and brain. Small entrance, wide exit; the inside of the young man's head had clumsily collapsed on the gray carpet.

Something popped. Like a car backfiring, a bone breaking. The frame of the couch cracked and splintered.

Ducking behind the couch, Izzy heard the rough *click-clack* of Mal pumping his shotie, ready to go again, and realized they were close to the front door. He pointed to it.

"Go," he told Eva. She paused in panic. Another blast shattered the couch. "*Go!*" Izzy shouted, and shoved her toward the door. Eva fell over the body, regained herself, and scuttled out the door. Izzy followed her on all fours, police sirens singing in the distance, and for once, he was relieved to hear them.

Chapter 4

There was no mistaking the three Albanian hardheads as they left Gate 27, squinting at foreign surroundings with a mix of confusion and hostility. Huna had last seen them three years ago, and they still all resembled Benny, minus his New York bullshit. They had broad, mountain-man foreheads, harsh and jagged like the rocks they grew up around. When they saw Huna they all embraced without a word, shaking hands and smacking each others' bellies and shoulders, wherever they could find girth. They were men of few words and fewer smiles, and Huna was pleased.

Years ago, the two families were on the verge of a blood feud. Now all had made peace and Arben's half brothers were in New York with better intentions. Huna had plans for Arben, or Benny, as his family called him. Not his mother and father, they called him Arben, but around Huna it was Benny, and Benny had a promotion coming. He wasn't especially bright, or motivated, more of an immediate gratification type of guy, seemed to prefer hookers to regular girls, and he did so many drugs his memory was shot to shit. Not serious drugs, just party drugs, a little coke, or yip, some ex, or Eleanor, maybe some Xanies or Vicies the next day. Maybe a lot of Xanies the next day. That was what worried Huna, when Benny would be so hurt from the night or nights before he'd take like, ten, Xanax, and walk around like a fucking zombie for the next week. One time, Huna was standing on the street in front of a bodega, and Benny walked right by him, didn't even know he was there. Huna stood about six-six, 280 pounds, that day, like most, in a full-length white track suit. Fucking guy's mind was obliterated.

But Benny could be trusted, and that was why he was about to step up in the game. Huna was going to give him a forty-pound-a-week chronic business, introduce him to all the out-of-state custies, have him make those 3:00 AM meetings Huna was sick of. Fucking bums driving in from bumfuck Jersey, could barely tell you within four hours of when they'd get there. Huna'd rather wait for Time Warner than those cocksuckers. Benny would clear at least a g per, and also handle some Eleanor's, if his custie was getting busy with that too. Benny was like family to Huna. He'd turn his back on him any day, and sleep soundly that night. Benny was about to make some real paper. But first, he had to be initiated.

That's why Benny's three brothers from Montenegro were in JFK with Huna. Whack jobs, ready to shoot anything that moved, with capped teeth, constant stubble, and dark, lazy eyes that looked at people like inanimate objects. Huna loved them. They reminded these pussy American Albanians what it's like to be hard—cocksuckers wouldn't pull their gats if a nigger spat on them. They walked past the luggage claim, their small carry-on handbags being all they had. Out in the parking lot, they murmured their approval of Huna's Benzo in Albanian. Sandro pushed his cream blazer back and put his hands on his hips, remarking how strange it felt to be without his gun.

On another cigarette break, Jacob lit up, smelled the butane flame from his shiny Zippo, snapped it closed, and puffed up the smoke. He thought of his mother's fine, dark-skinned client, wishing he had said something to her in the elevator yesterday. The trendy, mature women on Fifth Avenue strutted by, and he wanted to stop one, talk to her, make her laugh. Jacob was tired of young chicks; he wanted a woman, one who brought something to the table. He didn't understand why older women were always complaining that there aren't enough available men. He was available. It was just hard to talk to them. He didn't know how to not sound twenty-two.

He wanted to tell the woman on the elevator, "I'd never leave you waiting at Starbucks. Not even for five minutes."

But saying that would have caused more problems.

That woman was clearly dealing with issues of substance, unlike his ex, the frivolous Tiffané. T-I-double F-A-N—E accented, as she would say. Tiffané was the most beautiful girl he'd ever messed with, but that E accented thing should have sent him running. She said it the first day they met, holding up her gold nameplate at a bar by Columbia on Amsterdam Avenue, SoHa, like south of Harlem, aka HoHa. Known as a place to meet loose and desperate Barnard girls, the all-girls-school across the street from Columbia, Jacob wound up there alone on a lonely night. When he began talking to Tiffané and Melanie, he thought he had lucked up into an R & B video. He started up with Melanie first, the more outgoing, sexy mixed chick with a studded Baby Phat tail curled on her jeans. Tiffané sat beside her, a dark black girl with a gorgeous face, and slanted feline eyes; a thin five-ten with real 34 double Ds. They talked about how they couldn't believe Jacob was single, how he was such a catch, a relationship guy. Melanie got up and showed him the cat on her jeans, and Tiffané lamented, "She likes you."

So Jacob noticed Tiffané. She said she did some modeling, and had just started at Hunter, and Melanie at Barnard.

Then Melanie got sloppy drunk on Long Island iced teas and Jacob took Tiffané to another bar with a dance floor, where they linked and swayed to 112's "Only You," when she gave him a sweet kiss and confessed, "I'm only sixteen."

Tiffané and Melanie were seniors at Dwight High School. Melanie sold herself short by claiming Barnard; she got into Columbia the next year. Tiffané was so good-looking Jacob gave it a shot, until the night she tried to jerk him off and her rings left him with scabs. A couple of years later, fully aware of her eighteen-year-old status, he called her again. She was even better looking, had stopped talking with her silverware at meals, and dressed like she was sponsored by designers. On the negative, she didn't work or go to school, and Jacob couldn't afford her; single black female, addicted to retail. She would wear hats and sunglasses to restaurants, ducking behind her menu in hopes of being mistaken for someone famous. Jacob had to listen to her wail at her mother on the rare day she didn't buy her something from Bergdorf or Victoria's Secret, and bartend just to take her to dinner and go clubbing. She was too young for Jacob, but Jacob was too young for her. Well known among promoters and bouncers at chic meatpacking clubs, Jacob would follow her through the many corridors and floors of the burgundy Lotus, the open gray space and house music of Cielo, the powdery carpeted halls of Halo. Then the men. She had a hard time relinquishing any kind of attention, no matter how corny, bold, awkward, or blatant. Yet she demanded Jacob make her his girl, a status he wasn't eager for.

Once she was his girl she wanted to see his writing. She knew he wrote and that was a part of his appeal. Tiffané thought she was Carrie from *Sex in the City*, who was a writer. So Tiffané wanted to date a writer, pretending to read a book when Jacob picked her up on their first date. After he gave her the story he wrote about a hip-hop kid engineering a drug pyramid in college, she stopped calling.

Then came the rumors and reports about her everywhere with everybody. A friend of Jacob's explained to him, "Shallow people are fascinated with deep people. Only they're still shallow, so fascination means a few weeks."

Jacob realized he wanted to write when eavesdropping on his mother's sessions next door. His mom always came to his room telling him something was too loud, the TV or the radio or the CDs. So Jacob got very quiet and listened instead. Sometimes they were pretty dull, amazing only for their pettiness. Others, like the woman from yesterday, were outright fascinating, and made Jacob think of stories. One had a couple of personalities: a levelheaded bookkeeper and a mean-spirited dog hater who thought she worked for the post office. There was the crass garment district Jew, the gay-and-doesn't-know-it banker Jew, then the nymphomaniac Orthodox Jew. But the hot black woman, the West Indian from Connecticut, the intolerant social worker with the cracked-out cousin named Theresa, was his favorite. Jacob had a crush on her for years. Funny how for all that time, he had never caught her name.

Disease-ridden cunt. Dumb hooker. Bitch-made cock-sucker. Son of a crack whore.

Ouch.

Mal's wavering consciousness allowed a limited repetition. His aggressive current was occasionally interrupted by pain. Instinct by itself got him out of the apartment, with one silenced .22, one limp shoulder, and a duffel stuffed with cash over the other.

The back door of the town house led to a backyard area, unkempt dirt and grass contained by a small picket fence, likely installed by previous tenants. The Goodyear tires of a Range Rover, with disclike rims ready to twirl, dwarfed the small yard. Mal moved on down the back alley, passing more backyards, some with playground equipment; and tempting cars, some with leather and wood-grain interiors. He came to an opening onto the street, as a police car with wailing sirens raced by. A gas station was across from him, hosting a herd of yellow taxis. An idea formed.

He never jacked himself into a problem he couldn't jack his way out of.

With all the stealth he could manage, Mal crept up beside one of the taxis being filled, and got in the backseat. He exhaled and a momentary relief washed over him. He felt for his gun and took it out, wondering what he had grabbed in those hazy few seconds he was alone in the town house. Arben was by the wall, shot through his chest, bleeding on the TV wires, his gun in his hand. Two knuckleheads were under the couch, executed, no guns. TV was facedown on the floor. Unexpected dead girl in the bathroom. Izzy's gun on the floor.

Izzy's gun. He'd dropped it by the bathroom. Mal realized he was looking at it now. He also knew his truly favorite companion was gone forever. He'd left his shotie on the floor, by the kitchen. Maybe not the pinpoint instrument you would want a laser scope for, but it scared the shit out of people. That was his baby; he'd take one of them over a hundred bitch-made Izzys.

Charlie Brown was in the kitchen. Charlie Brown's .45 was also on the floor, by the kitchen. As Mal pieced the scene together, momentarily sober, he felt the bite in his shoulder and the dripping blood, reaching his leg with a cold chill. Charlie Brown's .45. That fucking *bitch*.

"You still got that forty-f—" Izzy paused, realizing that, to the person he was speaking to, a gun was either a big gun, or a small gun. As he drove to the Queensboro Bridge, eyes fixed on the road, Izzy surveyed a mental checklist of immediate, practical considerations. "You still have that gun you fired?" he rephrased.

Eva, reliving the unfathomable last twenty minutes of her life, barely grunted. The look of trauma and incomprehension on her furrowed, questioning brow wasn't ugly, but it wasn't cute. She was dry-crying, eyes strained and slanting toward her dire frown, without tears. Her body quivered and fidgeted like it didn't know what to do with itself, and she wasn't breathing. Eva's psychological state climbed a couple of notches on Izzy's list of priorities.

"It's okay. Let it out," he told her.

Her threshold broke, and she fell into sobs.

"Take me to Manhattan right now, goddamn it, Harlem. Move," Mal said through his pain, preparing to raise his gun.

No answer. Mal was alone in the taxi. He peeked through the partition opening and saw a shirt in the front seat. He grabbed it and threw it back behind his shoulder. With his other hand, he pulled the bottom of the shirt through his armpit and tied it over his bleeding wound with his good hand and his teeth. He looked for a set of keys up front, but didn't see anything. Reluctant to give up his rest, he got out of the cab.

A short Dominican walked toward him in an orange button-down open to his chest, revealing a neck full of heavy gold, above a round El Presidente belly. His elbows snapping as he marched, Mal, remembering his picture from the license inside the cab, had found his driver.

"Oye, what the fuck you doing with my car?" He got closer, and saw the shirt. "That's my fucking shirt, man! What is your fucking prob—"

Mal revealed the gun, aiming it between the cabby's eyes. "Shut the fuck up. My fucking problem is none of your business. Your fucking problem is obvious."

The Dominican slowed down, and raised his hands.

"Keys."

He tossed Mal the keys.

"Cell phone."

He tossed Mal his cell phone.

"Get in the trunk."

The cabdriver gingerly walked toward the trunk, as if his footsteps themselves might set the gun off.

Hoping Eva's sobs had tempered, Izzy tentatively returned to his list. "The gun. Do you have it?"

Eva looked about, patted herself, and then saw it on the floor by her feet. "Yeah, it's here. Why?"

"A person was killed with that gun. If you'd left it there, with your fingerprints on it, you'd be looking at double homicide."

She shook her head slowly, like she wanted to tell him he was wrong.

"Listen, Eva. Have you ever been fingerprinted?"

She was still shaking her head, finding a rhythm now, and Izzy thought she was going to cry again.

"This is important, okay? I need to know how much time we've got before they're after you."

She sucked in her breath, pulling herself together a bit. "We've got no time. I left my fucking purse over there. And yes, I've been fingerprinted. For a job."

Damn, she's condescending, Izzy thought, questioning what he had done back in that town house. Betrayed his partner, a man who, while flawed, had not betrayed him, but rather had enforced the loose terms of their partnership—*I kill one. We kill them all.* Mal had been there through many years, and they had killed for each other. Mal would say Izzy had betrayed him for a momentary fantasy, an infatuated glimpse of a girl Izzy didn't know, and a life that wasn't his. Pure weakness.

Yet Izzy had never regretted any decision that he was, at the time, sure about. His regrets came when he didn't listen to himself. Back at the scene, when he had looked at Eva, he knew he would not shoot her. There was little actual decision making involved. He held his gun. He looked at her. Nope. Now what? What followed was on Mal. Izzy drew a line. Then, as if Mal was the only one allowed to draw lines, Mal drew his own. It's remarkable their partnership lasted as long as it did.

So what if this girl has an attitude? You didn't kill an innocent person. You will know that until the day you die. So what if she'd rather get locked up than trust you?

Heading toward the Queensboro in his inconspicuous yellow cab, Mal made a phone call, steering with the thumb of his weak arm. He checked for police, knowing a lone cabdriver was a prime target for getting pulled over.

Dr. Strange's groggy voice answered.

"Wake your punk ass up," ordered Mal.

"This better be fucking important."

"I got work for you. And cash money. Meet me at the OR."

Mal hung up, wondering where Izzy might go. All he thought of was the scatter of ex-girlfriends around the city. He made another call. The phone picked up, but no voice spoke, only a raucous grinding house beat.

"Huna!" called Mal. He was familiar with Huna's method of screening calls.

A deep, Albanian voice rumbled over the strip sound track. "Don't blow up my fucking phone. Meet me at Privilege." *Click.*

"Huna? Fuck."

As he approached the Queensboro, Mal decided he had two advantages over Izzy: One, Izzy had the girl. Two, Mal had the money. Mal was sure Izzy wouldn't think to call Huna before his bitch ass took care of the girl. The first one to Huna lived.

Confident in his chances, Mal picked up speed, riding alongside a familiar construction van. As Manhattan emerged, a woman's profile registered in the corner of his eye, and an ache seized his useless shoulder.

"Bitch!"

Since 12:45 today the ordinarily tranquil ground of her predictable life began moving like a treadmill. Pulling away from her feet faster and faster, she kicked her heels up as best she could. She had abandoned all hope that she was dreaming, because while her inner demons were nothing light, she definitely wasn't this fucked up. Looking for something familiar, she flipped down the visor of the van and saw her face in the tarnished mirror. Eyes bloodshot, with swollen bags underneath. Dirty tear tracks streamed down sallow cheeks. She redefined her standards of "I look awful." Up until that day, she had actually never looked awful.

Who in the world was she riding with? Ex-con Mobil. While she was happy to be alive, she knew this aged stickup kid was a poor excuse for a savior. He was too eerily calm, waiting out her tantrum, contemplating moves, taking notes, a normal day at the office. He couldn't get her back to her cherished middle-class routine. A man couldn't put out a fire if he didn't know one was burning.

"Listen, could you just drop me off? Let me go to the police."

Izzy shook his head. "I'm not sure that's such a good idea."

"I won't say anything about you, I promise."

"That's not what I mean. The police are not your friends right now. Your fingerprints are all over a knife that, more than likely, remains—"

"I didn't do that!" she cut him off.

"I'm sure you—"

"They did." He had to bring that up. Her cousin's dead face flashed; knife in her chest, blood on Eva's hands. She looked down. Blood was still there. She couldn't have.

Izzy quieted, waited, and approached again, softly. "Anyway, there is something called gun powder residue. They will know you fired a gun for about another day."

"Sorry, I didn't know this," she snapped. "My experience with dead bodies quadrupled today."

His brown eyebrows lifted slightly in surrender. She liked that look, offering her control when she had none. His ethereal eyes suggested that dirty as she was, she might float away clean. The van quieted. Manhattan's vast skyline got closer. The towering shapes and myriad lit squares within calmed her. She welcomed the anonymity. Uncountable lights spread beyond her periphery, and Eva, with her situation, was just one of them.

Then her peaceful moment was violated. A feeling that would make her close her blinds when at home, or stare at an inconspicuous spot on the subway floor, snapped her private zone-out. She refocused on something closer, in the next lane, a hovering glare.

It was a taxi, and that same crooked-faced lunatic, staring at her with bloodshot, gunslinger eyes.

She said, "Izzy—"

The lunatic reached for something. A silver glint flashed. "Brake!"

Izzy looked up and stepped on the brake. A gunshot fired. The van's tires screeched on the asphalt, jolting them forward, seat belts choking them as they swerved into the next lane. Mal's taxi sped ahead. The cars behind them braked and skidded. Izzy glanced over at her. Her whole body clung to something—her feet pressed against the floor, her head flush with the headrest, her arm flat on the armrest, white knuckles clutching the seat belt buckle.

The taxi slowed. Car horns bellowed. Izzy pulled the van

into the lane behind the taxi. Mal pulled his taxi out of that lane.

"Give me that pistol," Izzy told Eva.

She looked at the gun by her feet, not wanting to touch it. She let go of the belt buckle and reached down to the floor, her seat belt restraining her. Her arm shook; maybe from the bumps in the road, maybe it was shaking anyway. Holding the heavy lump of metal between her thumb and fore-finger, she picked the gun up with her pinky high, as if she were cleaning up after a dog. She held it out, not wanting to remember how she had held it a short while ago, the fierce way it kicked back in her hands like something alive. Once it was close enough, Izzy snatched it.

Without taking his eyes off the road, he found the proper grip. He lowered the gun across his body, resting it on his driving forearm, pointing it out the window. A *boom* shook the van's frame, as Izzy swerved away from the concrete railing. Eva again clamped down on her seat. She closed her eyes. Another *boom* and she held on, closing her eyes tighter. Then shots, louder. Eva felt like a child hearing thunder for the first time.

She opened her eyes to see Izzy blasting out the window, handling the gun like it was an extension of his arm. Eva got the same impression of rehearsed virtuosity as when watching a professional musician, like Hendrix, live. She wondered what the difference was between the lunatic in the taxi and the lunatic in the van.

Izzy spotted something just past Eva. She followed his gaze out her window to a small break in the concrete rail-ing, separating them from the third, outermost lane. The break was just big enough for a car. Or maybe a van. She shook her head. Then tin thumps pelted the side of the van. Izzy's eyes flashed past her again; it was now or never. Eva hoped for never.

He slowed the van just enough and abruptly jerked the

wheel. The van turned sideways against the highway, and slid through the break in the shoulder, its front slamming against the beginning of the railing. Eva held on, amazed. The van tipped onto its right two wheels, the roof skidding against the bridge support cables, grinding as they drove with the screech of a braking subway car. The gun fell from Izzy's side of the van to ricochet off Eva's leg and slam against her passenger window. She looked out past the gun and couldn't even see the bridge, only the dark abyss of water below. Eva might have been screaming; she wasn't sure, overwhelmed by the roof's shrill scrape.

Then it tipped back. The van righted itself with a last *boom*, having a chance to echo in the ensuing silence.

Whoa. Can't believe that worked.

Izzy had seen that small break in the concrete railing year after year. Every time he would pass it, he would fantasize about switching lanes like that. Especially in heavy traffic, when that outermost lane was the only lane moving. Before it came up, he figured it was worth a shot. Now they were cruising, and the only thing separating them from the water below was that thin but evidently sturdy line of support cables.

Eva gripped her seat like her fingers might rip through the upholstery.

"You okay?" he asked.

Eyes wide, she nodded. Attitude or no, the woman was a trouper.

Izzy's phone rang. He awkwardly fished it from his pocket, and the flashing screen read MAL. Izzy was surprised for a moment, as if the man were dead and calling from the grave.

"What up, faggot?" said Mal, quite alive.

"You rang?" asked Izzy, unsure how to talk to his former friend.

"How's baby cakes?"

"How's your shoulder?" returned Izzy.

"Ooh. Your bitch got a bite, I'll give you that."

Antagonism it was. "Going to see Doc Strange for that? I might make a stop there. Light your punk ass up before I go take a shower."

"Bring your doggie with you. I got a nice bone for her."

Eva had dried blood on her hands, a disoriented scowl on her face. "Sounds risky," he told Mal, and hung up.

They rode along, the quiet only interrupted by the random bumps in the road.

"Going to see someone called Doc Strange?" asked Eva.

"Oh no," he told her. "I was just messing with him."

Chapter 5

Huna took the brothers over to the restaurant first, down to the basement. He showed them his guns, locked in a mounted box beside the dry food storage. Huna laid his gats out on a table, letting the brothers pick. Thirty-eights, .45s, nine millimeters, ten millimeters, old trey pound, new four pound, used duce-duce, all for sale. Huna asked the low wholesale price of four hundred, telling them to take whichever they liked, as though he didn't know or care which was worth more or less. Sandro, with a long, dimpled smile that rarely left his face like Benny's, gave Huna fifteen hundred for three guns, and they fought for fifteen minutes over the extra three bills. Those old-school Albans wouldn't take nothing for free. Finally, Sandro accepted three eight balls of Huna's raw Peruvian Gold in exchange for his generosity.

They all got blitzed out of their heads. Each of them ate half a prime rib, their appetites ruined. The brothers were anxious to party. Typically, after a plane ride one way or the other, they would binge for up to a week in a tele with escorts and ounces. So Huna kept them moving.

Privilege had just opened up, but the club was half-full, with a girl on a stage on either side, sequined legs wrapped around poles in acrobatic erotica. Louon, Huna's cousin, was there, his broad frame tossing back shots with his boys. Louon, heavy in the neck and shoulders like his namesake, a lion, made the tiny shot glass invisible in his huge hand. He then went up to the stage, feeding a dancing black girl bills and whispering to her.

Huna and the brothers walked up to the elevated VIP section, each sitting a space away from each other on the white leather chairs, making their territory known. A waitress took Huna's order, her gravity-defying breasts pressed together.

"Twenty Woo-woos," said Huna, surveying the club. "Give every motherfucker in here a shot, and give one to yourself," he told her, tossing a big-faced Benjamin Franklin on her tray.

Snickering, Louon came over to Huna, sitting next to him on the couch. Louon was so stocky he seemed upright no matter what, his bulging eyes lucid and yipped up.

"Yo, Huna, what up?"

Huna nodded and introduced him to the brothers, not mentioning last names.

"That girl up there? That's the one I was messing with, B. When she was over at Scores?" said Louon.

Huna looked at Louon sideways. Motherfucker talking like a nigger in front of the real Albans. Louon did at least dress better than Benny, though, with a crisp, bright Lacoste polo T, designer jeans, and spotless white sneakers.

"Shit, cuz, I didn't tell you? This girl's letting me touch her all over, right? The bouncer comes up and is, like, you can't touch the girl like that. I look to the girl and she's smiling with the fuck-me eyes, right? I know mad people who fucked this girl so I'm like my man, it's all love, ask the girl if she minds, right? The girl doesn't even look at this guy, I kid you not, your size, standing over us like he wants to do something, and I realize, he thinks that's his girl. The stripper is his girl. I'm like, oh God, this fool is getting possessive about a fucking stripper. So I touch her again and he comes over again, asking do I want him to touch me like that. I'm like look, I'm not like these other niggas around here, B, if you touch me I touch you back. I swear to God, bro, he put his hands on me and I knocked that nigga the fuck out."

Huna chuckled. He then leaned over to the brothers and translated the story into Albanian, and the three chuckled as well.

Izzy eyed the rearview as much as the street in front of him, making sure not to miss Mal again. The problem was all the taxis, too many to keep track of. He broke left at 59th Street, heading west.

Eva stared out the window, disheveled. She was trouble, the only evidence that he was ever in Queens. He wanted to help her. He thought he liked her. At the same time, she was extra weight he would just as well set down.

"So," he said casually. "Where to?"

It was a few seconds before his words broke through to her. She blinked and looked at him.

"Where to?" he repeated. "Where should I drop you?"

Eva adjusted in her seat, picking herself up by the armrest and resetting her weight to her left.

"I . . . I don't know," she said off to the side.

"Subway okay?" he offered.

"Subway . . . okay," she said, repeating the words as though to check if they were real. She pressed her head into the headrest, pulling her hair down with a long exhale.

"Which subway?" asked Izzy.

"Any."

"Any at all?"

"Yeah," she said.

"How's the N?"

"Good."

Izzy didn't want to go back to jail. Worst-case scenario was he'd get pulled over in the van, with Eva and that .45. Those three things linked him to Queens, and the sooner he separated himself from them the better.

"What did you say was on my hand again?" she asked, her voice shaky.

"Gun powder residue."

"For how long?"

Izzy was about to tell her a couple of days, then imagined her going to the police, and the story she had to tell. Likely she had enough details to unwittingly lead them back to Izzy—namely his name.

"You got a couple bucks for the train?" she asked in a low, shamed voice.

Izzy mindlessly reached in his pocket and brought out two singles, handing them over, thinking, *Wait.* It was dangerous to keep her, but maybe more so to let her go.

Eva stepped from the van with a good-bye nod, out into the yellow street light, where Izzy could see the blotted bloodstain on her blouse and hand. She might not even get home.

"Hold on, Eva, come back in here. Let's get you cleaned up first."

Eva paused and examined herself, holding the door, about to shut it.

"Sorry," she said. "I've had enough for tonight."

"Listen, you go back to Queens now and you'll be in the precinct by the end of the night. We'll get you a shower, okay? And figure out what's next."

"Can I just go home?"

"Your address is on your license, right? Likely there's already a uniform waiting for you."

Eva pondered, and for an instant appeared about to stomp her feet and cry. Then her stained hand adjusted from the outside of the door to the inside handle, guiding it shut as she sat back down. Izzy was glad. He really didn't want to go back to jail.

I had a wet pillow in prison.
I cried in the dark.
On the eighteenth floor of Bear Holliday Trading, Jacob mulled the lyrics of his new favorite mix tape song, trying to fit its rhythm and vibe into a new story. He tapped his silver pen, then stared at it, impressed with its shine, tapped it to the rhythm again, pausing when he heard another beat. A boss's wing tips approached with a swift creak, and Jacob gripped the neck of the pen, pretending to look busy.
Flashbacks of innocent kids.
Shot up in the park.
Imagine a dark jail cell, a man facedown on the top bunk bed, faded pictures of his family on the wall. He remembers a playground, kids twitching and fighting for their lives on the concrete. His kid. Praying for revenge, he counts the days until freedom, tears pooling in the prison pillow. No, not his kid. No pictures on the wall, no family. He's the shooter. High, out of his mind, creeping up on a rival, he doesn't see the kids until they're shot. It's too late, he drives off, never knowing if they survive. Now, in his cell, sober for days, he cries in the dark, among the desperate sounds echoing in the block.
Then what?
The idea of being a writer got Jacob through his finance internship. He wore a classic navy blue first suit every day and stiff black shoes without give. Poring over endless financial documents, he felt there had to be more to the English language. Not that he didn't like the suit—he noticed he had a new walk once he was wearing it, his power walk—arm swinging to the side in a light fist, hand flat against his stomach, angling his squared shoulders. He tried the walk in casual clothes and he looked gay. The suit was cool,

looking good with his shiny, silver Klaus-Cobert watch, which he bought mail order for $198, and looked like it cost at least a g. When he read magazines, he would save the ads for watches he liked, most of them Swiss and in the twenty-g range, and fold the paper up to use as bookmarks. He had to get paid. He wanted to be a writer, but he couldn't see himself pale and cooped up, unshaven and unshowered, writing day after day in torrents of unrecognizable brilliance. If he was going to be a writer, he would have to be a successful one.

This led him to his high school in the LES, where the sheen of popularity and success was ghetto chic. The guys who got the most respect, went to the best parties at the best clubs, popped bottles with models, always had their crispy sneaker in the door of some hip-hop scene. Not that that was Jacob. Jacob's mother would never let the boy in her life live so carefree.

Gail Glaser, a student of human behavior, and a natural overanalyzer, was all over Jacob.

Jacob would get home. "Hi, Ma."

"Oh," she would say. "I see."

Jacob's classmates came from either rich or hippie families, often both. The progressive parents insisted on independence at an early age, their kids calling them "Bill" and "Barbara"—mom and dad being too authoritarian. The rich kids had an umbrella of neglect to shade their lifestyles. Their parents, accustomed to spending money to eliminate inconvenience, would look the other way while their wealthy, entitled teens roamed the same scenes as up-and-coming hustlers, rappers, and bullshit artists. They all met with baggy pants and blunts, and Jacob wanted to be like them, walk with that swagger, talk to girls like he could take them or leave them, be up on what's hot.

More than anything, Jacob loved the music. He would

come home, still in his suit, and blast gangster rap, liberated. He always figured it gave him an edge at work. The most successful rappers, 50 Cent and Jay-Z, were also the most honest about their corporate CEO souls.

As a writer, he figured his loyalty was to write crime fiction, but to somehow merge the crusty old practice with a new, hip-hop protagonist. The same character who was embedded in the oversaturated music had to have a role somewhere in the oversaturation of PI novels. Right?

I had a wet pillow in prison.
I cried in the dark.
Flashbacks of innocent kids shot up in the park.
What next?

He decided to talk to his father, who never really knew he was alive. His father who had been to prison. His father who could tell him some stories, if he would return Jacob's phone calls.

After deceiving Jacob for most of his life, his mother recently confessed that his father was alive. The catalyst seemed to be the death of her mother, Grandma Glaser, who was at the top tier of guilt-provoking professionals. She grew even more effective after she passed. Grandma died, and Mom told Jacob, "Sweetie, your father's alive."

"Who?"

All Jacob knew was that he was dark skinned, since Jacob himself was far darker than anyone in his Sephardim family, and he died of lung cancer, which Jacob always suspected was his mother's invention to keep him away from cigarettes. Jacob met the man. They had coffee. His father seemed to defy everything he anticipated about someone uneducated, in and out of jail, and old enough to be his father.

First, the man was calm. He wasn't using the silverware as a mirror to watch over his shoulder or anything. Second, the youth in his face was chilling, like his café au lait skin was simply age resistant. Third, he was classy, moderately dressed, well spoken, with an almost slurred monotone that rumbled beneath Jacob's own spastic Manhattan speech.

He seemed ashamed when Jacob awkwardly called him "Dad." Any specifics about his life were notably unmentioned. He was shy. Jacob was more outgoing than ever. *My father's gangsta. Can you be authentic by blood?*

The telephone rang. "Yeah, Jacob."

"Jacob? It's Izzy."

Dad? "Hey!"

"I need a solid."

"Sure, what is it?"

Pause. "I need to use your shower."

Mal cautiously pulled his tattered taxi up along a string of Harlem row houses—just off Lenox on 118th, the block was one of Harlem's subdued nighttime pockets, shy of gentrification, with respectable, owner-occupied units. The nearby, round-the-clock traffic of fiends and hustlers avoided such strips. Mal got out of the car, pistol first, hyperalert, using his one good arm to open the car door and point. He checked every possible angle for Izzy's ambush. The quiet street wasn't helping his nerves any, as he reached back inside the taxi for the duffel bag, and slammed the door shut, echoing in the night. Swinging the gun over the railing, he pointed it down the stairwell leading to Doc Strange's Harlem OR.

No Izzy.

Mal rang the doorbell at the bottom of the stairs and waited for the buzz. The oversized door opened with a click and Mal crept through the darkness, pistol first. Beneath a tall hallway door was a thin line of light. He turned the knob, the light straining his eyes, trigger finger ready. Doc

*   *   *

Huna stared at the dancing ass but didn't notice it, stupefied by what Louon had just told him. His cousin's eyes swirled in his thick head and Huna knew the cocksucker was sincere. Louon nodded without a care.

"We worked all that shit out. I love Netta, I'm going to marry her."

"I don't believe my fuckin' ears."

"Huna, don't give me this shit, okay? I gotta run off and elope with the girl, then that's what I gotta do."

Huna shook his head, glancing over at the brothers. They were raising their drinks to toast, and Huna leaned in to pick up his, made eye contact, and touched glasses with each of them.

"I don't care if she's Muslim. I'm not religious and neither is she."

"She may not be Muslim, but she's had more in her than a fuckin' mosque."

"Hey!" said Louon like a sharp command, extending a stiff finger. "Not for nothing, Huna, you're my cousin, but that's my fiancée and I will take you outside and fight you."

Huna leaned in close to Louon's ear, unsure how much English Sandro really knew. "You know who these three are beside me? The same three that came to New York to put a hole in your fuckin' head three years ago."

Louon scanned the three men.

"So think before you do something stupid."

Benny's family was Muslim, and Huna's Catholic. Louon and Netta, Arben's cousin, had a thing. Louon proposed, she accepted. Then these three came from Montenegro to bury Lou. Fortunately, Louon soon found out that Netta was a whore and called it off.

This was why Huna was where he was. Instead of his

people hustling, thinking of new ways to get paid, it was this I love her and fuck you shit. Instead of a cash cow strip club like this one, he had a steak house. Instead of soldiers, he had fuckups addicted to Mega-Millions lotto.

Huna thought back to his father, the original enterprising Albanian who brought Huna up to build buildings. He beat the fuck out of Huna every other day of his life, and if he had to, he would have done it every day. The point was to be hard and never less. Huna didn't want to be what his father designated; he wanted to be his father. Huna didn't want to build things; he wanted to hustle, and never looked back. His father was a man of legend spoken of by wise guys he had never met, and those stories filled him more than the empty visions of skyscrapers. His father was dirt poor and worked as a busboy in a restaurant. Three made guys were abusing the owners, acting out, smacking waitresses, and never paying their tab. One night, the three guys were the only ones in there, coked up and crazy, making noise, and the restaurant manager didn't know what to do. So Huna's father removed his busboy vest, grabbed the gat he had seen behind the bar, set it down on the wise guys' table, and sat. With his few broken English words, he told them:

"With respect, I ask you to pay the bill, and leave."

He never put the busboy vest back on. Those men were capos in the Colombo Family, and Huna's father had found new employers, and eventually, partners. Huna had watched made men all his life, heard them speak and think. He knew about his father's half secrets, his crew of hookers and streetwalkers; the blow stash in his pinky ring, the ankle .22, the cigarette case full of tightly rolled marijuana cigarettes. He knew what he wanted to be before his father's mouth was shot off on Arthur Avenue.

Huna narrowed his eyes at Louon, thinking, *The chain's only as strong as the weakest link.*

* * *

There was heavy traffic on Central Park South. Horse-drawn carriages waited in a line, bulbous animals chewing and shitting with blinders on their eyes, indefinitely stalled. Tight-faced white women in beastly furs marched behind their suit-, hat-, and overcoat-clad husbands, masters of the city but seeming from some long bygone era. They passed ghetto shopping rats, talking on cell phones with tags dangling from their hats and boots, overextended by their crisp designer shopping bags. Tourists meandered, crisscrossing languages and filming everything. Just thinking about the property value made Izzy feel over his head. He had been standing in front of the building for about seven minutes. Would he get billed?

Izzy had thought that the third lane on the bridge was a bad idea. Seeing Jacob was worse. Being a stickup kid's father made that worthless pit in his stomach a chasm. Bona fide killers wanted him dead; he was bringing it to this sudden son of his. He was supposed to bail out his child, not the other way around. *Lowlife. Your kid is more of an adult than you.*

Izzy's earliest survival skill was shrugging off nagging voices, even stomach chasms. Being what he was, he had to be hard on command. So he stood tall, black jack boy outfit plaster stained beside Bear Holliday's immaculate glass tower.

Jacob came through the lobby, his tie undone, with a cigarette dangling from his mouth. He lit his smoke in a practiced pose, and saw Izzy.

"Hey." Jacob came to give Izzy a hug, and paused at the sight of his clothes. He then softly tossed the keys to Izzy. They shook hands. "Everything cool?"

It took Izzy time to recognize when he was nervous. He associated that anxious tremble with an inexplicable desire to smoke weed. He remembered the thin, pinky-length blunt of Sour Diesel he had in an otherwise empty pack of Marlboros, saving it for after the job was done. He had once been a regular smoker, and now enjoyed a smoke after accomplishing something, but it only beckoned to him when he was jittery. As he shook Jacob's lanky hand, recognizing his soft, dark features and full lips, he wanted to puff on something of quality, Northern Lights or better. "Yeah, everything is real cool," said Izzy, laid-back. "Just doing some construction."

Jacob nodded, and pursed his lips, saying, *You're full of shit.* Then he showed his upbeat, earnest smile, hiding a more analytical quality in his eyes. "Right. Need anything else? Money?"

Jacob didn't mean it as a blow. It still felt like one. "I'm good."

The kid raised one cigarette from his pack of Parliaments, and held it toward Izzy. Izzy paused, and then took it. Why the fuck not? Hadn't smoked a cigarette in over ten years, so tonight would be noteworthy in more ways than one. He felt the thin cardboard of the recessed filter against his tongue, and his body tingled with the old craving. Jacob lit it for him. The smoke filled his lungs, making way for more to come.

"So," Izzy began, awkward. "How's work?"

Jacob let out a long, tired exhale. "Kicking my ass," he said, trying to make his rapid staccato sound smoother, more like Izzy. "These old guys are fucking nuts. Every firm is different, right? Some are full of computer geeks who bitch if the radio is too loud. These guys? They have a refrigerator in the office full of exotic drugs. There's a keg in the coffee room. Look inside. That there's a bar in the lobby."

Izzy leaned in. Sure enough, through the ornate, marble molding frame of the lobby, in a room to the side, a bartender wiped glasses behind a working bar.

"How did you get this job anyway?"

"At a bar. Go figure, right? This guy was trying to talk to these girls, just making an ass of himself. The girls would give him just enough so he would keep on entertaining them. So I go up to him. Put my arm around him. I tell him, 'Listen, you want to get with those girls?' He nods, the guy is hammered. Red face, older guy, gray. 'Now, they can lead you on all night. You have to ask yourself, how far are you willing to go with this?' He looks at me, dumbstruck. 'Young man, that right there is the essence of trading.'"

Izzy laughed.

"I can't keep up. I work ten-hour days, then they make me go out with them, all night. Drinking aged scotch and eating onion cheeseburgers, challenging each other to arm-wrestle at chic clubs. Literally. I'm, like, it's four AM, you're over fifty, fer Christ's sake, your wife can't be that bad."

Izzy laughed some more. The kid was loosening him up. Then he coughed on the smoke.

"Not a smoker?" asked Jacob.

"Not for years. I used to smoke menthols. Things had teeth, man. Bite your lungs."

"I tried to smoke those. I'd walk around with a pack, impress all the black guys who'd bum off me. Now I got these Parliaments. They look at me like I'm a fag."

"High-maintenance beggars. They can buy their own smokes, then."

"Yeah."

"Not that you should be smoking," said Izzy, unsure how tongue-in-cheek he sounded.

Jacob tapped the ash out on the sidewalk, and tried to segue Izzy's pathetic fatherly attempt into a real one. "Really, though, I don't think finance is for me."

"Yeah? What would you rather do?" asked Izzy, glad to change the subject.

"Write, man," said Jacob, earnest.

Too earnest for Izzy. "Write?" he dubiously repeated.
"Like, novels."

"What kind of novels?"

Jacob paused. "Crime novels. I actually thought, maybe,
you could tell me some stories."

Izzy flicked the cigarette. He never green-lit this criminal
life conversation. He jingled the keys. "Thanks again for
the shower," he said, wondering if he had ever thanked him
a first time.

"No problem. I'll see you at home in a little bit," said
Jacob, sounding hopeful.

Izzy was just as hopeful that he and Eva would be long
gone by then. He wanted to tell Jacob he wouldn't be there,
but he couldn't be any more impolite, and he couldn't guar-
antee anything. He took Jacob's hand in a firm, broker
shake. "Yeah. See you."

"Hey," said Jacob as they released hands. He looked like
he wanted to say something else, and then covered his
mouth, glancing at the van behind Izzy.

Izzy nodded for him to speak, hoping he wouldn't ask a
private question about what he was up to.

Jacob smirked, uncomfortable. "Where'd you meet your
friend in the van?"

"What?" asked Izzy.

"Take my advice. Don't keep her waiting."

Eva wondered why on earth Izzy was talking to Gail's
son.

It would have bothered her if she hadn't been so busy
playing with her hair. It was an old coping mechanism for
when her mind shut down. It had been a while. She knew it
was an unproductive tic, using just enough nervous energy
to make her feel active, but she couldn't help herself. She
was thinking in circles; emotionally mired. She used to get
that way in Trinidad to deal with her manic household, but

back then she would pull her hair clean out. Father cheating, mother cheating, father in the house acting like everyone betrayed him. At nine years old she would pluck out her hair, and her father thought it was a silent protest. It got him crazy, and he hit her for it. But he couldn't stop her. She would then pull it out by the fistful. She had to do it. She had bad thoughts, and she wanted them out. Like now, spreading out her long, straight hair, rolling follicles between her thumb and forefinger. She wanted them out.

Izzy rejoined the somber van, seeing Eva with her straight black hair in front of her eyes, picking at it. He put the car in gear and backed up, throwing her head for a moment, without disturbing her long gaze. As he drove, sitting alongside Eva's distempered quiet, Izzy wished he was back joking with Jacob.

"Can you think of anyone you could stay with who the police would have no way of knowing about?" he asked.

Eva stared hard at her hair. "I have an old boyfriend I never speak to."

"He'll be one of the first."

"I have an aunt."

"Family is too obvious."

Eva shrugged. "Who were you just talking to?" she asked, monotone.

"My son," said Izzy, reluctant.

"Your son?" Eva looked back, as if she could still see him. "How old were you? Twelve?"

Izzy maintained focus on the road, hoping he wouldn't have to talk about it. Eva's glare, however, had forgotten her hair, and found Izzy.

"Well?" she demanded.

"Seventeen. Sixteen, maybe."

"Maybe?"

"Jacob's mother never told me about Jacob. Jacob told me about Jacob. Recently."

Eva raised an eyebrow. "Absentee father? He's not mad?"
Izzy shrugged. "I didn't know."
"And he believes you?"
"He doesn't have to. He knows his mother."
Eva laughed. "Yeah. So do I."

Chapter 6

Gail shut the front door to her apartment behind her, still tempering the competing surges of excitement and concern. She went straight back to her bedroom, dropping her keys on the dresser, to avoid forgetting which purse she'd left them in. Her downtown group had gone great that day—she had been talking about it all through dinner with Charlotte. But before she could really relax, she had to make sure of one thing.

Getting out of her overcoat, she reached for her bedside cordless phone, pressing 1 on her speed dial. It rang for a while, and a hushed voice answered.

"Ma, I'm still at work," said Jacob.

"Oh, sorry, sweetie. One quick question, what does it mean to 'get crunk'?"

"Excuse me?"

"You know my group at the school?"

"The young ghetto girls."

"Yeah. We had a great group today, and these girls speak so much slang I can't keep up. They started singing and dancing, it was great. But then one girl was saying, 'Let's get crunk. Crunked up,' and I got worried. Is crunk a drug?"

Jacob paused. "You're thinking of crank," he told her.

"Oh."

"Crunk is southern slang for a kind of music. Let's get crunk is like, let's party."

"Oh, great, that's a relief. What's crank, then?"

"Not sure. Some hard, nasty offshoot concoction your ten-year-olds have no business messing with."

"We had such a good group today, Jacob—"

"Ma," he interrupted.

"Yes?"

"I'm at work, I gotta go."

"Oh, right."

"I'll call you later. And, Ma, could you send me that mail?"

"Sure thing."

She hung up the phone and lightly pumped her fist, knowing she could now relax.

That day was a long one. First session was with her broker, then her Garment District Jew, or Garmento, as she referred to him in her mind. They both had the same problem: wealthy men who couldn't control or communicate with the princesses they were involved with. Everything else about them was different. The broker was classy; refined suits, subtle watch, practical, elegant shoes; articulate, thoughtful, nasal, and weak-willed. Garmento, even wealthier, strolled in as if it were the Jewish O.K. Corral, bow-legged to make room for his big balls; gaudy, with flashy suits and bright ties, a heavy diamond on his pinky and another in his ear. It amazed her how little class had to do with money.

Then Gail went downtown, to her group at the school for underadvantaged kids. Since she earned her PhD, she was able to run programs like that one. Not many psychotherapists with her status bothered with such a population, but the disadvantaged always interested her. Gail was motivated by research she read on the rhesus monkeys. These monkeys typically lived up to twenty-six years, and greatly resembled humans in their organized society. A long-term study showed that ten percent of the monkeys were complete fuckups. They got out of line, became alcoholics (when exposed by the study), were horrible, irresponsible mothers and often got beaten up or killed by the matriarchs. First, the study classified the different mothers from fuckup to the extraordinary. Then they took the fuckups' offspring and gave them to the extraordinary mothers. The mothers were tolerant beyond expectation, accepting of any behavior, and the offspring of the fuckups grew into outstanding pillars of the community. They were loving, cunning, sharp, and dominant, and they did not care for alcohol at all.

Inspired, Gail wanted to work with the offspring of human fuckups. Maybe they too could overcome their origins, harness their strengths, and make better lives for themselves. When Gail met her group she realized she was facing an uphill road. The ten-year-old girls were at war with each other. Two groups, not yet old enough to be considered gangs, plotted and conspired and fought against each other every day. On one side was the matriarch, Egypt, a gorgeous little black girl with hair piled on top of her head, riffing instigations in aggressive street slang. Her right hand was Belgica, a tiny Puerto Rican girl who beat up all the big-boned bovine girls when Egypt told her to. In the beginning, to maintain order, Gail's first ground rule was that no one could talk to each other. If they wanted to address another girl, they had to go through Gail. Egypt, as close as anything Gail had known to evil, was livid. They had to speak to Gail, so Egypt spat rancid insults from her juvenile-lockup-headed sneer. "You disgusting old witch." Or "What did you do to *that hair*, stupid?"

Gail took the insults with tolerance, like the patient rhesus monkey mothers, thinking how much harder it must be with your own children. Gradually, Gail allowed them to talk to each other, only no hitting, attacking, or cursing.

Egypt was unreachable, constantly inciting Belgica's minia-
ture fists of fury. Then one session, Egypt was gone. There
was peace, and the same big girls who still retained bruises
from Belgica's knuckles were nice to her. They knew the
source of all their misfortune was Egypt, and they tried to
get the ferocious yet slow-witted Belgica to see it too. "I
hate her. She's a b—bad person. Why do you like her?"

Gail interceded. "Don't talk bad about Egypt to Belgica,"
she told them. "You are putting her in a very difficult position."

The group got it. They loosened up and sang and danced,
stomping their feet and snapping their arms in wild, graceful spasms. Even the big girls were limber and joyful, losing
their stiff heaviness.

The next session was that afternoon. Egypt was back.
The girls returned to their sullen, divided circle, kinetic with
tension. The big girls picked at the rug, composing how
they would defend themselves.

Egypt made an announcement. "I'm leaving the group,"
she said. Gail knew but the girls were surprised. A mix of
relief and apprehension washed around the circle. Egypt
continued. "I hate you," she told the big girls. "I hate you,"
she told the others. "I hate you," she told Gail. "I'm not
going to miss any of you."

Gail showed tolerance. "You can hate me, you may not
miss me, but I am going to miss you."

The girls were quietly shocked. Gail wasn't lying. Not
quite anyway. All right, it was a white lie.

"Just because you hate us doesn't mean we have to feel
the same way about you."

Egypt had no answer. The group went on, eager to begin
its less divided future. They sang, danced, and got "crunk."
When time was up, they slowly filed out and Egypt made
sure she was the last one in the room.

She looked up at Gail, her face relaxed and even prettier.

"I love you," she said, and scurried out.

Gail stood there alone. So what if it was likely a sign of a burgeoning split personality disorder? Gail welled up and a tear slid down her face anyway.

"So you . . . and Gail?" asked Eva, incredulous.

Izzy nodded.

"You're going to have to explain that to me."

Izzy shook his head, squinting in the glare of passing headlights.

"It was a long time ago," he said.

"You say that like it's an explanation."

"And you sound like an ADA. 'Your Honor, please instruct the witness to answer . . .'"

"Fine," she said. "It's just a big coincidence."

"It's not a *big* coincidence."

"Whatever, I've been seeing the woman for eight years, and I just run into you out of the blue. I mean, how did you even meet her?"

"Eight years?" Izzy repeated.

They both watched the streets for a while, Eva slowly shaking her head.

Mal enjoyed the mild euphoria from the drugs, knowing it wouldn't last. His arm in a proper sling now, his duffel bag and a shovel from Doc Strange over his good shoulder, he left the corner bodega with two packs of Twinkies and two bottles of Gatorade. His fingers tingled with a pleasant vibration. He was together. He had his swagger back. He had *bank*. Look how he'd flipped shit—lost a partner, gained his half of the paper. He was a hustler for real. Fuck together, he was fucking fantastic. He heard the beat and walked to it.

"*You know I'm not no fronta. I don't talk shit, I just flip it on ya!*" he recited to himself.

He went to the trunk of the car, humming the ghoulish tune, and he opened it.

The taxi driver inside let off a Spanish barrage. *"Cono, puta maricon—"*

Mal tossed in one pack of Twinkies, one bottle of Gatorade, and slammed the trunk. *See, your man Mal's not even all bad.*

The tune was in his head and he walked to it with a ditty-bop. His shoulders swayed in rhythm, heels gliding across the concrete, popping his neck when he reached the car door.

He chomped on a Twinkie, remembering sharing Twinkies with Izzy on stakeouts. Honey Buns. Two-for-a-dollar chocolate chip cookies. Drinking bullshit like Boons or King Cobra. Wilding out, rehearsing, talking old boxing, old Knicks, old cons, bitches, snitches. Playing "How gangster is he?" Coming up with different criteria for rating people. "If he was training and fighting pit bulls, and his dog lost, would he shoot it? Okay, now, what if he was managing people?" Or sex routines. "Does he ever have one-on-one sex with women? Or only whores? Or strictly gang bangs?" Huna, for example, fell in with the latter.

Izzy and Mal had a lot in common. Most thugs seemed comical to them. They didn't care much for frills or flash. They kept to themselves, for the most part. But he was as good as anybody to pass the time with.

We got rules. Got to murk that fool.

He put the tune to his words and licked the cream from his lip.

Murk . . . that . . . fool. . . .

He started the engine.

Mal drove uptown on the West Side Highway, alongside the long, brown Henry Hudson River, and beneath the winding ramp leading to the George Washington Bridge. A desolate street ran from the highway to Washington Heights, past dilapidated residences. Beside that street, and just out of range of the echoing jumble of hip-hop, merengue, and reggaeton, was a flat bed of grass. Mal had filed it in his mental Rolodex long ago as a perfect hiding spot, exactly what he needed. Too late for a safe deposit box. Izzy knew about everyplace else.

He pulled the cab over and quickly got out. Too quickly. The drugs, a vibrating blessing just a few minutes ago, now stole his balance. Mal swayed, held a long blink, and caught himself on the roof of the taxi. *You're close, motherfucker, real close,* he told himself. *Take a couple breaths. Deep ones. Walk over there and dig a hole.*

He took two breaths. Deep ones. Then he folded his arms on the roof of the cab and dropped his head between them.

Izzy opened the door to Jacob's tiny Morningside Heights one-bedroom apartment, seeing the transition from college student to ambivalent trader. Columbia University BA diploma framed beside a pile of hip-hop CDs, jazz posters, unread issues of *Barron's*, the *Wall Street Journal*, *Vibe* magazine, nice ties haphazardly lying on the couch. The wood floors had thick, gaping spaces between the slats, baseboards showed the wear of generations of student tenants, and the furniture didn't even pretend to match. Eva eyed the bathroom and went to it.

She turned and informed Izzy, "I'm getting in here."

She closed the door and sighed with relief. Finally alone. She turned the knob up hot, and steam filled the small, cracked, mildewed bathroom. The tub, with a rust ring around it, looked as though it had never been cleaned. It was a rare day that Eva didn't care. She got in, the heat relaxing her muscles as she watched the water, soap, and blood swirl down the drain.

*   *   *

A little excited, Izzy turned on the game. It was just the fourth inning. Both pitchers had been tested, both worked out of trouble. Pedro had thrown forty-seven pitches for the Mets. Leiter, the more stubborn pitcher, had thrown almost sixty. Bernie Williams popped out and the score was still nothing-nothing. Izzy was grinning as he watched, and the rhythm and sounds of baseball filled the room. The unhurried announcers. The *swap* of the ball into leather gloves, the wood crack of a solid hit. It was the comfort food of Izzy's daily routine, the nonviolent familiar. He wondered what kind of baseball player he would have made; he had never played a day in his life.

Izzy lay on the floor. He stretched his back out against the carpet and put his hands on his head, thinking. Mal could keep the money. It was a small price to get the prick out of his life. Izzy would call him, tell him keep it, all for you. *Just bounce. Be out of the tri-state. 'Cause I'll shoot you on sight. No questions, no convo. Just bang, bang.*

It wasn't a bad plan, if not for the Albanians. Clanlike fuckers with a severe notion of family. Mal was a secondary problem. Once it got to Huna that Arben was dead, at least a couple of heads would have to roll. Izzy could imagine that pale whack-job hearing the news, his big face tensing up, getting red without him knowing it, saying Albanian curses mixed in with "cocksucker" every few words. Mal might go to Huna first, try to blame Izzy. That was just as well. A nigger was a nigger to Huna. He'd pop Mal just as soon as roll with him.

He couldn't believe that Gail was Eva's shrink. Gail was so many years ago, and as much as he had forgotten her, she was indirectly back once again. First Jacob, now this. People say first loves never die, but Izzy always thought that was bull. He wasn't even really messing with Eva's head in

the car when he avoided talking about how they met. He
recalled Gail well, but the specifics of meeting her at one of
the few Harlem outreach programs he darted in and out of
escaped him. The more immediate, visceral experiences that
filled his memory made Gail feel more like a movie he'd
seen. Yet when he met Eva, the coy and analytic way she listened, their rapport felt familiar.

He thought of Eva in the shower, no longer regretting
saving her, but still not knowing what to say to her. Her
haughty, semihostility was amusing back at the bar, but
now it felt antagonizing. He wasn't sure if Gail was the
same, but she probably was; intelligent women want men to
know it; they are challenging and witty and ask questions.
With Izzy, such relationships went from good to bad in a
blink, as that same aggressive prodding that opened him up
could, in the wrong tone, close him down completely.

Eva was so easy to talk to back at that bar, though. Sweet
thing, with that healthy smile and slanted eyes, thick lips,
and Indian hair; all Izzy could think about was taking her
home and playing corny eighties love songs. Prince, he had
wanted to hear "I Would Die for You" since he met her. It
was only that evening, Jesus, it felt like a week ago. What
had he said to her? The aquarium, then the shellfish. She
said there was something wrong with him for that. But she
wanted to go. Maybe to see if the aquarium would make
her want shellfish too.

Then Jacob, that still made Izzy cringe. Practical thinking
figured Jacob's apartment to be the perfect spot to lie low.
The determining factor was simple: Mal knew nothing
about Jacob. Not his mother, not his existence, nothing. So
the choice was made, regardless of the consequences. Lying
on Jacob's floor, under a mounted Miles Davis poster, his
black skeletal hand holding a single *shhh* index finger to his
black lips, Izzy understood what bugged him so much. Izzy

used to bail out his mother and her habit, before he understood what her habit was. Now Jacob was bailing Izzy out.
Why did his family seem to get younger as they grew older?

As Izzy's mother's habit worsened, her suppliers became
close. By the time her money had run out, a dealer named
Knuckles was using her spot as a base of operations. He
was a lanky, cruel hustler with dull gold teeth and dark,
cracked skin that reminded Izzy of raisins as a kid. She
could pay the rent, but the thugs terrified Izzy. As far as
those characters go, they weren't so bad, Izzy knew that
now, but back then they scared him. They called him "Cool
Breeze" and gave him money if in a good mood, but he always anticipated watching his mother smacked, tooled,
prodded, injected. If he said anything they didn't like, then
he would get smacked, and what they didn't like was arbi-
trary, so he never spoke. His mother never hit him, so
Knuckles's hard smack was brand-new, now a physical
memory—his young skin swelling with shame. His mother
would make him read and study, the only times he could be
home without holding his breath.

For her birthday one year, he had run off with a sleeping
homeless man's shopping cart full of cans off Eighth, turned
them in, and bought her a gold bracelet from Chinatown. It
turned green after about six months, but that day he felt
like a man. Maybe that was the problem. If you're too self-
sufficient too young, you stop growing. Maybe feeling like a
man on that day robbed him of needing to feel like a man
later on. Here he was, thirty years later, still stealing veritable cans from veritable junkies.

Using the shovel as a cane, Mal made his way to the
grass. He tapped the ground with the metal head, searching
for a soft spot. With his one good hand, he raised the shovel
and struck the dirt, leaned all his weight into it, then
searched for the strength to lift it back up. Motherfucker

was hard as hell. And Mal had nothing. His foot found the wedge along the head and he tried to push it farther down instead. He stomped a few times. The thing wouldn't budge. *Fuck it,* he thought, deciding on his usual recourse.

He ambled to the taxi and took the bloody shirt from the front seat. He went back to the trunk, quickly opened it, tossed the shirt inside, and closed it.

"*Cabron,* fucking *puta*!" the Dominican yelled, muffled from inside the trunk.

Mal drew his .22. "Listen! Tie that shirt around your head, you hear me? So you can't see a goddamn thing. I'm going to open this trunk in five seconds. If I so much as see an eyelash, this trunk'll be your coffin. Comprende? Four . . . three . . . two . . ."

Mal opened the trunk, holding the gun on the body inside. The driver was well blindfolded, with blood from the shirt on his face.

"*Cono, puta pendejo diablo.*"

"Shut that mida, mida bullshit."

As the driver sat up, Mal took him by the arm, guiding him from the trunk and over to the shovel, standing upright in the dirt. Mal put the driver's hand on the worn wood handle. "Now dig, nigga."

The driver stood for a moment, confused. Mal pressed the gun against his head to clarify. "Dig."

He dug.

Confident the Dumb-inican was doing his job, Mal backed away and lowered the gun. He sat down in the driver's seat with the door open, and exhaled with relief. The gun in his lap, he leaned up against the headrest, eyes drifting shut.

Felipe only drove a taxi because he hurt his back and couldn't bartend anymore. Driving all day hurt his back too, but not as much as bending and twisting to grab bottles and glasses. All he did as a bartender was drink anyway. He would get shit-faced *borracco*, go to his friend the Negrito's spot on 158th, and do coke until morning, then crash at his girlfriend's, because his wife wouldn't let him sleep if he came home like that. He'd seen enough guns, between DR and *El Casa de Negrito,* to know not to panic when one was in front of him, and he'd known enough lowlifes to know when one was crazy enough to shoot him.

Sweat filled his beady hair and trickled down his forehead, creeping inside his bloody blindfold. With his forearm, he wiped the sweat away, and slightly raised the shirt from his eyes, just enough so he could see the grass, and highway road, and support pillars for what he knew was the entrance ramp to the George Washington Bridge.

In the top of the fifth inning, Cliff Floyd stroked a 0–2-breaking ball clean into the black seats in dead center Yankee Stadium. Izzy liked Floyd, a perpetual underachiever with huge talent. His towering, muscular frame strutted around the bases, and the score was 1–0, Mets. Izzy was happy.

In Jacob's dresser, Izzy found a V-neck undershirt and a pair of baggy straight-leg jeans that fit. In a lower drawer was a pair of baby-blue cotton sweatpants that had to be for a female. Eva came up behind him, smelling clean, with a towel wrapped around her body. Izzy held up the sweats. "I think you're in luck." She took them, as Izzy rummaged through the drawer some more, and found a tiny white tank top. "I think Jacob's getting lucky too," he muttered.

She made sure Izzy caught her expectant look.

"Oh," he realized, tossing the tank top on the bed. "Right," he said and left the room.

Eva waited a moment before taking the towel off. There was a short, black Ikea bookshelf with cold, trumped-up titles like *Hard Boiled, City Primeval*, and *Hell to Pay.* Then on another shelf were equally trumped-up titles like *Infec-*

tious Greed, Liar's Poker, and *Blood on the Street*. She had a feeling she would find no body lotion whatsoever.

Wait, was that . . . ? It was. Palmer's Cocoa Butter Cream, in a tube. She tried not to think about why it was beside the bed.

Being alone was nice. It was more like normal than being around a stranger. Still, she felt one step away from chaos, as though the room were so fragile it would crumble if she breathed wrong. She sat on the bed and let the damp towel fall. She wasn't breathing. She squeezed her fists, told herself to trust, and let out a full breath. The room was still there, and she half smiled.

It had been a while since she had thought about her father, and the recollection bothered her. Eva liked to think her mind was clean of him. The last time she thought of the man was when he, through her aunt Carol, had invited Eva to his third wedding. Eva proudly refused. Tonight she felt back in Arima, the small village she was raised in. Her father's nasty moods passing through the back rooms, hoping he wasn't heading for her. Having to tiptoe around the tenuous peace, afraid speaking or breathing might spark rage. Eva unraveled the tight bun she had her hair in for the shower, and began straightening it, combing her shaking fingers through. She wanted to go out into the yard with the chickens to get away, drink peanut juice, play with the flying cockroaches that would swarm after the rain, plucking off their long wings. She looked again at the hair in her fingers, wondering if plucking it would be as easy as when she was nine.

Eva dragged her dry fingers across her dry palm and thought about the bodies. That day was a blizzard of corpses, seemingly more unreal than a dead body already was. First her client, blue and stiff with rigor, on her neck a choker of bruises. Then Theresa, glazed as always but now with tiny pupils looking past Eva, mouth caked with dried puke but still with that half smirk, as though amused at her ability to complicate Eva's life, even through death. The other bodies were too many and too fast for Eva to recall, except for that bullet track she had stared into, a reminder of the earthly stuff minds are made of. The two women, Theresa and her client, were stuck in her head. She wrapped her arms around her body and felt the dry skin behind her armpits. Her client's boyfriend couldn't remember killing her, couldn't explain how his prints were on her crushed windpipe. Eva was revolted by that reaction, and now her cousin's death was much like her client's: final moments gone with the dead and forgotten by their killers. Her own words to Gail rang in her head, *I'd have to kill her*, and she wondered if her client's boyfriend had been heard making similar threats.

Shuddering, she let go of herself and went for the moisturizer, sitting down on the bed and rubbing it in, first her legs, then up to her neck. With the cream, her skin came to life, as though breathing on its own. She put her nose to her shoulder and inhaled the smell of a delicious pastry. The sweats and the tank top actually fit. As she looked at herself in the mirror, she heard a knock.

"Already?" she said.

Izzy came in, a towel around his waist. He was a well-built guy, without an ounce of body fat on his mostly unblemished skin. She thought of the excess just above her hips and sneered, jealous.

"Listen," he said in that calm slur, managing to pronounce every syllable, "I got about forty bucks. What do you say I put some clothes on, and we go get some food?"

Eva smiled involuntarily at the thought. She hadn't realized she was starving. "Pancakes?"

They were inside New York's most famous exterior, Tom's Restaurant having graced every episode of *Seinfeld*. The inside looked nothing like the show's Left Coast set, run by dark, coarse Greeks with hair in their ears. Attractive, single middle-class women in canary-yellow fifties uniforms were nowhere in sight.

Izzy had bacon, four eggs, and hash browns. Eva had blueberry pancakes. She poured the syrup on with a happy anticipation that startled her. It was like when her uncle would take her out, just her and her uncle, and not tell her painfully high-maintenance cousin or aunt. He would always get her some treat, cookies and cream, or yogurt-covered raisins, just between them. It gave her such a warm feeling, and as she cut the pancakes with the side of her fork, she quickly felt ashamed and chased the pleasant thought away. *All this chaos, and you're grinning about Uncle Richard?*

Then she took a bite of the pancakes, the squishy, sweet dough and blueberry bursting in her mouth. *Fuck it*, she thought. *If it feels good, then feel good. You've earned it today.*

She looked up at Izzy, almost wanting to share the memory with him. He looked weary, as though talking to her were like approaching a minefield. She knew that look, and wondered who was high maintenance these days.

She smiled. He smiled back.

"One thing's for sure," he began. "That plasma TV won't give you no more problems."

She laughed, thinking of the gaping gunshot wound suffered by the television back in Queens. "That was my first laugh in a while."

He shook his head. "Damn it, when I saw you there, man. I just couldn't fucking believe it," he said, sounding odd in a voice that conveyed an inability to be surprised. "I was just shocked. Shocked."

"Yeah," she said, not wanting to think about it. She was enjoying her time away.

"Honestly, I froze. I've never froze before," he said, not seeming upset about it. Eva believed him.

"So, what do you think happened back there?" she asked.

"You mean, with your cousin?"

She nodded.

"I was going to ask you. I mean, they called you, right? Told you to come over and get her?"

"Yeah. They gave me something to drink."

"A drink? What, you wanted to party with them?"

"I was just stressed, okay? The only way I can take being around those people is if I'm working, or drinking," she explained.

"'Those people,'" repeated Izzy.

"Anyway, I took a sip, got real dizzy. I saw a knife. Next thing I know, I'm on top of my damn cousin, and she's not breathing," she said quickly, and blinked several times, as if to put things in focus.

Izzy thought until he finished chewing. "Your cousin was sick. They called you. Before you show up, she ODs," he said, doing his best to make it sound plausible. "Scared of a murder charge, they drug you. And set you up." He shrugged, like it was simple.

Eva squirmed. "How does that sound to you?"

"It's a bit extra. But you know you didn't stab her. I guess those guys were just that stupid."

"I guess. But I blacked out. I mean, who knows what they gave me?"

"You thinking, maybe you really lost it?"

"No. Definitely not."

Izzy raised his brow. "You sure?"

She flashed back to childhood, how she tortured those flying cockroaches, pulling off one wing at a time. The good wing would flap, sending the fragile back skeleton around in circles. Eva could be cruel. Her mother used to tell her so. And she had wanted to be cruel to Theresa for so long.

Eva poked a blueberry with her knife, watching the jelly

bleed into the fluffy pancake. She felt queasy. "You shot at your partner," she stated.

"Yeah, he was about to pop me. That'd have done him too, if you didn't start blastin' off like a damn cowgirl."

"How do you know?" she asked, coy.

"I know."

"Um-hmm, you're a professional."

Izzy dropped his fork and gave Eva a sober look. "It's a bit late for us to bullshit, don't you think?"

"All right, then, no bullshit. What if he was turning to shoot me? What would you have done?"

Izzy picked up his fork and went back to business with his bacon, looking at her like, *Don't ask.*

She asked anyway. "Would you have shot him?"

"I can't answer that. He was gunning for me."

"Are you sure?"

Izzy scooped up the last bits of egg and ketchup with his toast, not bothering to finish chewing. "You were unconscious. Are you sure?"

Mal snapped out of a daze to see his Dominican blindly digging. The hole was deep enough for the bag, maybe four feet. "That's good," he told the taxi driver, who dropped the shovel on the grass and stood in place. Mal walked up beside him with the duffel bag and dropped it in the dirt hole. "Now dig it back."

The round Dominican felt about the air, touching nothing. "Señor, how can I do this if I cannot see?"

He had a point. "Fine. I'll do it. Get back in the trunk."

"Okay," he said, and just stood there, facing dead ahead. "Again, señor, how can I . . ."

"Shut the fuck up," Mal cut him off, and grabbed him by the arm, leading him back to the trunk. Once he was safe inside, Mal, with his good arm, filled the hole back up himself.

Chapter 7

Sandro, Sergay, and Samic Rukaj all anticipated Arben's initiation so eagerly they barely gave two shits about Louon or the dancing hookers.

Huna sat with his arms folded, without expression, as a stripper dry-humped his giant thigh. Her sweaty body and balloon breasts quivered and gyrated like she was in the throes of passion. Huna checked on the brothers to make sure their drinks were full.

Also stone-faced, they nodded back to him from a sofa beside his, raising their glasses in another toast. They loved toasts. Huna grabbed his own glass and raised it back, sure to hold eye contact with each of them as they touched glasses, so as not to disrespect them. To toast without eye contact would be an insult.

Huna sipped his drink and sat back as he remembered his own initiation, all those years ago. He followed his connection, a big, hairy Alban named Anton, into a tiny room with the lights out, and felt the squish of plastic beneath his feet and the hot, cluttered smell of men close by. The lights came on and he was looking at four Albanians, all holding guns to his head.

"You're a rat!" they said in Albanian. "You sold us out!"

"No, never!" said Huna.

"Liar!" they said.

"Fuck you. Fuck you and your mother!" said Huna. In Albanian, this was the single worst insult possible.

They cocked back their hammers, drew back their slides. And laughed. They lowered their guns, and laughed and laughed, and Huna laughed too.

Now it was Arben's turn. As soon as he got back from that ghetto bullshit, jumping out of vans with niggers, and this stripper stopped boring Huna. He wondered, when the four of them pulled out on Arben, would he say "Fuck you and your mother" to his own brothers?

That was when Mal came in—slinky little cocksucker looking around the room with his crooked face. He spotted Huna and came over.

"Why are you here?" asked Huna.

Mal sat beside him, unwittingly distracted by the stripper on Huna's lap. "I got bad news," said Mal, his eyes on the girl.

"What?" Huna rumbled gravely.

"It was Izzy."

"What?" Huna repeated, the same as before.

"Izzy let Arben get shot. He's dead."

A quiet, disbelieving rage burned in Huna's eyes as he stared at Mal. The song ended. The stripper stopped dancing.

"You want me to stawp?" she asked in heavy Staten Island–speak.

Huna's eyes didn't leave Mal. "What?"

"It was Izzy, he went for the money."

"You dumb cocksucker monkey motherfuckers!" Huna growled through clenched teeth.

The stripper had not caught on to what was happening. "Twenty a song. You want me to keep going, sweetie?" She was either tough or very dumb.

"Get the fuck off me, bitch," Huna said like an after-thought.

She got off his lap and took a step back.

"Dead?" Huna said.

"That's twenty, then," she said, her glittery face pissed off, holding out her hand.

"No, bitch, you move like a dry fish," he told her, and pinned his eyes on Mal. "Are you fucking lying to me?"

Mal knew this was an important moment. He had to get Huna to believe, if only for a short while, that this was all Izzy's fault. Mal wasn't looking for a friend. He knew Huna would try to kill him just for being there when Arben was shot. But if Huna wanted Izzy worse, he'd use Mal to get him. Then maybe Izzy and Huna could take care of each other.

Mal returned Huna's eye contact with a solid look, and held it there as long as Huna wanted to. He knew those Albanians were funny about eye contact. As if only a liar would look away or blink, and only an honest man could actually look in your eyes. When he felt the time was right, maintaining the contact, Mal slowly shook his head.

"I'm gonna break that kyke-nigger in half!" Huna declared.

Mal knew he had succeeded as an unfortunate black bouncer approached Huna, leading that pissed-off, bleached-haired, tanning-booth stripper.

"I think you better pay the lady," said the bouncer, defined pectorals twitching in his tight Armani red tee.

Mal scooted away a bit, preparing for a show. Bless this nigga for stepping in front of this grenade after Mal had only just pulled the pin.

"What," cracked Huna, pointing at the bouncer, head cocked to the side, "I don't have a hard-on, so now this faggot gotta act like one?"

The bouncer was stunned, trying to maintain his tough exterior, while glancing to Mal as if for an explanation. Mal shrugged. *You on your own, nigga.*

The bouncer lunged to grab Huna, who grabbed the man's chiseled arm as soon as it was in reach and pulled him down into his sweeping fist. The bouncer's meaty back hit the floor as fast as Huna's fist had hit his head. The whole club shook. Dancing stopped. Necks turned. The other bouncers—Mal counted five—began speaking into headsets and moving toward Huna like a military unit.

Then about two-thirds of the men in the club stood up, moved in front of the bouncers, and squared off. Nothing at all happened for a moment, just a lot of staring and calculating. The strippers looked on like they wanted to cover themselves up, actually seeming naked. The bouncers were quickly and badly outnumbered.

The three nasty-looking Albanians next to Mal decided to take advantage of the downtime. One of them had a gram bag of coke, and ripped a few bumps up his nose with a key. The others joined him, apparently confident now the bouncers wouldn't mind. Huna rose, spat a green slug on the unconscious, muscular lump in red on the floor, and began out the door. Mal followed.

Izzy and Eva strolled the peaceful, privileged college streets of Morningside Heights. They passed bookstores and restaurants, students eating and chatting. To Izzy, their futures seamed so bright. They were in programs that led to more programs that enabled them to do better things. Their lives had definite, upward-moving phases, while Izzy meandered sideways.

Eva was awkward in her baby-blue sweatpants and stiletto work heels, but she pulled it off. The streets were so tranquil; it was difficult for Izzy to reconcile his hypervigilance with the neighborhood's lazy sanctuary. Eva was having a similar problem.

"Somehow, people look different to me," she said.

"Like how?"

"Half of 'em, I expect to pull a gun or something. Like, that's something that seems to happen now, in my life."

Izzy smiled. "And the others?"

"They seem petty. And I'm a social worker, I deal with people in dire situations all the time. Middle-class concerns have always seemed petty to me, unless, of course, they were mine. But now? Shit."

"New league?"

"Like Payless to Jimmy Choo."

On the corner of 12th Avenue, Albanians filed out of Privilege's glass hotel doors. The red carpet in front had been pushed off center, and the rope poles had all been knocked over, heavy round bases rolling on the sidewalk. Maybe nine Albanians stood outside the club, each processing the news of Arben's death differently. Most smoked cigarettes, shaking their heads with their hands in their pockets, muttering to one another in disbelief. They formed a quiet barricade around the three brothers, whose tirade sucked the violence out of the rest. One in a black and red Adidas track suit put a dent in a mailbox. Another in a light blue paisley collared shirt was weeping. Another in a cream sport jacket pulled his gat on Mal.

"Ho, easy—don't kill the messenger," said Mal, sidestepping toward Huna. He was regretting this visit. Huna was a logical enough guy to predict within reason. These other guys were another story. White nigga with a trey-eight on 12th Avenue.

Huna spoke to the man in Albanian, whose pained eyes sank with despair. He lowered the gun and stared at Mal. Then spat at his feet.

"Nasty fuck," replied Mal.

Huna shoved Mal back against a building. Mal hit the wall hard, losing his breath, outweighed by close to a hundred pounds.

"These are Arben's brothers, you understand? *Straight* from Montenegro. If I tell them you were even there, they will gut you. Understand? Dangerous fucking men. Help them find Izzy. And watch it," Huna said, patting Mal's stomach. "They might take yours on the way."

Huna turned and spoke to the brothers in Albanian as Mal rolled his eyes. These East Europeans thought they were the hardest fuckers on earth. He remembered Arben's stories, how they grew up on a mountainside hunting deer with nothing more than a knife and a loincloth or whatever. Came down to civilization like he-men and murdered cock-suckers until they were running shit. Like how Huna said *straight* from Montenegro, as if that made them bulletproof or something. Please.

Huna turned to Mal with sweat on his forehead and a sneer. "You know where to find him?"

"Not exactly," said Mal. "But I can. I know he got a soft spot for females."

"Fine. These men are going with you. Watch them. They don't speak English. And they don't understand that guns are illegal."

It was the top of the fifth. Pedro had walked A-Rod and now Sheffield was up, whipping his bat back and forth like it was made of rubber. Izzy loved Sheffield, the most no-nonsense gunslinger in the group. He'd do a job with Sheff any day, the reason he wore Sheffield batting gloves. The right-handed hitter would pull foul balls so hard that third base coaches would sit in the stands when he was up, scared they might get killed. Then Sheff would get charged with negligent homicide.

Izzy was back on Jacob's floor, staring at the ceiling again, hoping the pain in his back would go away. The only position that helped was flat on a floor, as if the stiffness straightened out all those twisting knots he worked into while on his feet. It felt as though his vertebrae were gradually realigning, preparing for when he might have to stand up again. This position was his favorite one to think in. All the blood rushed to his brain and the muscles in his back relaxed, taking a break from supporting Izzy's damaged spine.

The many times Izzy had told it over the years rescued the story from his forgetfulness. He told it at bars sometimes, if his drink was strong enough, but most often to women wondering why he was on the floor.

He was shot in the back. Literally. He was eighteen. Joined the army, another uneducated inner city child scoring low enough on the placement test to see live combat from jump. 82nd Airborne Infantry. Infantry—foot soldier. Airborne—in the air. Izzy wished he knew what "Infantry" meant back then; catching the oxymoron could have changed his mind. Basically, after a rigorous six-month training in Fort Bragg, North Carolina, they would strap a gun and a parachute on him, put him in a plane, and point at someplace below. He would have to jump down to that place, and kill just about anything that didn't come off the plane with him. In the Grenada invasion, Operation Urgent Fury, he was shot by a sergeant in his own battalion. The bullet went through his side and lodged in his vertebrae, narrowly missing permanent nerve damage. As he went down, he turned and fired, assuming he was being attacked. Just about took off the sarge's leg. The sergeant's father being of some importance in the Army, he was discharged for doing what he was trained to.

Izzy knew how to use a gun. The other servicemen were in awe of how he handled and shot with intrinsic competence. Not that guns turned him on; it was more remarkable how they didn't turn him off. When he had one, he felt normal; when he didn't, something was missing. He didn't show them, or try to scare people with the sight of one. He scared people by shooting them where they would live, but would never forget him. He regarded guns with the ambivalence a young, prodigal violinist might regard his instrument—he was pleased that something made him special, but resented that he had been unable to choose what it was. When he got back to Harlem, his credit had plummeted on account of a Plymouth he'd leased before he knew any better. He needed money bad. It was the Reagan years. Crack was a spawning business and ghetto youths were flossing in the streets, stacking paper without a clue what to do with it.

He wished that Won in the BK with Mal was his first. Sometimes he felt like he was. But Izzy had taken his first lives when he was just eighteen, in the haze of dust kicked up by helicopters, grenades, and mines, shooting by pure instinct at moving shadows. When hit, each hunched, creeping silhouette became human. Each fell and grasped for his life with the same ferocity that Izzy would. Each resembled Izzy as much as the men he fought with. Each was a world onto his own. Each was something Izzy took but didn't want.

Men made it through life to spend their last moments with an apathetic, utter stranger like Izzy. Had to figure his last would be no different.

He thought about the female in the next room who might as well be in the next continent. When he was with her, talking to her, she seemed so close to him. Like she really was right there, like he could just reach out and touch her. But the minute he remembered who he was, she was out of his orbit. The only way into her life was to get locked up again, maybe develop a drug problem and wind up in her Catholic Charities program.

Sheffield struck out. Two hard foul balls followed by a nasty, diving changeup. Sheffield swung through. Izzy groaned, and thought about the blunt in his pocket.

*   *   *

Eva closed her eyes in a deeply optimistic attempt to sleep the night off. She had a few things going for her—she was finally showered and clean, she had found some clothes that fit her, and her tummy was full with comfort food. But the moment she shut her eyes, she saw rag doll Theresa again. Gaunt face, pocked complexion, eyes open, creepy, pinpoint pupils. Eva wished she had shut her cousin's eyes. Then maybe Theresa would get out of her head. Theresa was a sister imposed upon her, indifferent to the preference of Eva's stepparents. Eva's childhood was full of nights wishing that monstrous princess dead. Now she wished she wasn't. Now, instead of draining Eva's and her new family's patience, she was nagging Eva about a very suspicious and convenient blackout. Like always, Eva wished Theresa out of her life. Now she wondered if that wish made her a murderer.

They gave her the drugs and the knife. Or maybe just the knife. Left it on the sink without thinking. Maybe there weren't any drugs in her at all, and a rage seized her. Maybe the blackout was a defense, protection from the unthinkable. Killing Theresa was unthinkable. But you don't have to think to act.

Eva's eyes snapped open and she shot up in the strange bed. She saw a digital clock read 9:07 PM. Fuck this. Why was she trying to sleep anyway?

She went in the other room, finding Izzy lying on the floor with his knees to his chest, his hands on his thighs, and his feet dangling in the air. It wasn't the very last thing she expected to see, but it was close.

"I haven't been in that position since I saw my ob/gyn," said Eva.

Izzy dropped his legs. "Oh, hey," he said, seeming uncomfortable, really for the first time. "I try to only do that stretch when I'm alone."

"What's it for?"

"Bad back."

"Sucks to get old, huh?" she said.

"For sure."

She went and sat on the couch beside Izzy, her feet by his head.

"Can't sleep?" he asked.

"Nah."

"I thought you were tired."

"I thought so too. Until I closed my eyes. Seems my mind was playing a trick on me."

Seen from the floor, her supple curves were more pronounced. "Maybe your mind's got a lot on it," said Izzy.

"Yeah . . . Are you going to talk to me from down there?" she asked.

"Oh. Okay," he said, and slowly got up off the floor, his body creaking. He sat beside her, stiffly holding himself up.

"I . . . I don't know what to think about my cousin," she confessed.

Izzy didn't expect that. He examined her, thin fingers playing with a loose thread on the couch. He remembered Eva in the Queens town house, how during his argument with Mal she had snagged that .45 without them noticing. Got the idea her life was in danger and bucked wildly at Mal. The girl had heart.

"But why would you—" began Izzy.

"Not to speak ill of the dead . . ."

"But . . ."

"The girl was a parasite," she said flatly.

"That's what happens when a person is an addict. You know that."

"You don't know Theresa. She was nasty before the drugs. She stole before the drugs. The lies were the worst." Eva spoke with her hands, letting them dangle as she finished.

"Big 'L' liar or little 'l' liar?"

"Big 'L.'"

"I'll take a thief over a liar. A thief is after my salary, a liar, my reality."

Eva raised an eyebrow. "*You're* a thief," she reminded him.

"Who steals from liars," he said, easy.

She rolled her eyes. "Anyway, Robin Hood, Theresa was just a bad seed. I don't know how else to say it."

"I'm not sure I believe in bad seeds." He shrugged.

"I might say the same thing, if I hadn't known her."

"Seeds, if I'm not mistaken," said Izzy, "need sunshine, water, soil . . ."

Eva brought her legs up on the couch, tucking one under her butt and facing Izzy. "You're saying her environment had to help. Her environment being her family. She had a great family. She was well loved." Eva could feel a nice friction in their conversation, like when they first met, when they could speak their minds and the back and forth kept rolling along.

Izzy's arm rested on top of the couch. Eva thought if she happened to fall forward, they would embrace.

"Every family got at least one person that's not right. The family's face looks good, but then that one person is just everything that's wrong."

"What are you, a social worker?"

"Not licensed," he said with a one-shoulder shrug.

She laughed, and stretched her arms over her head, slightly lifting her shirt. She saw Izzy trying to look away, scratching his goatee. She knew it. After all that craziness, just give her a shower and a meal, and she looked good. When her stretch finished, she was closer to him.

"Theresa's mother? My aunt? Took me in when I was twelve. She brought me over from Trinidad to live with Theresa, her and her husband. He was the nicest, tall, goofy Jewish man. Compared to my father, he was a goddamn saint. He owned a golf store in Connecticut."

"From Trinidad to Connecticut?"

"Darien, Connecticut. From one of the world's poorest places to one of the richest."

"I feel like that on the 4 train."

"Let me tell you, they did not understand this little Trini. Imagine all those young princesses, at the age of twelve, all knowing what their parents are worth. 'My fah-ther traded three million six in the last two days,'" she said in her best, eerily accurate, martini-swilling socialite voice. "'My fah-ther just closed the Peterman account.' Then me. 'Me fada be welding all todey, an me don't paint de walls 'ow 'ee like it," she said in perfect Caribbean patois, "'so de man beat me wit him tool belt.'"

Izzy laughed. "Wait, so your cousin—that girl, the addict, she was a princess?"

"A little demon princess. She was sixteen, and I'd tell her I was worried about her coke problem. She'd say, 'I do coke. I don't have a problem with it. Do you? Then you have a coke problem.'"

Izzy laughed some more.

"That girl could take diamonds and turn them into coal."

Eva felt good, riffing on Theresa, the corrupt cousin, the other who was wrong and made Eva right. It was a familiar routine for her; any old friend or boyfriend knew most of those lines. As she found comfort in that familiarity, it suddenly evaporated, thinking of her cousin's brutal death. Eva dropped into a frown. She didn't want to think about Theresa anymore. She let out a long exhale, and swallowed rancorous bile.

Izzy responded to her quick change in mood as though something just fell and he jumped to catch it. "You . . . okay?" He put his arm around her. She put her face where his shoulder met his chest.

"What did I do?" she asked into his shirt.

He spoke softly to her. "We don't know. But whatever it was, you're human, either way."

Eva picked her head up. Their mouths were close.

This man confused her. He looked more like her father but acted more like her uncle.

Her head dropped onto his shoulder.

Not just her uncle, but Gail—he had her patience, her forgiveness. Eva recalled yesterday, sitting across from Gail, struggling to sort herself out. She tried to remember why the session was strained, why the last fifteen minutes were so quiet. It was because of Theresa, of course, it always came back to her. Eva trapped in her bedroom, unable to visit her own apartment; the living room perfect and untouched; only inhabited by the smoke seeping through Theresa's door. Eva trapped in her bedroom like back in Trinidad, terrified of their father. Eva was supposed to be strong now; being scared and trapped was supposed to be over; she was a woman now, better than her mother, cheating and breeding more half-Indians above her chicken coop; better than her brothers, sullen and addicted to hard labor and harder drugs; better than that whole island of hip-gyrating, ca-lypso-listening, sex-crazed, former-slave half-breeds. Eva was a woman like her aunt. She would go back to the island with white boyfriends and suitcases full of New York presents, swooping in like the flying ants and leaving the village with the same bitterness. They were jealous of her power, stature, and craftiness to achieve them. Most of all she was better than Theresa, the Trini-Jew born into every reasonable advantage possible, and wound up more devious, glut-tonous, and soulless than any dirt poor junkie loser in Trinidad. Eva was better than Theresa; she had been telling herself that through high school, college, and social work school, and through those frustrating nights awake and tossing in her own weakness. Even before high school, when not a single child could understand her patois, and

Theresa, a year younger but already feral and popular, led the spoiled children in hurling insults. Her cousin was the only one who did understand her, and even then, Eva would tell herself, *I'm better than her.*

It was Theresa's born privilege that made Eva refuse to believe it; Theresa's ability to revoke her family's love with a dirty look, revoking everything Eva would hope for herself. Aunt Carol and Uncle Richard loved Theresa so much as a child they would have done anything for her. Her failure as a daughter was their failure, her wild debauchery evidence of their hidden shortcomings, so when she spoke for them to Eva, *They don't love you, they're just glad you're not me*, Eva believed her.

I'd have to kill her, Eva had said. She had meant it as a joke, but Gail hadn't laughed and neither had she. Now it was even less funny.

Of all the things Theresa was, she wasn't that: princess, junkie, hooker, bitch, parasite, lowlife, loser—never that.

Eva spoke the word. "Murderer."

"What?" snapped Izzy.

Eva's posture sank into a morbid and uncomprehending slouch. "It's such a condemning word. Up until tonight, I never thought about it like that. Someone can be a murderer, and they're not a person anymore. I keep thinking about it. I'm not a Trini, not a social worker, not a woman, not a friend. Murderer."

Izzy's brow dropped and he cracked his neck. "But you don't know for sure."

Mal drove with the three Benny brothers in the backseat of his taxi, like he was a cabby and they were his fare. The Albanians said nothing to each other for the whole ride. Preparing to get busy, Mal guessed. They were, for the time being, not trying to kill Mal. They had an easy shot at it from back there.

He pulled over in front of a brownstone on 137th Street. All four of them quickly got out, and Mal led the way up to the door. It was at least ten feet tall, heavy dark wood, with an old gargoyle face holding a round metal knocker in its mouth. Mal grabbed the iron ring, rocked it back, and banged it against the door a few times. He smirked, feeling like some old-world nobleman. They waited. He pulled it back again and banged louder, preparing a snooty greeting. Correspondence for Madam. Or just stopping in for evening tea. He then heard something rustle behind him.

What looked like a Smith & Wesson .44 pointed at Mal. It fired before he could get out of the way.

"Ow!" yelled Mal, holding his eyebrow. The shot had singed it. "Crazy, dipshit motherfucker!"

Ignoring Mal, he kicked the door on the lock where he had shot it, and nothing happened. He kicked it again, but the door just shook, heavy knocker rattling. The Alban took a couple of steps back, preparing to shoot again.

"*Tranquilo!*" said Mal, one of the few non-English words he knew, realizing too late that Spanish was a long way from Albanian. Then he drew his .22 with its silencer and shot the lock again, one for the upper, and one for the lower, and the heavy door drifted open. The others marched past him.

Mal followed. He saw Tess in a nightgown, with braids, still looking fine, rushing out of a bedroom.

"What the hell is going on here?" she demanded, outraged.

The Albanian brother in the cream sport jacket cold-cocked her, hard as he would a man. Tess spun around, crashed into a sofa, and flipped over onto the floor. A baby was crying in the other room. The brother in the red and black shoved his gun in Tess's mouth. The brother in the paisley collared shirt emerged from a side room holding a toddler, with a Ruger automatic to its head, talking in Albanian.

"No. Not his," answered Mal.

He stood over Tess and squatted down, looking in her tearing, swollen eyes as they quivered, teeth clattering on the gun in her mouth.

"Hey, Tess. Looking well. Seen Iz?"

Chapter 8

Jacob couldn't understand it. His father and his woman. Maybe not his woman but his fantasy woman. Of all the fine thirty-something women out there, he knew that one the best. Now he would have to give up on trying talking to her, before the situation got any more Oedipal. "I eavesdrop on your confidential therapy sessions" probably isn't such a great pickup line anyway.

It was getting late and difficult to focus. Jacob began thinking of girls he could call. He pulled out his Razor phone and scrolled through the names. Lyn Chin, the Chinese girl who lived to give him head. She didn't even want to be in public with him, steeling him off to bathrooms and taxis. She made a good story but got tiresome and a bit spooky. Carolina, the Colombian girl—pretty but on some rocker shit; went and dyed her hair red and purple. Lana, Irish girl; she liked Jacob a lot but he never really enjoyed kissing her thin wiry lips. Then Tiffané.

Her personality was annoying as a mosquito but he couldn't get the image of her naked out of his head, riding him with rhythmic confidence. Before he could stop himself, he was calling her.

"Oh, hey," she said when she knew it was him, as though surprised he continued to survive without her to notice him.

"What's up?"

"Nothing, I'm, like, on my way *out*, yah," she said in her overmedicated slur.

"Out"—that high school term for doing stuff way cooler than whatever you were doing "in." Jacob said good-bye before she could sneer "It's over" with more than just her tone.

Ever since Eva said what she did about being a murderer, Izzy had been thinking about Won. He had killed before. But he was a soldier at war. To not kill in that situation would be to abandon his brothers. He had thought the same thing about Won. Izzy had to shoot him—otherwise Mal would have been at risk. But Mal's risk was of his own making. He didn't have to kill that woman who manhandled him; he wasn't under threat of live fire. So Won was the difference between killing and murdering.

Izzy couldn't get over Eva's audacity, strolling so haphazardly into his condemnation. For her it was a terrible possibility, for him an identity. Though if she had killed, it would have had nothing to do with convenience or practicality; hers would have been a rage so blind she blacked out. Izzy wondered which was worse, killing because you care or killing because you don't.

"What's the plan for me, Izzy?" Eva called from the bathroom, over the sound of running water. "I can't just be on the run. I mean, that is really not me."

"I'd say wait until the powder marks have faded. Go talk to the cops in another day. Your story will be more convincing if they don't have evidence that you shot someone."

"Why did we come here? Aren't you worried about your son?"

Another question. Izzy answered rationally. "Jacob is the only part of my life Mal knows nothing about. No one knows anything about him. Except you."

Eva came back in the room and sat down beside him. "Still. Are you worried?" she asked.

Now she was rifling questions, turning things back on him like it was her nature. "I had no choice. I don't have money for a hotel. Mal would find us anywhere else. Jacob always wanted to be my friend."

"Worried?" she repeated.

"Why are you making me say it?"

Eva lay back on the couch like she'd won. "I guess I just don't get you."

"Yeah? How's that?"

"You seem like a decent guy. How did you end up . . ."

"Robbing people for a living?"

"Yeah. And don't give me another hard luck story, 'cause I've heard them all. What you got against paying taxes?"

Izzy wished he didn't like how she pushed and prodded; then it would be so easy to blow her off, and not talk about himself. But the way her mind worked, she might understand him.

"It was never about hard luck, really, not entirely, anyway. I was a badass. I was in the Army, and good with a gun. Got home and couldn't get a job. Again it's not about hard luck, it's just I was good at something. I mean, you can't tell a broke kid on his own who's good at something not to do that something, right? I know the hood's poor but there's so much money in it for someplace that's poor. Think about how at any given moment, someone is giving someone else a boatload of cash for a boatload of something else. And that cash doesn't belong to either of them, not legally anyway. It's the accumulation of thousands of junkie's selling ·cans and pipes, petty thefts, dishwashing. Coins from a city's couch cushions. As far as the government goes, that cash doesn't exist. Those hustlers got no more right to it than I do. Least I use a real skill to get it. . . ."

Izzy paused, ready to go on, until he saw the Eva's blank look.

"I'm wasting my breath," he concluded.

"No. It's just an interesting way of looking at things. It's different. I'm trying to keep up."

"It's about territory. The only thing that makes this money belong to anyone is that it's in their territory. Like with animals."

"Animals."

"Like in Africa. On the savanna. Now, a leopard, let's call him Jeff."

"Jeff."

"Yeah, Jeff will go around, spraying piss in a clearly defined line around his territory. Every other leopard knows that's Jeff's territory. They smell Jeff a mile away. They don't hunt where they smell Jeff, 'cause Jeff'll fight them. Jeff don't hunt where they hunt, right? But a lion, now, that's different. A lion, let's call him Ed, may smell Jeff, but that's just a pansy-ass leopard to a lion. Ed goes in and out of Jeff's territory all he wants, and if Jeff doesn't eat up quick, whatever he killed will end up in Ed's stomach. Jeff knows that. Turns out, Jeff's territory and Ed's are the same piece of land. But different species don't recognize each other's territory, there isn't enough space. That's how it is with me. See, I'm not a hustler. A hustler's a different species to me. So if he doesn't eat up quick . . ."

Eva's face was slightly less blank. It was dubious. "So you take what you want. Because you're the biggest animal."

Izzy thought his version sounded more eloquent. "Well, not animal, like, *you're an animal!* Animal, like, we're really all animals."

"Izzy, however you rationalize it, you're using a gun to make an illegal living. Every time you jump in on somebody, your life and theirs are at risk. You have to know, what happened with me . . ."

"What?"

"It was a matter of time. You've been doing this how long? Are you going to tell me you've never had a problem before?"

Izzy thought of East New York again, Mal pointing a gun at him while he pointed his at Won on the floor. Not as planned. But he did him anyway. He was ready then. He had to have been. All those bangs, he'd have killed, if it came down to it.

"We were real good. The best. Anonymous, never hung anywhere near the clicks we ripped off. Got it down to a succinct transaction. Hospitals, never the morgue."

"That doesn't sound like it could last for long."

"It did. It lasted a long time. Just not forever. I never froze like that before."

His phone rang. MAL flashed on the screen.

"Hey, Papi Chulo, guess who I ran into?" Mal happily said into the phone, holding it beside the woman with a gun in her mouth. "Check this. Tess. You believe that shit? Here. Scream for me, baby."

She did her best to scream, choking on the nozzle of the gun.

"She can't scream too good. She got a Smith & Wesson four-four in her mouth right now."

"Fucking bastard," said Izzy.

"You know it. No cops, just you," said Mal, and hung up, pleased with how that went.

The apartment was nice; Tess was doing well for herself. Unless the father of that kid paid for the kitchen. Some nice stones in there, and top-notch, stainless-steel appliances. Living room had a handsome, brown leather sofa set, gathered around a faux fireplace. Maybe it worked; there were pokers beside it. The rug Tess lay on looked like those crazy expensive Persian rugs they sold in warehouses on the East Side. But hell if Mal could recognize a knockoff. Three hundred or ten grand, he'd believe it either way. Since either way, it was a ridiculous number for anything you walked on.

He then got in between the Albanian and Tess, pushing the gun out of her mouth. The Benny brother was surprised. He grunted some nasty language. Mal wondered how many times tonight he'd been called the Albanian word for "nigger."

"Relax, Boris."

The man pointed to his chest with his thumb. "Sandro!"

He turned to the woman. "Tess, honey. I want you to tell me everything you know about Izzy. Even what you think I know. Start from the beginning."

Izzy's fist sailed through the air.

"What is it?" asked Eva.

Izzy marched into Jacob's room and grabbed a coat hanger, letting a shirt fall, then took his shoulder holster from the pile of his dirty clothes on the floor. He slipped on a baby-blue Columbia hoody from the closet, and he took the .45 from under a *Barron's*, quickly releasing the clip, seeing it had six rounds. He jammed the clip back in and slid the gun into the holster by his left arm. He rolled up his sleeves, took a note pad from beside the phone, and wrote on it.

"What? What happened?" demanded Eva.

He went to the front door and turned the knob. "My number's by the phone. Stay here. If I call? It'll ring twice, then hang up. Then you call me back. You hear anybody with an accent? Sounds East European? Run."

Out the elevator, through the lobby, and on the street, Izzy picked a black Impala a few cars down; he was always good at wiring those. He slid the hanger down the door and was inside in about fifteen seconds. He pulled out the wires from under the dash and without looking, his fingers found the ones he needed. He exposed them, flicked them together, and heard the warm sound of the engine turning over.

Tess's place was a quick ride from Jacob's, and as much as he didn't want Mal to know how close he was, he had no real choice. Especially with those Albanian voices in the background—he couldn't waste another second. He raced across the brightly crowded 125th Street, and over to Eighth Avenue, where the buildings were residential and the traffic was drugs. He passed Tess's familiar street, where a taxi and two Albanians stood out front. He drove to the next block, pulled over, and spent the next sixty seconds feeling his pulse, hearing nothing but the beating rhythm. And he was ready. He got out and pulled his black Sheffield batting gloves on his hands like a hitter coming to bat. He turned down the side street just before Tess's, and cut through a narrow break between the buildings, into a strip connecting concrete backyards. He passed a few masks with long horns, plaster drying on the ground, made by Tess's neighbor, a sculptor. Tess's short porch, which he had helped to build, was one story up. He climbed the wire fence in front of it, making it over the top, fingertips just reaching the second-floor short porch, and he scurried up onto it. Then he used the fence on the porch to boost himself up to the roof.

Tess used to complain about people breaking in, thinking she might get robbed. Izzy would tell her not to worry. "If it hasn't happened yet, it most likely won't. You know these fiends have tried most everything around here."

Izzy paced, giving himself a moment to catch his breath. He walked around the little brown structure housing the stairwell. He stood just on the ledge and peeked down.

Two Albanians, neither of whom he knew, waiting, chests puffed out, barely concealing their guns. Izzy pulled out his .45 and aimed.

Mal was listening to Tess ramble, casually holding his gun on her, trying to keep the names she mentioned straight, and think if he knew them. All of them sounded familiar.

"Glaser, also. G-something, Glaser. Izzy was a kid, she was an intern, a social worker. She was his first, they were tight."

That name did not sound familiar.

Then a loud *pop* from outside. Tess stopped talking. Mal looked up. The Albanian in black and red ran inside, his eyes tearing with rage, carrying on like he was on fire, pointing to his head, pointing outside, and pointing up.

"The roof," said Mal.

Izzy pulled the .45 back from over the ledge. He faced the door in the little house, as faint footsteps climbed from inside. He checked the clip, five rounds left. The footsteps louder, like a gallop, at least two people, maybe more. Izzy backed up to the roof's edge and looked over. Long fall, three stories. Footsteps louder. Izzy dug his heel against the ledge, raising his gun in the firing position.

The door flew open. A big Albanian in black and red aimed his gun dead ahead and fired. So did Izzy. The Alban missed, Izzy didn't. Gave the man a third eye in the middle of his forehead. His other two rolled back, and his wide body followed them, crashing into those behind.

Izzy faced the ledge, put his gun in his holster, then turned, grabbed the ledge with both hands, and dropped down, his body dangling alongside the building. He looked down. Bad idea. A long drop; the glance momentarily took him out of sorts. But he saw the decent-sized window ledge he was counting on, about half a foot from his feet. Maybe a foot. Foot and a half, at most. Whatever the distance, the footsteps on the roof above were coming on fast.

He let go and dropped that half a foot, foot, and landed well, but off balance. As his body sailed backward, he grasped and caught his fingers inside the grooves of the deeply indented brick face. Tentatively secure, he let out a long breath and felt his pulse rate skyrocket.

His foot reared back and kicked the window, hard, and through. He tried to pull it back out, but it was stuck in the glass. He gave it another good yank and the glass all fell, shattering around his ankles and cutting him. He glanced up and saw Mal swinging his arm over the ledge with a silenced pistol. Izzy jumped through the window, head first, landing with his gloves on the glass, rolling over, cutting his back. He tumbled across the floor and into the bedroom closet door. Cut up, his back killing him, he adjusted into his comfortable position without trying to—flat on his back, knees bent. If only he could have stayed like that.

Izzy rushed to beat Mal and whoever else downstairs. He breezed through the ground floor, past Tess holding her child. He continued out the front door, feeling horrible for putting her at risk. He was feeling like that a lot lately.

Outside, an Albanian was on the ground with his head split open and leaking on the pavement. Izzy stepped over the lump and went for the taxi. He tried the door. It opened.

Izzy got in and closed the door behind him, shuffling his back against the far door, and leveling his pistol sight on the brownstone entrance.

Mal flew down the stairs. Jesus, Iz fucked that Albanian up. He needed a perfect head shot to reverse that big guy's momentum like that. Had to be a high-caliber gun too, hollow tips, from the spray. Maybe that .45 that killed Arben.

Mal reached the ground floor with the one in the cream blazer behind him. He thought of asking Tess where Izzy went, but there was no reason to. He wasn't in the house. Likely watching the door.

Mal paused. Why was he going first? He pretended to look around the living room, hoping the Alban would walk ahead. He noticed a thick, oozing red chunk on his sling, a piece of that Alban's skull, and quickly brushed it off.

Benny's last living brother had stopped in front of the front door, waiting for Mal. Must've been the smart one.

"Not here," he said with a thick accent, the first English Mal had heard.

Meaning, stop looking around and open this fucking door. Mal inched toward him.

"Go," he said.

"Right behind you, partner."

The man raised his gun. "Fuck . . . You . . . Go."

The Albanian's stare was ruthless as the barrel of his gun. If he'd had his way, CSU would be chalking Mal on 12th Avenue right now.

"You want me to go?" asked Mal, rhetorically. "Want me to? Fine. No problem!"

Benny's brother didn't move. Mal grabbed the heavy handle and pulled it open, glancing outside. He considered saying "After you," then thought better. This man would pull his trigger.

Finally the door opened, and an alert Mal pointed his silenced pistol in every possible direction, even up. Then another Albanian in a cream blazer, Izzy hoped the last. Mal crept east, pointing west to the Albanian, who started that way, and then paused, looking at the taxi. He moved toward Izzy. He couldn't have seen Izzy; he would have been shooting already. He slowly shuffled his feet, gun ready. Izzy leveled on the Alban's head, realizing what the man was looking at. Izzy's blood. Must have bled on the door as he got in.

As soon as a shot was clear, Izzy pulled. The window shattered. Another Albanian took one in the head.

The back window shattered too. Right. Mal. With the silencer.

Izzy reached to the handle behind him, got out of the cab, and ran, sirens ripping through the distance, bullets singing by, kicking up pavement chips as they missed. He made it to his Impala.

He drove east toward Second Avenue and headed downtown. He soon saw Mal's taxi in the rearview, as expected. Izzy picked up his phone.

Four brothers killed by one gun. Three Albanians. Three head shots. *Something had to be said for that*, thought Mal, as he drove away from yet another crime scene, cruising behind Izzy's new Impala.

Mal wanted that woman, the one back in Queens who saw him execute three men, then shot him. He wanted her bad. He wasn't planning on worrying about police or being a wanted man. If Mal didn't get to her, he'd be ducking an All-Points within days. He didn't want to leave New York with his money for the Caribbean or anything. The Caribbean was nice, but he couldn't live there, always in the sun, gangsters wearing linens and sandals. He hated sandals. He hated the sand, always ruining his Reeboks or Timbs. Damn flashy Jamaicans with their bright yellow and green, couldn't understand a word they said, always figured he was being insulted. Vegas was okay, for a visit. Get some quality hookers, not have to pay too much. Mal had some family out there. But he couldn't stand those country-ass cowboys, calling Mal "Yankee" like it was still the eighteen hundreds. They all thought they were pimps, and put metal in their teeth, which Mal never understood. They didn't like Mal 'cause they thought he looked down on them, him being from New York. And they were right. No, fuck a vaycay. Mal was going to finish what he started, and get back to his life, tiger of the concrete jungle, with a bit more money. Get that track lighting for his hallway. A couple of plasma screens. Nothing crazy. Ass every night for a year. Only problem was Izzy. Getting rid of that fuck might be tougher than he'd thought. Huna would have to get involved, personally. Now that more Albanians were dead, Huna's help was a given.

Mal's phone rang.

"New recruits?" asked Izzy.

"Party crashers."

"What, you tell them I did Arben?"

"It was convincing. Not that those hotheads needed much. I'm not mad you took care of them, tho," said Mal. "Pretty sure, they had their way, and I was going to get it right after you."

"You following me?" said Izzy, more of a statement than a question.

"Nah. But I got to ask, how'd you get up on that roof?"

"I used to live over there. You tried to ambush me on my home turf. I know my way around. Mal, you going to push this?"

"Yeah. One of us got to go."

"I like the odds," Izzy said, a smirk in his voice.

Mal thought of the three dead Albanians. Then shook the thought off. "Ain't no excuse for that shit you pulled in Queens. Freezing like a pussy. You got the heart of a fucking chicken."

"Quit clucking, then. Come test me."

Click.

Test you? No problem, pussy-eating fuck. I'll put holes in

you, you fuck. Leave you bleeding all over your little cunt
bitch. You fuck.

Where was Izzy going? He had turned east on 117th and
pulled over on Pleasant Avenue. A ghetto block. Couple of
do-rag kids out on the street. Could see the cars zip by on
the FDR. The goodfellas' hole-in-the-wall laundry spots,
drinking spots, Dominican gambling spots, ass spots. Nothing over there. Except that Alban's spot.

Chapter 9

Izzy remembered the last time he left Tess's home, when back pain had him dragging a laundry basket full of his belongings by a canvas belt. Tess had thrown him out because of his distant, foggy emotional reactions. Tess had had a miscarriage. In the following weeks, Izzy was unable to keep pace with her wild moods. Pain had attacked Izzy's back. After he slept it off on the brown shag rug, and had a horrible dream of shooting Mariano Rivera in the shoulder, blood soaking his white pinstripes, Izzy woke up to stifled sobs. Tess was locked in grief, convinced that Izzy was glad she had lost the baby. She went into the sort of righteous tirade that made Izzy miss white women. She referred to the day she told Izzy of the miscarriage, while he was cooking sausages in the kitchen.

"They should have burned!" she insisted.

Eventually, she forced Izzy to do the one thing he couldn't— get up. Dragging the laundry basket down the sidewalk by his khaki belt, a kid on a stoop with a skateboard saw Izzy and cracked up. "Where's your wheels, man?"

Izzy gestured to his skateboard. "Give me yours," he said, deadpan.

The kid giggled, and then paused, Izzy giving a long, serious look.

Then Izzy smiled.

Ignoring that same back pain, Izzy descended the narrow, dark staircase leading down from street level. It smelled humid and stale, like the block's concrete armpit. Just off Pleasant Avenue, a notorious "thing of ours" territory, Huna had greased enough hands and made enough friends for an Albanian business. Izzy stopped at the bottom of the steps, before the door, released a long exhale, and took his pulse.

Taking his pulse wasn't the monitoring necessity he had told Mal. It was his mantra. Izzy didn't want to know his pulse as much as control it. Remind his body what it was time to do. Focus. One beat, one bullet.

The action from before still raced in him. He could feel the vibration from the gun down his forearm as he pressed his finger to his throat. It was all over so quick. Then the thoughts came back like a crash. He wanted more of that wild immediacy, like a smoker wanting a cigarette.

Izzy knocked, the cracked paint flaking against his knuckle. The eyehole clicked from the other side.

"Huna sent me," he announced.

A few locks slammed back and the door opened. A hunched, fat Albanian with one eye squinted and his belly showing shook Izzy's hand. Sneering, he turned and walked inside without looking at Izzy, who followed.

Izzy was tired of being on the run without money. He never took bank cards, or anything that could ID him on a job, and his petty cash was down to $32.16 after the pancakes. Poverty was the reason they had gone to Jacob's place instead of a hotel. Seeing Tess, beaten, holding her baby, was a reminder. Izzy did not want anything to happen to Jacob. It was time to get proactive.

Incense burned; cheap red stuff draped everywhere—red scarves on the walls, and hanging beads for doors. Diverse girls were sprawled about; cheapened by flaws—gap teeth, burn marks, scars, obvious wigs, tracks. Some smoked hand-rolled joints, smelling minty, like Dust. Izzy crinkled his nose.

"You want a girl?" asked the sluggish Albanian.

"Nah, man. I'm good." *Really good.*

"What does Huna want? I have to pay another point?" He made a gross guttural sound. "Now he send niggar. We do less business, I get smaller cut. Motherfucker. Look around, I have family to feed, *zazak*."

Izzy couldn't get used to the Albanian's casual racism, the way they said "nigger" to his face, like it wasn't an insult. "You call these dope-fried chickens family?" Izzy asked. He'd get the slug-man for that "niggar" shit later.

"At least one, yes, is my daughter. That I know of! Ha, ha! When I was your age? Fifteen times a day, at least," he said, pumping his fist to the side.

Izzy was getting impatient. And queasy. "Where's your muscle?"

"Yes, yes, over here."

Izzy followed the man into a back room. On the wall was a sheet of paper with a chart on it, listing names of girls— Brittany, Jessica, Riana, Nicole—and beside the names were tick marks. Another Albanian was at a solid, thick oak desk, with a long, misshapen head, a cigar burning between his fingers as he ate Chinese. The slug sat on a couch.

"If you don't want a girl, what do you want?" asked the man at the desk, between bites of takeout.

Izzy spied his food, and walked over, interested. "Beef with Broccoli?"

"Have a seat." The man leaned back, an offended boss. "Get your face out of my food."

"I'm good," replied Izzy.

"What, you want me, faggot? We only offer girls here." He swallowed his food and gave his best hard stare.

"You don't know shit," said Izzy.

"I know Huna wouldn't send me no goddamn nigger for nothing."

"So he hasn't told you, then."

"What?" he snickered.

"There's a war going on."

"Yeah?" he said, laughter a bit nervous now, glancing around. "Who's at war?"

"Me. And your crew," said Izzy, simply. "So I need your bank, and your guns."

The Alban quickly rose, off balance, pulling a gat from somewhere under the desk.

Bang.

The man fell to the floor. The desk toppled over. A hole burned in Izzy's pocket. The man was writhing, holding his leg. Izzy stepped on the wound, and crouched down, pulling the .45, putting the nozzle against the man's Achilles' tendon.

"The artillery, the bank, and the keys to whatever you're driving. Believe me, you don't want to lose this."

This guy wasn't a problem, whimpering and nodding on the floor. Izzy heard some rustling behind the desk; panic, the heavy Albanian breathing hard. Izzy peeked, and a gun fired. He ducked back down. The shot hit the desk. The slug had a gun.

"Hey, put that thing down!" called Izzy, peering at the slug with a revolver in one hand, his other arm around the neck of a girl, his shield.

More shots hit the desk.

Izzy put his gun to the wounded man's long head. "What's your name?"

"What?"

"Your name," repeated Izzy.

"T-Tony."

"What's his name?" He nodded toward the desk.

"Sam."

Another shot.

"Hey, Sam! Listen up! Drop the gun, okay? I'm gonna pop your man Tony here in his head, Sam. All right? Drop it."

Tony concurred. "Drop it, you fat fuck!"

More shots. Maybe Sam didn't like being called a fat fuck. Maybe he didn't like Tony, either. Izzy peeked again. The slug had a satisfied grin, enjoying himself. His head was beside the girl's. Tough shot.

"Come out, you mutha fucka!" Sam yelled, getting a taste for it.

"Old man doesn't have much regard for your life," said Izzy.

Tony was petrified, moist eyes pleading. Like Won was in the BK. Had no intention of dying over a little cash. Izzy was stuck. He didn't want to do Tony or Sam or the hooker. So why had he come in? He had to be ready. He looked up again at the girl. Young pale face, scared like Tony. Far from innocent. Everyone was far from innocent.

"Fuck him," said Tony.

"Somebody got to go, here."

"Sam!" gelled Tony. "Drop the fucking gun!"

Another shot. This one broke through the desk and whispered between Izzy and Tony.

Izzy waited a moment. He raised his gun above the desk, aimed, and fired. Sam and the girl dropped.

Fuck. Izzy rushed around the desk and kneeled next to them. She was bleeding. *Fuck.* She was still. Exactly fucked. Blood on her head. *You can't control this shit, dummy. This is beyond your control. If you weren't so damn arrogant. If you weren't such an arrogant prick. You could stop being here. Feeling bad. Doing anyway. Feeling bad. Doing anyway.*

Izzy took off his glove and reached his fingers to the girl's soft, pale neck. He couldn't remember feeling for any-one's pulse other than his own. And there it was. That faint flutter.

She blinked, and coughed.

"Hold still," said Izzy, taking her head in his hands and turning it slightly. There was a cut across her head, like a long, lipless grin, drooling red. Sam the Slug had a crater burrowed through the bridge of his nose.

Too close.

Mal never liked stakeouts. They were necessary, but he got restless. He would down coffee after coffee, crazed in the car while Izzy calmly watched the spot like a home plate umpire. That night was no different. Fifteen minutes in that taxi, and Mal was sick of smelling himself, staring so hard the street and brick entrance blurred. It wasn't the time spent that bothered him. If he knew Izzy would be out in forty-five minutes, he would sit still. It was the not know-ing—an hour, two, all night—that made him want to cap himself.

Couldn't imagine Izzy going there to hide, or to twist out a girl. Was he going to bang them? Even that seemed like a stretch. Some bold, wild cowboy shit. Izzy wasn't that thirsty. Was he? Then again, he might as well. No talking his way out of anything with Huna. Iz must be stopping through for some quick bank. Either way, Mal was hungry as a mug.

He jogged across the street to a corner bodega, his eye on the stairwell across the way. Mal grabbed some more Twinkies, a couple more Gatorades, a Sprite, and four fifty-cent Salsa Doritos bags. He popped a bag open in the store and started eating. He had finished one by the time he got back to the cab. He remembered his cargo, wondering if he should dead that cabdriver right quick. Needing a better reason than idle time, Mal popped the trunk and tossed in a Gatorade.

Izzy emerged from the stairs. Mal caught it in the corner of his eye.

"Fuck," he screamed.

Mal jumped in the driver's seat and started up the cab. He watched Izzy walk around the corner, turn, and get into a Navigator. He started the car up and drove. Mal kept his distance as they went farther and farther downtown. The scattered Dunkin' Donuts gradually became scattered Starbucks, as the property value improved.

Mal wished he had learned how to hot-wire a car. Izzy once offered to teach him. Mal couldn't remember his reason for refusing. Must have made sense at the time.

For now, Mal was stuck with that wreck of a taxi. As Izzy approached the Queensboro Bridge, Mal turned around and lost him.

He called Huna, wondering how safe it was to be the bearer of bad news twice in one night.

"Yeah?"

"We got problems," said Mal.

"Keep it in person."

"Meet me on the Upper West Side. I think I know how we gonna get this motherfucker."

Izzy shrugged it off. Feeling bad. Doing anyway. Shrugging off.

Izzy glanced at the Queensboro Bridge from his new, wood-grain, butter-soft leather, GPS Navigation equipped vantage point, and thought about what Eva said. She thought he froze back in Queens because he wanted to do something different with his life. But it was easy taking out that slug back uptown. He didn't feel that bad about it anymore, either. The girl, yeah, he felt bad about her. He could have killed her. Didn't. Could have. Didn't. Izzy could shrug that off. Izzy could shrug most anything off. Eva thought Izzy froze because he wanted a new life—Izzy thought he froze because of Eva. He had a little crush on her. Izzy would get those from time to time.

It was difficult for Izzy to reach through his foggy calm to grasp his own motivations. With the adrenaline still running, he felt lucid. Flipping the script on Mal was something Izzy had wanted to do anyway. Sure, he could have just disappeared, and dissolved the partnership, but then he wouldn't have gotten to see the little wacko bug out. In that way, yeah, Eva was right, he wanted a new life. A life without Mal.

If he had really wanted a new life, what he just did back at that little whorehouse wouldn't have been so easy. Or fun. Izzy sat high in his new Navigator, still feeling the rush from the gunplay, still congratulating himself. He had a couple of new guns. He had a bankroll he still had to count. Felt good.

Or he was clinging. Rationalizing. Shrugging off. The same "shrugging off" that was as much a part of the "feeling bad, doing anyway, shrugging off" as the "doing anyway." Izzy wasn't sure what he had more talent for, the "doing anyway" or the "shrugging off."

He made a phone call. Then hung up.

His phone rang, an electronic, office ring.

"Hello?"

"Hey. Everything okay?" asked Eva.

"Yeah. Just had to straighten a few things out."

"What happened?"

"I got some sick crazies coming after me. They took it to my ex's house."

Eva was concerned. "She all right?"

"I think so."

"You didn't check on her?"

"I couldn't."

"*Couldn't*," she imitated him. Sarcastic.

"Listen, you weren't there. I make one misstep, and you on your own. Might want to withhold judgment."

"Just keep my mouth shut, then?"

"I didn't say all that."

"This is your world. I don't know the rules, don't have the instinct. If I don't have judgment, I have nothing."

"I got to argue with you about the instinct. My old partner still got his arm in a sling on account of you."

"Aw," she said. "You sure know how to make a girl feel special." Still sarcastic.

"I'm going to come get you soon, get you out of that spot."

"Where are you now?" she asked.

"Don't worry," he said. "I'll see you in a few. Got to make one more quick stop."

"I'll be okay," she said. "*Blind Date* is on."

"Bye."

She giggled. "Bye." Maybe at him. Maybe at *Blind Date*.

Izzy checked his rearview for conspicuous, window-shot-out taxis, and saw none. He thought about Eva, laughing at *Blind Date* in sweats, and the slug, bleeding on the rug, the images both simultaneous and incongruous, like Izzy was watching two different TV sets.

He made another call. Tess's hushed, pained voice answered, "Hello?" surrounded by buzzing police radios and official muttering.

"You okay?" asked Izzy.

"Yeah. Fine," she said, quickly and quietly.

"Okay," he said. She hung up.

Bless Tess. She always was a trouper.

Huna hung up his phone, pulling the Benzo up in front of Benny's Steakhouse. Louon was in the passenger seat; Huna had grabbed him outside Privilege to make sure he kept his mouth shut about Netta. Although from the sound of Mal, it might not matter.

There was an ache in his stomach for Arben. Those other three hardheads, fuck 'em, last time they were in New York Huna could've been the one that killed them. But Benny was like a son. Fuck Muslim, Catholic—that bullshit only went so far, an excuse to get rid of bad blood. Huna wouldn't ever have laid a finger on him, not even for Louon, who was family. Louon was tough but a fuckup, letting some hooker dictate his life and his family's lives. Huna had Benny's back all growing up, gave him his first gun and taught him how to shoot. Huna would watch on the sidelines as Benny drained Threes on West 4th Street, that absurd smirk tattooed on him, pissing off all the niggers. It was Huna who squashed the playground beefs, knocking niggas out so another one would pop up and get knocked out too. Huna was the muscle behind Benny's mouth; he protected him, gave him the confidence to stick niggas up, grab their stash, and run. Then the motherfucker got off on it; worked it too much, and like anything, it killed him. Not it, though. Cocksucking Izzy, supposed to be the best around. Huna would carve out his heart and keep it frozen in cold storage, so Benny's memory could rest.

The emotion began to set in as Huna walked up to the steak house, pausing to look at BENNY'S on the sign. His stomach devastated by the sight of the name, he went inside, thinking he must be coming down because he shouldn't feel so bad. Mad as all hell, sure, but not so bad. The bar and the dining room were full, and Huna blew past the regulars into the kitchen, leaving Louon out at the bar.

The pastry chef had left his station and was taking off his apron. All Huna wanted to do was go downstairs and rip a couple for his nizzle. The head chef, or Chef De Cuisine, was in the pastry station, squeezing raspberry sauce on a fallen chocolate cake. He looked up at Huna, his busy dark eyes shrugging. Fucking pastry chefs. He was the fourth one this year.

The pastry chef was packing up his set of knives in a leather case.

"What's going on?" asked Huna.

"I quit," said the Moroccan in his French-Arabic accent.

"No, you don't. There's a full dining room."

"I tell the waiter no substitutions on the special. He make substitution, I cannot do it. The Chef De Cuisine tell me to do it, I say no. You hire me because I know pastry, I know what's right," he said as Huna sized him up, a tall, wiry man with a goatee, clutching his case of knives. "Chef tell me I have to make it, I tell him—you make it."

First, Huna smacked him, with his other hand grabbing his knife set. He wasn't sure what the man was talking about, only that there was some kind of "fuck you" behind it. Huna then removed a long, thick knife, grabbed the man's wrist, and held it against the counter.

"Listen, cocksucker, you go make whatever desserts they tell you to make, or you have a cooking accident. You can quit now, but you'll be going to the hospital carrying a pinky."

All of the man's weight pulled with futility against Huna's grip. He lowered the knife so it broke the skin between the pinky and forefinger, and the pastry chef stopped struggling. The whole kitchen got quiet, and Huna wondered how anyone ran a restaurant.

Chapter 10

In the kitchen, Gail Glaser wore silk maroon pajamas, brewing her nightly chamomile tea. She hoped, as always, the tea would calm her down enough to get a good sleep. She saw her toughest patient tomorrow, her multiple. By definition, Gail didn't know what to expect from her multiple. As far as multiples go, hers wasn't too bad. She could function, hold a job, and a moderate social life. Gail wouldn't deal with full-blown multiple personality disorders requiring hospitalization. She wasn't thirty anymore. Plus, since she saw patients in her apartment, she was extra careful about who knew where she lived.

When she was very young, she believed intimacy was the only way to understand the people she dealt with. Gail had very little self-control. She worked at a group charity program, where there was a young biracial man with light eyes, who was just gorgeous. And he was Jewish. She wanted to eat him up. So she pretty much did.

It was her only such indiscretion, give or take some harmless dates. As if the ethics committee imposed the retribution themselves, she got pregnant. Gail kept the baby and never looked back. The father joined the Army and fell out of touch. She was happy that way. She adored her Jacob.

He was the man in her life, but she never stroked him. She had seen single Latin mothers calling their only son "my savior," which made her nauseated. Instead of pampering, she worried. She wanted him to be the best, hardworking, independent, successful mench he could be. She worried because he was rambunctious; all that violent music coming from his room; always reading those violent books. He had some of his father in him.

Gail remembered the manila envelope she had put aside for Jacob, and went into her office to get it. The room was freshly painted, with gorgeous, off-white designs swirling against the cream walls. She had two couches and three chairs, if a client wanted to lie down for analysis, or for group therapy. She wanted to keep her desk better. It had stacks of work, notes, and bills. On top of one pile was Jacob's envelope, full of the bills and offers that still came in the mail. She brought it into the living room and set it down on her table so she would remember to mail it in the morning. She then went into her bedroom and curled up into bed with her *Psychology Today*. Hearing the traffic mingle and a bus stop, sigh, and roam 85th Street, Gail thought she could do better. She reached for her remote and clicked a few buttons to hear Billie Holiday's strained and lyrical meow surround her.

She opened her eyes. The magazine was on her face. She had forgotten to turn the lights off. Something woke her. She groggily got up, went to the light switch, and flicked it off. Then she heard it again, the sound that woke her, her doorbell. She thought she'd woken from a dream.

Gail expected no one and no one ever dropped in unexpected. She was nervous, but her curiosity led her right to the front door eyehole. She saw a thin black man with his arm in a sling, and a crooked face, making puppy dog eyes.

"Ms. Glaser? My name is Mal," he said sweetly. "I'm a friend of Izzy's."

Gail was perplexed. The lock made a clicking sound. "Uh, yes?"

"See, I was wondering if we could talk. I know you're a psych—counselor, and I was thinking . . ."

Gail was gone at "psych—counselor," hurrying for a phone. She heard the door creak open behind her. She reached for the living room phone, but Mal came on strong. He grabbed her wrist, shook the phone to the floor, and wrapped her arm around her back in a police hold. She cried out.

"You don't want to do that," he told her, throwing her on the couch. Her eyes were wet and swollen with tears. He pulled a gun—*oh God.*

"Look, bitch, I don't have no fucking time to play with you. Where's Izzy?"

"Ezekiel?" she said, stunned. "I . . . I have no idea. Why would I? I haven't seen that man in . . . over twenty years."

"I ain't buying it. I have it on good authority that ya'll are close. As for me, I'm a bad man. I will put a bullet in your tit. I already got one in the shoulder today and I'm not happy. So spill it quick."

Mal then seemed distracted by something. "What the . . ."

He was looking at her picture of Jacob from that summer a few years ago when she got that cottage in Maine. The gun was still pointed at her, but the man stared at the picture, smiling in disbelief.

"Get . . . the fuck . . . outta . . . here!" he said, and laughed, a young, sinister cackle.

Izzy pulled up in the Navigator outside Benny's Steakhouse. He surveyed the greasy-haired, pseudo-Jersey gangsters, mingling and smoking cigars in front of the restaurant. He surveyed his artillery—.45 in one holster, a new Walther .38 with a full clip in the other, and the old slug's dinky revolver on the passenger seat. He wasn't thirsting for more violence, but he had no plans to be a sitting duck.

Izzy knew it could be crazy in there. But he wanted things settled, either way. Things were crazy in Queens. It was crazy in Harlem. It was crazy in Clinton. It was crazy in Grenada. It was always crazy. The chaos was a part of him. He was never more aware of that. It was that thread of control he could manage within the chaos that gave him satisfaction. No woman ever came close. He thought of Eva's suggestion to give it all up and it scared him. Dying never scared him. Eva scared him.

Izzy left the Navigator double-parked, strutting past the shiny suits, catching nasty glares. Maybe they knew who that truck really belonged to. Maybe they just gave nasty looks. Six men. Likely six guns.

In the steak house, the whole bar of open-neck collared shirts and heavy gold turned to look at Izzy wearing jeans, T-shirt, sneakers, and baby-blue Columbia hoody. Fat men looked up from their expensive plates and young, plastic dates. Dangerous, shadow-eyed bodyguards in well-worn suits held up the walls all around. An older hostess with heavy makeup and a tight dress approached him with one thin eyebrow raised.

"Mister . . ." she began in a heavy Albanian accent.

"I'm cool at the bar," Izzy said, turned, and sat on the one empty chair before she could deny him.

The bartender, in a bow tie and suspenders, pushed the glasses back on his nose and wearily tossed a bar napkin in front of Izzy.

"Huna here?" asked Izzy.

"He was. I'm guessing he'll be right back. You want to wait?"

Izzy scanned the bottles behind the man, and spotted Johnny Black. Izzy shrugged. "Couldn't hurt."

* * *

Mal's cell phone rang. The caller ID was blocked. Normally, Mal would never answer a blocked ID. Tonight was different. He picked up.

Huna. "I'm here."

Mal stared at the photo. The kid was lighter, a few dashes of milk to Izzy's café au lait. Same mouth, same shape of his eyes, with those easygoing eyebrows.

"52 West 85th Street. I'll buzz you in," said Mal.

He thought he knew Izzy. They were both loners who spent a lot of time together. They would ramble on; exhaust topics like funny cons and baseball. Mal had heard about Izzy's mother, Grenada, his girlfriends, and recent taste for Dominicans to excess. Izzy was never private. How could that sneaky fuck have hidden this? Izzy wouldn't ignore his kid. A kid for Izzy meant time spent. Money given. And lips tight enough to beat a grand jury.

"Does your son live with you?" asked Mal.

The woman had no intention of answering. She didn't even look up at him.

Mal turned away from the photograph and lowered the gun, hand on his hip. Then he saw the manila envelope on the dining room table. A smile brewed wide across his face. He laughed again and the woman behind him began to sob.

The doorbell rang. Mal went to let Huna in.

Before the big man could speak, Mal was into his agenda.

"I know where he is. Tie her up, cut the phone wires, and call me," said Mal, breezing past, before Huna could mention the absent Albanians.

"What's the fucking rush?"

"He might not be there yet. Got to beat him."

"A-Rod's going to ruin you bums," said a grizzly gangster at the bar, wearing the only collarless shirt in a row of pomade-slicked heads, in the thick smell of intermingling cologne. His skin was slightly darker than the other removed Mediterranean characters'.

On a plasma screen mounted above the bar, Alex Rodriguez was up at bat.

"You fuckin' nuts, Frankie?" asked another, this one paler, with a wide forehead. Albanian, for sure. "Check the numbers. Guy's the AL MVP this year, guaranteed."

With the posture of a matador, Rodriguez adjusted into his batting stance, the head of his bat making small, controlled circles.

"Douche bag only hits when it don't mean nothing, Frankie."

Pedro Martinez then hung a breaking pitch chest high, which Rodriguez calmly stroked into the Yankee bull pen, clear out of the ballpark.

"You know somethin', Frankie, I think you got lost in some Harlem cuchie, got you smoking crack."

Because only people in Harlem smoke crack.

These men were both named Frankie, and Izzy was curious how dark Frankie would take that one. Would he turn it on light Frankie's sister? Mother?

"Can't help it, your little mixed daughter's up on 145th giving it away free."

Daughter. Close. And he managed to insult Izzy indirectly as well.

"Besides," said light Frankie, "Yanks go down, and this guy's the reason." He pointed to the screen as Gary Sheffield stood at the plate, violently waving his bat front to back, in striking contrast to Rodriguez's coiled control. "Loose cannon, can't get along with nobody."

Izzy jumped in. "Only people Sheff doesn't get along with is reporters. Teammates like him just fine. Opposing pitchers are scared shitless of him."

Izzy's comment hung in the air, as he had addressed nobody, and the Frankies hadn't realized he was eavesdropping. Izzy thought maybe he should have kept his comments to himself. These were far from friends.

Dark Frankie scratched his thick stubble. "Got that right."

Izzy took another sip and noticed his drink was still half-way full. There were too many balls in the air for him to enjoy Johnny B. The steak house, except for the body-guards, had basically forgotten he was there. He kept checking the Navigator, making sure he didn't get a ticket. Which made no sense, because the truck wasn't even his. Too many balls in the air. Huna, Mal, Eva, Jacob. The base-ball game. A jolt shook him. He was pretty sure it was anxi-ety because he wanted to smoke his blunt so bad he could taste hydro. Izzy paid for the drink and left.

He paused in front of the restaurant, hearing the cigar-smoking, silk-laden degenerates spit at the sidewalk by his feet. Likely the gesture was for him, but he paid it no mind. His attention was just past the Navigator, across the street. There was a temple. A fitted-cap, low-jean, XXL-white-T Harlem soldier climbed the stairs, with a large gold cross hanging by his belly, and appropriate disrespect in his swag-ger. He spat and walked in. The temple was plain and mod-ern, with a large Star of David above the entrance. Izzy touched the symbol around his own neck. He took the *hamsa* from under his shirt and kissed it, thinking of his mother.

"Goddamn chronic, fried my memory," he said to him-self, wondering how he could have forgotten the temple was there. He had walked past the Navigator. He didn't want to smoke anymore.

He thought about Green Haven Prison, where he learned how to be a Jew. Izzy was always defiantly aware of his Jewishness, but until he got his transfer from Clinton, he had little knowledge of what that meant. The jail at Green Haven was famous for having the only hot kosher food in

New York State. Prisoners from all over applied for transfers and converted for a decent meal. Rodrigo, a heavyset Guatemalan, went so far as to grow ear locks and wear a *yarmulke*. Green Haven even had its own rabbi, who was convicted of kidnapping for taking a kid to Jerusalem for his bar mitzvah. The mother filed a complaint when she learned she would stop receiving money from the temple once her son turned thirteen. Izzy spent time with the other Jews, except for when the knives came out, and he preferred the company of those who looked more like him. Izzy even worked at the kosher cafeteria as a volunteer (to avoid being harassed by COs as an employee). There was even a doctor there, Dr. Hertz, a heavy-jawed, deeply stubborn man with a hairlip, who let a woman bleed to death from a botched abortion, refusing to call the paramedics. In the shower, where religious secrets were exposed, Izzy would joke that Dr. Hertz should complete Rodrigo's conversion, and cut his goy foreskin. It got picked up by the guys, and everyone began to joke about it, until Hertz took a hot slice of tin can, what they used for a knife in the kitchen, and Rodrigo whipped out his gentile member, laying it on a cutting board. Everyone screamed, "No!" getting in between the two of them, the only two who didn't know it was a joke.

Izzy remembered the East Coast Zodiac Killer, reciting his trial in his cell every night, doing all the voices, every objection, and every witness. The guards got sick of him, and set a fire in his cell, which made no difference, because after twenty-plus years, his entire trial was committed to memory. He went on reciting every night and was certainly doing so to this day. Izzy never remembered the particulars of his case, which never went to trial, or cared to think about them. It was another curve in his winding past of unpredictability and inconsequence.

Except Won. Won seemed real. The difference between killing and murdering.

Won, who looked exactly like the man who had stalked outside the East Side Temple, climbed the stairs, paused, and spat on the *Mezuzah*, which you were supposed to kiss. It was the same squat, bulldog face that Izzy saw now on the temple roof, emerging and fading into darkness like a fish drifting from the cover of a cavernous reef. He was there, and then he wasn't. Then again, red bandana, screw face. Then gone, and back, this time with his arms flapping at his sides. And gone again.

The date was over. A goofy law clerk with blond hair and brown roots leaned in as the aspiring-actress-administrative-assistant with the nice rack turned her cheek. His thin lips planted just below her ear, in what would be a sincere kiss to an old friend. He took advantage of the embrace and squeezed, as though she really were some old friend, and the verdict was in. On his date with national television, the law clerk was rejected.

He stood with a desperate grin, holding the girl's hand as she tried to go home, searching for eye contact. Eva bit her lip in delicious voyeuristic embarrassment. The girl finally made it inside and Eva let out a long exhale. She waited out the commercials to hear what they had to say. The guys were always predictable after leaning into a turned cheek. They were either desperate or they compensated. "We can be friends and I'll hope for something more," or "She's not my type anyway. Excuse me while I call my hos while the camera's rolling." The girls were unpredictable. One could give a guy the cold shoulder, flirt with every service professional throughout the episode, turn her cheek, and then say he was the man of her dreams. She could give the guy a lap dance, get drunk, and shove her tongue down his throat, tell him to call her, and then confess that she really never wanted to see him again. Eva had long ago decided she would never understand women; it was hard enough understanding herself. She wondered how guys dealt.

The couple came back, and predictably the law clerk was ready to get married and the actress was ready to find someone who could actually help with her career. Eva was disappointed when the show ended, and surfed the channels aimlessly, picky about her inane television. The rest just reminded her of her circumstances, and she brought her knees to her chest on the couch, though she wasn't cold.

She didn't want to process what had happened. Not now, anyway. She knew it was too soon, yet she could not turn her brain off, thinking like she was in session with Gail. Theresa was everywhere. In Eva's apartment, her suffocating blunt smoke constantly wafting from her room in the back. If Eva ever went in, she could see the smoke suspended in front of the TV, thick enough to cast a grainy shadow. Theresa's razor dismissive voice would tell her to get out. She didn't care if you could smell it in the hallway, in the lobby, if the co-op board complained, if Eva asked her to leave. Theresa was queen, and Eva couldn't dethrone her, even as her name was on the title and she paid the mortgage. Eva was in the country to help Theresa, fix Auntie and Uncle Richard's problem. Otherwise she'd still be in Trinidad, beheading chickens and most likely getting beaten and cheated on by some vague replica of her father. If not for Theresa, the poison, there would be no Eva, the cure.

So she cured her for good. Eva felt ruthless, and convinced herself she knew what had happened. She could stop wondering. Eva had stabbed the bitch. All there was to it. Long time coming.

This acceptance brought less comfort than Eva hoped. She would work on this kind of thing with her clients. *Try to accept the worst. Now go backward. Find yourself. Okay, then.* Eva had found herself. She was a repressed do-gooder from Trinidad still trying to prove that she was worthy of her new family's love, who finally regurgitated all that swallowed aggression. Years of letting Theresa have her way finally caught up to her. First, she met Izzy and felt comfortable with him. Then, her drink still going strong, she strutted up into a thug den, feeling confident. Her aggression was just building. She saw these violent characters and felt comfortable again. She joked with them. She relaxed with them. She felt like having a drink with them. Forgot the repressed Trini. Saw who was left. A rude bitch. A switchblade sister. Fucking murderer.

Eva was in tears. She picked her face off her knees, her cheeks sliding from the slippery wetness. She got to her feet and woozily sidestepped, struggling to balance. She went to the kitchen and looked through the worn cabinets. Cereal, Ramen, and pancake mix. In the fridge was soy milk and crusty old white Chinese containers. She went back to the couch.

Izzy passed a liquor store, insufficient booze in his blood; slightly impaired, but not enjoying it. He drove over to Broadway, where he would pass another liquor store in ten blocks.

Izzy pulled over on West 97th Street and jumped out, leaving the hazards blinking. He scanned the bottles behind the counter.

"Give me that fifth of Jack," he told the clerk, switching his drink for Eva's sake, and hearing radio static, cheering fans, and John Sterling's fuzzy, jumping voice. "It is high . . ." The game. Izzy stopped, put his hands on the counter, and leaned in. "It is gone!" Who? The crowd was cheering. That didn't matter, the crowd was equal parts Mets/Yankees fans.

"They turned him loose on a three-oh count, that'll be the last pitch from Leiter, sailing over the Yankee bull pen." Who? Who hit it? What was the score? "Mike Piazza struts the bases and the Mets jump to a three-one lead."

Izzy didn't like that. He never liked Piazza. The man should have learned to play first base years ago; maybe he'd have helped his team.

Out on the street, he looked around for Mal's taxi. Yellow taxis were pretty much everywhere.

Mal ran his third red light. He knew it was risky; he was excited and didn't care. Yellow cab with two shot-out windows running red lights. *So what? Tonight might be the night I pop a cop.*

Mal played with the rhyme. Pop a cop. Pop a cop in his top.

Then he saw a cop car. The light was red. Mal stopped. Waited. *Patience. Patience.*

The Eastern European was the biggest man who had ever been in Gail's home. He almost hit his head on the French door frame. His mass increased with maybe a bulletproof vest beneath his platinum sweatsuit. He looked at Gail like another piece of furniture, pulled the phone wires, searched the kitchen, and asked if there was any duct tape around. As if she would tell him.

"I don't have any," she said.

He thought. "Just don't go anywhere or I'll break your fuckin' tooth, bitch."

Another charmer. Gail would have cried if she wasn't so scared.

The man made a few phone calls, muttered some aggressive Eastern European language—throwing in a couple of "cocksuckers"—slammed his phone down, and stood up. Gail sucked in a breath and held it. He reached in his pocket, pulled out a little green baggie, and tossed it on the table, sitting back down. Gail breathed.

"Was that . . . Croatian?" she asked. She figured her only prayer was to loosen him up. He looked like big-time sleaze, but her profession was people. "I'm Gail," she said.

The Albanian pulled a switchblade from nowhere and flicked it open. Gail yelped. He snapped the seal of the baggie with his other hand and maneuvered the blade inside.

"Huna," she said. "What kind of name is that?"

Huna scooped a small pile of powder on the tip of his blade and shoveled it up his nose, the stiff snort filling the room. And then again, the other nostril. He glared at her with bloodshot eyes. *Shit*, she thought. She shouldn't have said his name.

"Huna," he said, his nostrils red and raw, "is 'nose' "— *sniff*—"in Albanian."

A small pile of CDs was on Jacob's floor by his Toshiba five-disc DVD changer. Eva squatted and looked through them. Nelly, 50 Cent, No Doubt, The Killers, Lauryn Hill. She shut the TV off and put on the Lauryn Hill CD. The downbeat rushed in and a dynamic rhythm bounced over piano keys. Eva shut it off. She couldn't listen to music; it was too intense, like jumping into a cold pool immediately after the sauna.

Then she spotted the PlayStation beneath the TV stand. She pulled it out, shaking the stand, and something fell from on top of the TV. It was a film case. Eva thought she had seen a digital camera in the kid's room. Before she put the case back, she snapped the lid, releasing a rich, floral, green smell. She pulled out a small bud of weed, with shiny white crystals and fuzzy red hairs. She smirked. Checking on top of the TV, she saw there was also a glass pipe.

The hot smoke burned down her throat and she coughed a lot. Then she laughed at herself for coughing. She considered another hit, felt her pulse race, and set the burning pipe down. It filled the room with an almost chemical-smelling smoke, different from the dirty, cheap weed and cigar smell she was used to from Theresa. She sat, needing to focus on something, remembering the PlayStation. She turned it on, awkwardly holding the controller.

It was a fight game. Eva chose the badass girl. She fought a guy with a green face like a monster. She took a couple of swings and quickly got disoriented. It was too vivid and made her dizzy. She shut the thing off.

The TV came back on. The guy from *Chips* in an info-mercial ad, with poor lettering in front of a fuzzy-looking suburb. Erik Estrada, that was his name.

"Hot Springs Village, Arkansas, is on the rise. Come join this emerging residential community, for a one-time low price of six ninety-five down and one ninety-nine a month. Don't wait any longer. Own your own home for a total of twelve thousand dollars."

Something rattled. Eva's eyes shot to the doorknob. It shook.

Got it. The door made that satisfying click as Mal eased it open. He put his tools away and drew his gun, as the room gradually came into view. Gray carpet. Clothes and junk on the floor. A red couch. Coffee table with a little glass bowl of weed. The TV on. Erik Estrada talking.

Mal stepped in, pistol first, seeing no one. The door was about all the way open. He took a step toward the kitchen, the door swinging back closed behind him. An excruciating shot of pain stabbed his shoulder.

When the little guy stepped toward the kitchen, Eva coiled her stiletto heel back over her head. The door shut. She saw his back. She struck. The heel went clean into his

bandaged shoulder. Must have been right around where she
had shot him.

Mal yelled and dropped his gun. Eva saw it bounce by
the couch and her eyes lit up. She let go of her shoe, raced
around him, and picked it up. The door shut. She held the
gun with two hands and quickly pointed it at Mal.

He was on his knees, muttering. "Goddamn motherfucking cunt bitch whore . . ."

The gun made her manic. Her impulses conspired this
way and that as she held on, aiming, pretending to know
how.

"Fuck!" said Mal, reaching back toward the heel, unable
to get to it. The shoe was in good.

Eva giggled, surprising herself.

Mal began to regain composure. "You think this is funny,
bitch?"

She shrugged, holding on. Swaying. Holding on.

"All right. Laugh all you want. But give me back my
fucking gun."

The gun. It was longer than the other one, with a heavy
metal extension on the barrel. "So you can shoot me with
it? Do I look that stupid?"

"You're not going to shoot me with it."

It was long. She couldn't aim it. She wanted to.

"You sure about that?" she asked.

"Yeah. You don't have it in you," Mal told her, getting to
his feet.

"I did it once," she said. "Why wouldn't I do it now?"

"Do it, then."

It was heavy, and getting heavier. When she did it before
she wasn't thinking or feeling, she was just acting. She remembered how the kick sent her back into the wall, her
hands vibrating to the bone.

"Longer you wait, the harder it'll get."

Mal reached back to get the shoe again, coming up short.

The gun had lowered. Eva's heart raced and the weed smoke swirled in her head as she raised the gun and closed one eye, aiming.

Mal began to laugh. Hard. A creepy hyena laugh. Eva hated hyenas.

"You really don't know shit," he told her.

"I know enough," she said.

"Sure, then shoot me. The slide's not racked, tho."

She had no idea what a slide was, or what racking it meant.

"Means you don't have a bullet in the chamber, genius. You know what that means?"

She wanted to shake her head. But she didn't. She held on to the gun with two hands and hoped she wouldn't drop it.

Mal spoke slowly, like she was a child. "That means you are going to pull the trigger, and nothing is going to happen."

He took a step toward her; she took a step back.

"Bullshit," she said, sounding unsure, even to herself. "You would have already tried to take it from me."

"I got a goddamn shoe in my back!"

He became blurry. It was the weed. Eva felt fast and slow all at once—she thought too fast and moved too slow. She hated weed. She glanced at the bowl on the table. Then quickly back to Mal.

"The slide is that chrome-looking thing on the top. It looks like the top of the gun, but if you pull it toward you, it's going to bring a bullet from the clip and into the chamber." He came closer as he spoke, soft and conversational. "The chamber is where the bullet takes off from when you pull the trigger. Chamber the bullet, you'll be good to go, you sexy assassin. If you got it in you," he sang like a schoolyard taunt.

Eva was unsure if she wanted to have it in her. The

thought took her mind off track, and she followed his instruction, reaching her weak hand up from the handle and toward the slide. Mal's chest almost touched the extended tip.

Then a noise. Keys jingled. The lock clicked and opened. Izzy stood in the doorway with a bottle in a brown paper bag.

Mal grabbed the gun, sidestepping. Eva squeezed.

The handle kicked. A bullet whispered from the long barrel. The bottle in Izzy's hand shattered.

"Shit!" yelled Izzy.

Mal wrenched the gun from Eva's hand. She let it go but grabbed her shoe and pushed the heel deeper into his back. He wailed. He had the gun, but held it by the slide and couldn't transfer the grip with his bad hand. He shoved Eva down on the floor with his forearm, and turned to see Izzy draw with his left and aim.

Mal jumped sideways into the kitchen as that big .45 blasted twice. He rolled on the tiled floor, and rested against the refrigerator, adjusting the shoe in his back. He guided the pistol handle into his good hand and gripped it properly. His shoulder was limp and numb. Whatever anesthetic Doc Strange had used was probably keeping him conscious.

Mal took a few breaths, then spun into the kitchen doorway, pistol first. The room was empty.

Izzy watched his shooting hand bleed fresh on the elevator floor, by where Eva's feet stood in a pair of men's ribbed socks.

"Fuck, fuck, fuck," Izzy repeated.

Izzy took off his jacket, then his shirt. He wrapped the shirt around his right hand. Eva tied it up tight.

"I'm sorry," said Eva.

"Baby, you got a real habit of wounding men," he said.

He noticed the "baby" afterward. He hadn't meant to say it.

"I'm so sorry, my God."

They rushed out of Jacob's lobby, Izzy putting his jacket back on. He flipped open his cell phone and made a call to his son.

Chapter 11

Yet another late night, and Jacob was at the office. Winthrop paced behind him as he tried to look busy. Winthrop's face was already red. He seemed awkward, unsure whether to compliment or insult; an older man relying on money for confidence. He hovered over his employees, perpetually impressed with his status, quick with a "to make it in this business" speech, working well into a fourth martini or brandy. The whole company had an adolescent obsession with doing what they weren't supposed to, as long as they made money. Jacob had yet to decide whether or not this was a virtue.

Winthrop shook the keys and change in his pocket.

"How's it going?" he finally asked.

"All right," said Jacob, cool, affable. "Just got all this filing to do. You know, time-consuming."

"Actually, I don't know. I haven't filed anything myself in over twenty years."

No shit.

One of Jacob's coworkers passed with a stack of papers and a chip on his shoulder. Jacob could hear him from the other side of the cubicle.

"Valedictorian. Honors business," he muttered. "Ivy

League, all the way. Three sports for four years. Now what do you do? I file. Pretty much it. Eat, sleep, shit, file."

Winthrop leaned in close to Jacob, eyes on the disgruntled employee.

"See him? He will never work here."

"He does work here," offered Jacob.

"Didn't you hear him? He doesn't work. He files. Tell me something. You got plans for tonight?"

Jacob cautiously shook his head.

"Come with me. I got a party to go to."

Jacob pointed to his work.

"Yeah, put that shit down."

He sauntered out of the office and Jacob followed. Winthrop made him uneasy, but clout was clout. Jacob breezed past his coworker in his amateur business shuffle, ignoring the phone ringing on his desk.

"No answer," said Eva, closing the phone.

Izzy's hand didn't hurt. It oozed. The bullet had gone through and through. The splintering glass cut him. But it didn't hurt. The life was emptying out with the blood, as though in time his hand would be useless. His shooting hand.

"He have a cell phone?" asked Eva.

"If he does, I don't have the number. Fuck. I guess Mal will most likely clear out of there, after those gunshots. Cops'll be coming."

"He following us?" asked Eva.

Eva looked back. Izzy checked his mirrors. No sight of him, but he was there. The worst possible scenario. Mal knew about Jacob. Of the reckless indifference Izzy had shown himself, making a living jumping out on armed felons, here he was, no worse for wear, a bloody hand but okay. Others might not be so lucky, who might not have his catlike knack for survival. Mal was now his shadow, a step away from him, and whoever stood beside him.

"He wants to kill me," said Eva, as if to herself.

Izzy nodded. "He figures, you already got a body over your head. You could be a witness against him, for what he did."

"Yeah, why not? Izzy, maybe I should just go to the police. I could get killed out here."

She was scared, holding her elbows, hunched against the cold.

"You got to do what you think is best. But you had better come up with something to explain the knife, and those powder burns."

She was shaking her head. "I'm so fucking stuck!"

"But really, who's going to believe you killed all those people?" asked Izzy, trying on optimism.

"I do not want to risk meeting him."

Huna pressed his fingers on the remaining powder, sucking it and rubbing it on his teeth, feeling that hypernumbness. It was a good session. He needed it, no question. Arben was gone. No word about the brothers. His plans for the night had changed drastically.

Privilege was just the warm-up. They were going to initiate Benny, then go back out and hit Scores, where another of Huna's cousins was a manager. Feed those hookers twenties all night, see who stuck around at sunrise, take them back to the station, and run a train. All five cars. Huna would be the caboose, the family could go first, it was all love. He didn't even mess with girls without his boys.

There would be no girls tonight. Fucking Izzy. Last night of that cocksucker's worthless life. Mal too. Huna was good and ready. Murder those two at least.

The doorbell rang. Huna checked the woman in her silk pajamas, and went to get it.

Mal rushed past him again. Huna grabbed him, his meaty hand wrapped around Mal's thin biceps.

Mal winced.

"You missed," said Huna.

"Yeah. I fucking missed."

Huna let go, and gripped the bloody bandage on Mal's shoulder, digging into the stickiness.

Mal's scream was satisfying. Little cocksucker always acted like he ran things. Like he was better than Huna.

"Leggo, let go!"

"What do I look like to you?" rumbled Huna.

"Leggo my fucking shoulder, bro!"

"Your shoulder? No. My fucking shoulder. My fucking arm. Only reason this is still connected to your body, I didn't take it yet."

"I swear—"

"I asked you a question."

"Man, I swear I'm the only one here using my fucking head!"

"I asked you a fucking question!"

"What?

"What-do-I-look-like-to-you?"

Sneering mouth, eyes squinted, Mal stuck between pain and resistance, Huna's pressure overwhelming. Mal surrendered.

"You look like, you, man, what?"

Huna loved to get high and dominate little cocksucking punks like Mal. "This"—he pointed to his face, red and glossy—"is what my last nerve looks like. Once it's gone? That will be the last face you see." He spoke slowly, with long, agonizing breaks between his words. "What . . . happened . . . to . . . my . . . countrymen?"

"Izzy got them. All of them."

"Not possible," said Huna, squeezing deeper, earning more moans.

"He did. I saw it. They all took head shots, man. One by one. He's mean. He's mean with that gat. Believe me, man. No lie. I want this dude. I want to murk this dude worse than you do. I swear. No lie."

Huna let go, bulging eyes roaring at Mal. His fist swung into the drywall, coughing up dust. Then he lowered his head, leaning up against the dent.

"He's got the money from the job tonight," said Mal, rotating his shoulder, trying to shake off the pain.

Huna picked up.

Family was family. Money was money.

"I thought you might like that," said Mal.

"Now I see why you went ahead without me. From now on, you don't leave my fucking sight."

"Well, you were wrong about my instinct. I don't have it," said Eva, feeling some minor relief as her naked toes played with the clean, carpeted interior.

Izzy took a moment to get what she was talking about. "You sure about that?"

"Yeah. I had a chance to end it, and I didn't. I had Mal's gun," she exclaimed, remembering the heavy, long steel, tilting in her hands.

"You didn't have the heart?"

No. She didn't have the heart and didn't want the heart. "I guess not," she said, trying not to sound emphatic. She recalled Mal's hungry look as he calmly talked her out of shooting him, for no other reason than so that he could shoot her. She was afraid for her life. Yet she didn't want her spastic reactions to insult or hurt Izzy. Not that she found him sensitive. Izzy was cool. His world just scared the shit out of her.

Eva had known every kind of fuckup, delinquent, and sad story. She interviewed scores of them. Every last one was eager to tell his life, couldn't wait for a soapbox, camera, or spotlight. She had heard uncountable, carefully cropped heroic tales about suffering, unfairness, and loss. Some would curse her out. One mangy, toothless former felon sporadically called her "Skinny Bitch." Some came on real strong. A six-foot-nine man with a high-pitched voice tried to sing R. Kelly's "Ignition" to her in her office. Some wanted mothers. A squat tenant used to only do exactly what Eva had told him not to, gleefully lapping up her scolding. Some seemed like good guys gone a bit astray. Drugs took over; bad parents, worse friends; desperate lives with resilient smiles. One man named Donald, who she knew from a clinic she used to work at, would see her in the street all the time. Hopelessly addicted, he worked the shopping-cart and garbage-rummaging assembly line. When he saw Eva his dignity took over. He stood up straight and called her "Teacher." She would advise him about shelters and programs, and he would wave a hand and gently smile, like a willing martyr. "The street's my life," Donald told her one time, and when she got home, she got in bed and cried for him.

Izzy was no Donald. She didn't feel sorry for Izzy. She wanted to, but she didn't. She had never met anyone like Izzy before. He was unflappable like the affluent Darien trust kids, yet he had no air of entitlement. Even the way he froze when he saw her back in Queens seemed more unwound sluggishness than a crippled shock. Eva thought that Izzy was still watching some pivotal moment of his life, and the daily wildness was an amusing subplot. Part of her wanted to smack him. Snap him out of it. *The world's on fire, stupid. You're roasting marshmallows.*

But Izzy was her guide. His calmness was unsettling. She still needed it.

"He told me to 'rack the slide,'" exclaimed Eva, shaking her head.

"He was messing with you," said Izzy.

"Asshole."

"He came to shoot. He racked the slide before, believe me," Izzy said, glancing at his hand, then staring at her.

She felt flushed. She lowered her head, and then faced him. He actually wasn't looking at her. It was something out the window. He pulled over.

"There. The Duane Reade." Izzy reached into his pants and pulled out some cash. He gave Eva a twenty. "Get some gauze, some tape—"

"Wait, why am I going in there? I don't have any shoes, they'll think I'm nuts!"

"I don't want to bleed in there," said Izzy, holding up his hand, the shirt tied firmly around it, a heavy spot of blood dripping through. "Blood drops anywhere is a no-no."

"This isn't a crime scene, it's a pharmacy."

"You go in there, and they'll just think you're homeless or broke. Show them you got money and it's all good. I go in there, people will think I got shot. People might panic. Security might call the cops."

"So you want me walking on that concrete with my bare feet," Eva said, folding her arms.

"Who shot who again?"

Jacob could see his reflection in the oak desk's sparkling finish. He could see himself again when he looked out the window, a thin, dapper young man floating above a muted Fifth Avenue, thirty-seven stories below. The tiny streetlights shone as Fifth stretched uptown. Everything was shiny. And Jacob could see himself in all of it.

Winthrop was rummaging through his desk drawers, looking for something. Pinkish cheeks glowed in his red face. Winthrop's jacket was off, revealing the circles of sweat beneath his armpits. The lingering strings of hair on his scalp were soaked and stuck together. Jacob was stuck on the view.

"Wow. You must just get a boost every time you look out there," he said, realizing as he spoke that the opposite was most likely true. Winthrop probably didn't notice it at all anymore.

The older man shrugged, his search becoming a bit more frantic.

The silence made Jacob self-conscious, thinking he should be making conversation. He was intimidated by the distant ceiling, the window twice his height, and his smug, shady boss.

"I mean, I've been standing here five minutes, and I already feel better about myself," he said, again the opposite being true. "It being yours makes all the difference."

Winthrop turned and went over to a corner of the office, where a small black refrigerator was dwarfed by a grandfather clock. The fridge was stuffed with clear plastic Ziploc bags. Winthrop sat down on the floor and began taking handfuls of the bags out, looking at the different substances inside—white, gray, and brown powdery stuff, and fluffy green weed. He dropped each one on the floor between his knees, until he found the one he wanted, his smile long and greedy. He held the bag out to Jacob, who recognized the long, sticklike stalks and brown caps inside the frosted baggie. Mushrooms.

Alone in the Navigator, Izzy scrolled through the static of AM stations to find 880. Three to one, Mets. Bottom of the seventh. Bases loaded for Derek Jeter, the Yankee captain and poster boy for New York's interracial glamour. The Mets manager, former longtime Yankee player and coach Willie Randolph, was taking no chances and pitching lefty-lefty, righty-righty. Meaning for every righty hitter, a righty pitcher would throw, giving the pitcher an advantage, because it's more difficult for a hitter to see the ball when it's thrown from the corner of his periphery. Izzy always loved

Willie Randolph, from when he played second base for the Yanks. Now he was way on the other side of things. So Izzy supported the person, instead of the uniform. Made sense to him. Even though uniforms made rivals of teammates.

Unsurprisingly, Jeter poked a 2–1 pitch into shallow right field, scoring a run. The crowd went crazy. It went crazy for everything that happened. It was all New York. An eruption of boos and cheers followed anything at all.

Eva left the Duane Reade with a shopping bag, feet in a pair of disposable foam hospital slippers. Izzy chuckled. She opened the Navigator door and set the bag down on the passenger seat, without a word about her footwear. She found the gauze pads and opened up the box. Izzy unwrapped the bloody shirt as she opened packages of thick pads, getting them ready. As soon as he removed the shirt, Eva stamped the pads on each side of his hand, pinching them in place with one hand, and reaching for reinforcements with the other. It was the calmest Izzy had seen her. Having a task seemed to focus her, and she had never looked so pretty. Her heavy lips softly parted and motioned as she worked, almost speaking to herself, wrapping layer upon layer of white tape around his hand. He could not see her eyes, only her lashes, curved back toward her like long, manicured fingers being admired. She squeezed his hand to test the strength of the bandage. Izzy closed his hand over hers. Eva looked up at him and he winced, as though she had hurt him.

"Sorry," she said.

He nodded.

"So, where are we going?" she asked, slowly, reluctantly releasing his hand.

"A hotel."

"Oh? You got money?"

"Yeah. We've got money."

Out on the street, Izzy noticed a young, trendy woman

closing the gate to a small, designer boutique. "Any chance you want to get yourself some clothes that fit?"

Eva turned and saw the girl. She broke from Izzy and ran to her. The door still open, Izzy realized the game was still going on. Tied 3–3. He lowered the volume and heard Eva barter.

"Hey," she told the girl. "Hi, I'm sorry, but I really need your help. I need some clothes, and shoes."

"Oh no, see, I already shut down the register and set the alarm. I can't open up the store now, no way. Sorry," exclaimed the girl, too tired of retail to sound sincere.

"Wait," said Eva, and rushed back to Izzy. "How much money we got?"

Hesitant, Izzy reached for the heavy wad of bills.

Eva's eyes lit up. "How the hell did you get all that?"

Izzy shrugged.

Mal's shoulder burned like all hell. He wanted to pop Huna in his fucking grill right now. Open that nigga's brain up. Spray it on the wall.

He couldn't. Mal pulled out his gun and couldn't even look at Huna; his glower and enormous body consumed the room.

Mal was cold. The pain throbbed from his shoulder through his body and quickly cooled. He should have been hot. He should have popped Huna for that. His hand shouldn't have been shaking. Mal aimed at Gail Glaser, and didn't understand why he shook. He squeezed the handle tighter to make it stop. Didn't work.

"Where is your son?" he managed. "I won't ask twice."

"Honestly," the woman said with a forced patience, "I don't know."

"But you know his cell number, don't you?"

She slowly shook her head. "Of course I know his cell

number," she responded, labored and deliberate. "But I'll never give it to you."

She was possibly in her late fifties, her skin taut around her cheeks but loosened as it draped over her throat. Mal focused on those hanging wrinkles below her chin. *Saggy bitch.* "You would die first?"

Gail held her head up as her eyes welled. "If I have to," she said, sucking in her tears and composure.

Cunt. Dumb cunt.

Mal's backhand sailed and snapped her head around. Before she could recover, the long nozzle of the silencer was against her jaw. Though dignified, she cried.

"The number, bitch. That's all I want. Just want to talk to him."

Her head was wedged between Mal's gun and the canvas armrest, tears pooling in the fabric. It felt good to Mal, the fantasy becoming real, like seeing a beautiful woman taking off her clothes. Excitement raced inside him. Fuck Huna. Mal was in charge here. He thought of the men he had killed that day—all the weeping and struggling like a gradual coil for the snap, pop. He did it like it was nothing. He made people pray for their lives, and then he took them. It was what he did, who he was. Not that squealing piglet he was with Huna. That wasn't him anymore. His shoulder flared at the thought, pain stabbing down through his lower back. He remembered the feel of Huna's thumb pressing inside him and he remembered his mother.

Gail chewed on sobs as she tried to speak. "I . . ." she stuttered. "I—I know you."

Mal was surprised. "Lyin' ass."

"From years ago, Harlem Outreach. Yes, you're Cookie's son. Malik, the kids called you Mouth."

Bitch wasn't lying. Malik. He hadn't heard that name in years. He was shocked but he tried not to show it. He just remembered his mother and here was this woman, speaking her name, and the name she called him. He could hear it in his mother's shrill, exploding voice, *Malik. Malik!* His ear pulled to the floor, nails stabbing him, scratching his lobe. All he could hear. *Malik.*

His mother was long dead, barely skinnier than when she was alive, beneath a nub of a gravestone, no higher from the ground than a knuckle from a fist. She was rotting in hell and he was sure to see her there someday.

"It's just Mal now. And my mom's long dead."

"I'm sorry."

"Don't lie, bitch. You ain't got no feeling for me."

She squirmed and the gun relaxed a bit. She got her body beneath her, supporting herself with her hand. "No," she admitted. "But I did for her. Cookie had a very hard life."

Hard. Life. "Yeah, no shit."

Her voice grew soothing. "I know what you've been through, Malik," she said, emphasizing that name again, like it made them friends.

"Look, don't try that shit with me. We got a problem at hand," he exclaimed, pushing her head farther back toward the couch. "Stop trying to distract me. Tell me where your son at 'fore you lose yo head."

She sniffled. "You're not going to do that, Malik," she said, settling down and finding some authority.

Mal felt the cool go away and heat rise again. "Don't call me that. It's Mal."

"You're not going to harm my son, Jacob, either."

Mal thought of his mother again, chaining him with a bike lock to the radiator one winter. Hot steam whistling like the heavy whistle from Huna's nose. Huna breathed behind him. Above him. He didn't look.

"I don't think you know who the fuck you talking to." Mal was enunciating, projecting, trying to sound stronger. *I'm a goddamn killer.*

"I know. Periodic abuse. Mood swings. Watching your mother decline. I don't know everything. But I know that much."

"You trying to get inside my head?" She didn't know. She didn't know shit. His mom could seem like a victim to a cunt like Gail but she wasn't. Mom would make Mal hers, and probe his young body with hard props for places that gave. All these cunts wanted to get inside him. Now it made him laugh. Of course they did, that's what cunts did, but he would win, like always. Like when his mom needed his shit so bad and he wouldn't even give her a taste. *I. Will. Not. Lose.*

"I'm just trying to get you to see," she said, still measured in her awkward position. "I'm a human being. So is my son. We have done nothing to you. Please, don't hurt us. If you need money . . ."

Mal dropped his arm.

She exhaled.

He slid down to the couch beside her, his eyes quivering. "You know, lately—I have been feeling like I need someone to talk to."

She wiped her face, brushed her hair back, and sat up, feet bumping Mal's ankles.

"It's just been so rough."

Gail nodded, sympathetic but weary. She was professional. Very professional.

"And Ma? She did beat me," he said, averting his eyes from Huna, knowing he watched closely. "She beat the hell out of me. Broke my jaw, my arm. She did some *things*, man. Sometimes, I get so mad, you know? I feel, like, rage. Just thinking about it, I want to hurt . . . I want to hurt somebody, you know? Like how I've been hurt."

"That's okay. As long as—"

"Yeah," he said with a jolt. "That is okay. It's natural. I mean, there must be studies, right? I know there's other people like me."

Gail squirmed and shuffled a bit farther away. "Mal, I don't expect you to suddenly reform yourself. Only to see that me and my son, are people. Like you."

Mal dropped his head into his lap and held still. The room fell quiet. He sensed Gail's and Huna's confusion. Gail examined him, coming closer and closer. Her hand rose and inched toward his shoulder, a tentative consolation.

She touched him.

The gun flashed and Mal opened up and fired at her face. The back of her head shattered, spraying on the wall as she jumped, and quietly slumped over.

Just like that and she didn't exist. For a moment, none of them existed anymore.

Mal stood. "I know you're people. That's what I do to people. I fuckin' erase 'em."

Chapter 12

Izzy waited through the radio commercials of endless pitching changes, alone in the car, thinking about women. His track record was reliable. Gooey infatuation, followed by swift disinterest. He had love for all of them. The relationships themselves, however, had only lasted at the most two years. Women were always drawn to him. Even when he was into a girl, his unhurried swagger drew in many gorgeous hood chicks used to being hollered at and harassed. Izzy loved hood chicks, so long as their attitude was cut with a bit of class and decency. Hood chicks were the sexiest females in the world. Keep your frail, pouty-lip, inflatable-boob models. The right girl in the wrong neighborhood could flip a billionaire on his ass, make a broke man spend, turn a gay man straight. These women would stroll through the sea of mishapen, overweight, hustling minorities, a mass of attention swept in their wake. In the most jaded hoods, they were a breath of amazement. They were simple and knew how to have fun. They had seen a lot and nothing much surprised them. And they didn't make Izzy feel guilty.

Adina was Izzy's first black girl. She had memorized every Rakim song, loved to shop, and had ass for days. Izzy would hold it when they slept. She loved hip-hop a bit too much, getting lost backstage at a Big Daddy Kane show, and Izzy slipped out of her life without a word. Then there was Penelope, or Princess, another black girl, this one a bit classier, who inspired Izzy to learn how to cook. To this day Izzy made a mean manicotti. He had wanted to learn to make Jewish food, but he didn't know what it was.

Penelope had wonderful breasts and made so much noise during sex upstairs that neighbors would interrupt to complain. It built Izzy up, but her regal superiority would knock him down, and her bad temperament and vicious self-involvement pushed Izzy to a white party girl. He honestly couldn't remember her name. He always referred to her as his white party girl. He must have known her name at some point, but he couldn't be sure. He had some wild sex with that one, often with another of her many white party girl friends, all intent on reviving their idea of risqué free love. Got old quick. Plus, her heroin habit became more and more obvious, reminding Izzy of his mother and thus numbing sexual feeling.

Izzy tried another white girl right after her, a twenty-eight-year-old virgin, and cousin of Evil Knevil, named Amy. Amy Knevil was a strict Protestant from Pennsylvania. Izzy told her he was in the music industry. They dated for three months before they got naked together, and Izzy discovered that though she was a virgin, Amy Knevil could still reach orgasm by minimal rubbing of her pious clit. He still wanted to deflower her out of some urge for conquest, and one night while spooning, the erotic frustration peaked and Izzy penetrated her. Though she was dry and tight, Izzy found relief, and didn't realize, from the disorienting sensuality of her jersey sheets, that he had fucked her in the ass. "I'm a vaginal virgin," she insisted, defending her purity the next morning, and Izzy decided white women were weird, black women were annoying, and all women were crazy.

So he tried going alone. It was tough to get through the

brutal daytime hours, from that last newspaper to the first pitch, without a female to at least think about. Before the season ended, and Izzy faced real time on his hands, he met Tess. Tess was the first woman who knew him. She knew what he did, who his mother was, she knew Mal. She watched baseball. She was a chinky-eyed black girl with naturally straight hair and mysterious Belizean background. From their first night in bed, Izzy swore off all kinky sexual experimentation, convinced by her oceanic Caribbean rhythms. Not that she even had an accent, Harlem had cured her of that, but heritage alone rocked her hips like boats in saltwater. Her moods were like the tide as well, pushing and pulling with the consistency of the weather. When she pushed, and Izzy was able to ride her raging energy, they coasted through a more compelling domestic life than Izzy thought possible: hours of laughing and cooking, watching baseball with unending subplots, a party every time they went out to dinner, or to hear music. But when the weather changed, and she pulled, Izzy could barely stand. His back worsened, the hateful quiet drained him. She didn't mean him any harm, she just receded, and if she happened to be holding Izzy's hand at the time, he had no choice but to resist, or be dragged. The abortion heightened her volatility and she threw him out, dragging his own clothes in a laundry basket down Lennox Avenue.

Tess was the beginning of Izzy's infatuation with Caribbean women, which, after a couple of frightening encounters with likely bipolar Jamaicans, led Izzy to the Spanish Caribbean. Puerto Ricans, Cubans, and Dominicans had a similar intoxicating rhythm but with different accents. Izzy was darker than some and lighter than others, and he noticed he did better with the latter. A haughty Puerto Rican named Xiomara from Spanish Harlem introduced him to the culture. She was lovably quick tempered with sharp cheekbones, a lilting, singsong accent, and a weakness for romantic gestures. Izzy inexplicably cheated on her with Sugeri (su-hati), a wild Dominican with thick lips and a cowboy stare who fucked him relentlessly. During his first visit to her Washington Heights apartment, surrounded by her friends and neighbors speaking aggressive Spanish, when Izzy asked for the bathroom, Sugeri showed it to him and followed him inside, politely suggesting in her thick accent that he show *it* to her. Izzy, being more concerned with a different function at the time, declined. But it was a sign of things to come. She was nasty, but Izzy grew addicted. She had that good Caribbean motion, but there was always a violent storm over her waters. She told him how when she found out her baby's father was cheating, she broke four El Presidente bottles over his head. Izzy was scared to cheat, but did so anyway, once he was sure Sugeri was doing the same. It was with a black, wealthy, dynamic Dominican girl, tall and thin with a great rack and lush lips. Izzy didn't know why he was cheating so much; he never cared for it before. He figured he had caught the Latin-man compulsive-cheating syndrome from all those Latinas, who tended to be drawn to the spoken for. Izzy had never experienced a more vibrant, compelling, gorgeous, and deeply competitive group of women.

The wealthy Dominican, with her hormone-fed ego, obsessed with posing and celebrating herself, used to stroke his guns and wanted Izzy to hold one to her head while he fucked her. The request sent Izzy running to a waitress from one of her Paramus, New Jersey, backyard parties—a married, quiet, unassuming, beautiful light-skinned Dominican with soft lips and minimal English. From her to her darker, spicy best friend counterpart. From her to a taller one across the way with that long, proud native frown. All the Latinas grew dizzying, and Izzy began to forget who was still talking to him, and confuse the names of women as he slept with them. He would take trips to their native islands and buy gifts for other girls. He would have felt bad about it if he wasn't confident that all of them were scheming and creeping just like him. He began to want to feel bad about it, in a small cabin on the shores of PR, waiting for the girl he had flown in with to finish in the bathroom, sitting on the bed, scanning the incomprehensible channels, hearing the rush of water. When the water stopped, and the girl emerged, she was three shades lighter than the one he had expected. It was a different girl altogether, but she acted like she knew him, like they all did, and Izzy felt a profound loneliness. He came back to the States, changed his phone number, spent $425 for an ounce of Sour Diesel, went to Barnes & Noble, and spent $279.15.

Before all of them was Gail Glaser, the compassionate social worker and only Jewish woman (unless the white party girl was Jewish). She would steal looks at him in the group home. One day, she boldly asked him if he was Jewish. He didn't wear his *hamsa* then, and was amazed that someone could know just by looking at him.

"Your jaw has that Sephardic slope," she told him. They spent hours talking. She brought him home and showed him her bookshelf, stuffed with psychology textbooks, Freud, Jung, Carl Rogers, Nietzsche—names he remembered longer than those of his recent girlfriends.

"Are you intimidated?" she had asked him with her knowing smile.

"I think I better just keep my mouth shut," he said.

She laughed.

Izzy was always off balance with Gail, never knowing if he should make a move, if he could, or how he would, since he had never made one before. There were sloppy playground gropings and puckered lip kisses, but no moves. He knew many guys who were twisting girls since they were twelve, but Izzy wasn't ever aggressive enough for that. The hood rats that came on to him were too obvious, callous, or funny to turn Izzy on. Gail was this angelic, motherly enigma from another world. Across the street but another world. That first day in her apartment he did nothing. He sat and talked with her and she gave him books. The neighborhood kids clowned him.

"You supposed to get ass, nigga, not homework."

Gail introduced him properly. She had him over again, and their conversation of Civilization and its Discontents led to quiet stroking. Strictly missionary, she would tenderly hold him between her legs, breasts flush against his chest. Pillow talk sometimes saw the sun rise, as she fed off the grisly details of his childhood. Gail would tell him about her own upbringing, her resentment toward her cold and unpredictable mother.

"There was no point in asking her for anything. All she gave freely was guilt."

Izzy listened respectfully, never trivializing her problems with the dramatic weight of his own. The secrecy of their relationship opened her up, and Izzy believed he was responsible for her first orgasm. She was grateful, and slightly embarrassed. "You're supposed to be learning from me."

But Gail perpetually fought the inappropriateness of being with him, refusing to see Izzy in public. If anything reminded her of her lack of ethics, or her proper face, she refused to see him at all. Izzy knew only slightly before she did that it wasn't much more than a delicious rebellion for her, a dreamy departure from her more rigid persona. But when it was over, he fell into a deeper depression than when he lost his mother. He was in control when his mom died, because he had to be. He was on his own. When Gail was out of his life, his control vanished and he despised being seen. Seeing people led to confrontations, which led to violence. A shoulder brush caused Izzy to stab a kid in the gut with a shard of broken window glass. Izzy became acquainted with Harlem's most desolate, private spots, and after a while, he knew more public, private places than longtime junkies. He soon joined the Army.

Izzy looked around at the lush security of the butter-soft leather interior, and the easygoing sounds of the baseball game. Torre was about to make another pitching change.

The most sensible shoes in the store were a pair of open-toed, high-heeled sandals with cork platforms. Everything else was meant to show out in the city—six-inch snakeskin stilettos, knee-high suede boots with Old West stitching, hard cherry pumps with impossible sharp toes. Eva would have gone for the sandals, if not for the fall chill in the air. She would have loved the suede boots, if she were trying to show out. So she went with the lowest heel she could find, a black shoe with an Asian floral design. She put on a pair of two-hundred-dollar jeans and stepped onto the floor to admire them.

"That's killer," said the white salesgirl.

Eva put her hands on her sloping hips. "Yeah?"

Shopping was a sudden, unexpected pleasure. Eva was at times trying to enjoy it, and at times trying not to.

"Sure you don't want to show your boyfriend out there?"

Eva smirked. "He's not my boyfriend."

"Husband."

"Strike two."

"Oh. Okay," said the white girl, failing to hide a smirk.

"Wait," said Eva. "What does that mean?"

"It's all good, girl," she said, trying on a sister-to-sister, wink-wink voice. "I been there."

Meaning, she'd fucked a guy for shoes before too.

Eva was prepared to embarrass this white girl with an indignant rant, as she often would. But she couldn't. She thought about the reality of her situation, and it was too ridiculous to say a word. Who was she to look down on this trite little gold digger anyway?

"Why not get it while it's good, right, honey?"

High five.

Boyfriend. The word by itself made her feel like a crusty spinster. She wasn't a man hater. But she wasn't that big on loving them, either. Her first two boyfriends were white. If you could call them boyfriends in high school, her first three were white. Once she trained herself out of patois, a couple of guys paid attention to her: the experimental, rebellious Bob Marley white boys, or other minorities, often in school because a parent worked in maintenance or athletics. Eva liked the white boys. Open and unafraid to look like assholes, she liked learning about their culture. Plus they were more like her uncle Richard, the best man she had known in her lifetime. Hank was a caddy at Richard's golf course, a redheaded stepchild. Literally. He insisted he wasn't treated as badly as was rumored. Eva let him kiss her, which was a big deal to him, though it seemed petty to her, compared to the way kids danced in the Caribbean. She didn't give it up until college, when she met her first bass player. Luis Costanzo introduced her to George Clinton, Earth, Wind, and Fire, Shuggie Otis, and Stevie Wonder, being the first in a long line of American white boys to teach her about black American culture. Luis played a mean electric bass and his band had school shows and eventually found some local gigs. They lost touch when Eva moved to New York for social work school, but she always remembered his sly, Sicilian smile fondly.

"What do you think of this blouse?" asked the salesgirl, holding it up to herself by the hanger, and then holding it against Eva. "I think that blue is just terrific for you."

It was a pale sky blue, and it *was* terrific for her. It had a swooping neckline with white stitching tracing the lines of the shirt. She felt the soft, synthetic cashmere. *Ooh.*

"Vera Wang," said the salesgirl, with a shrug. "Daddy wants you looking nice, right?"

The girl was pushing it. But that blouse was hot.

Eva remembered her first mature relationship, studying at Hunter School of Social Work, spending nights listening to live music. Brian Berg was her second bass player, another soulful white boy, this one into jazz, and serious about the upright bass. He was broke, so was she. They stayed in a lot and her social life consisted of going to his shows. She didn't have to worry about groupies; it was thirty years since jazz musicians had any groupies. Eva learned a lot from him; he read philosophy and his grasp of music was beyond her. After a while, his weed smoking and circular thinking became too much. Eva began making money, and he was still broke, and Eva realized that was how he liked it. She would miss him, especially how he could play her clit like his thick bass strings. But she moved on. Another bass player, but this one was black. Eva was tentative with Rodney. He played electric bass at Café Wha? in the village, which was well known enough to feed Rodney's raging ego. He was cheating, but that wasn't even the point. It was his indulgent nature, how he could forget about Eva even if he was just playing a pickup game of basketball. That day wasn't a big deal. Or it shouldn't have been. Something clicked in Eva, and she found Rodney at the playground, watched, waited, and then politely told the sweaty narcissist to never call her again. Since then, Eva gave men almost no chance. She decided bassists were a bad idea, but never seemed to like anyone else. The Swiss banker didn't even get five minutes.

Eva left the boutique with the jeans, the black shoes, the blue blouse, a cream poncho over her shoulders, and a tan bag with tassels, $978.19 lighter.

"Wait," said Izzy, raising the volume on the radio.

Eva had thought she looked good. Figured good enough to be greeted by better than a baseball color man. The crowd's ruckus, mingled with radio static, grew louder.

"And the pitch," said the announcer, his voice swooping and drawn out. The crowd erupted. "He struck him out swinging!" Yelling.

Izzy pumped his fist, nodded, and looked at Eva. "Hey."

"Hey yourself." She looked straight ahead, arms folded, lips pursed together, her tongue tracing her gums. Jesus, was she pouting?

Izzy turned down the volume on the commercials and pulled out. The man just gave her some cash to get dressed because she had no clothes or shoes. He wasn't trying to be anybody's sugar daddy. *So relax.* Though, if Eva was pouting, Izzy hadn't noticed.

Eva folded her legs, adjusting her poncho. "Who's playing?" she asked, sugar in her voice. She didn't know why she asked it. She had dated sports fans, and had never asked, never cared. Sports were just a man's excuse to ignore her.

"Yankees and Mets. New York versus New York," said Izzy.

"You a Yankee fan?"

Izzy shrugged.

"How can you like the Mets?"

"I don't, really. But there are plenty or reasons to like them."

"What are you, a politician? What's your team?"

"Can't say I have one."

Eva leaned back. *Okay. He shushed me to listen to his game,* she said to herself. *Only he doesn't care who wins.* All right, then. She turned to him. "What was that little celebration just now?"

"Oh, I just like Tom Gordon. Like to see him get outta a jam," he said with a shrug, eyes on the road.

"So you root for players?"

"Basically. Players change teams every year. Managers

too. Manager of the Mets this year was a coach for the Yankees last year. So what, I'm supposed to like him then, dislike him now? Or vice versa?"

"I don't know. You men seem to work all that out."

"Fans are fools," said Izzy. "They say all kinds of shit to support a loser, just 'cause he's on their team. Or trash a top player, just 'cause he didn't perform when they wanted him to. Then they get their hearts broke when they lose. Or gloat when they win. I'm like, you didn't win nothing. Go to your mailbox tomorrow. See if the Yankees sent you a check."

"Isn't that why men bet on sports? So if they win, they really do win?"

"Yeah. That makes sense, in a sense. The way spending seven dollars on a pack of cigarettes makes sense. Losers finding a new way to lose."

Izzy's words had disdain, but his voice had that barely awake creak, like they were losers, but it's okay to be a loser. Eva thought of her uncle, taking bets on shots at the driving range. He never seemed like a loser, smoking cigars and holding cash like he could hit someone with it. Even when he lost he didn't seem like a loser. That was how you could always win, if you didn't care when you lost.

"So, you don't gamble?" she asked him.

"I gamble, just not on sports. I test my luck every day. Got none left over for games. I've used up so much luck, Eva. You don't even know. And every time I get lucky, I get nervous. Like I'm using it all up. Say to myself, you might need that later on."

"But at least you've got some luck, then. After tonight, I'm not sure I've got any at all."

"Could've been a lot worse," he said.

Eva had wanted him to commiserate, and she almost retaliated with "how?" or "I'd like to see that," but something stopped her. Maybe it was her Caribbean superstition resurfacing. Or the memory of Theresa, stuck like an hors d'oeuvre, bathroom stinking of vomit. Or that canal tunneled through the young man's head, revealing the matter within his mind.

Chapter 13

Jacob trailed the squat, surprisingly nimble man in a dark blue suit and shiny black shoes. Jacob had worn brown that day. Earth tones anyway. Brown pin-striped pants, tan blazer, chocolate loafers, and a light green button-down. They both held their heads down to keep the misting rain from their eyes, and Jacob kept losing track of Winthrop. He tried to keep up, kicking his feet quickly to stay above the moist sidewalk. Then he got distracted by the rain, the silky white strings within, like guitar strings, violin strings. He thought he could see each individual drop encased in a glistening enamel, exploding to the ground like a struck match. The shrooms were likely kicking in.

Winthrop slipped into a huddled burgundy lounge, very classy, with dramatic drapes, viral Roman columns, and a large mirror framed by ornate gold. The space was thick with patrons all in black suits and dresses, who seemed to know each other and speak in restrained voices. Winthrop got stuck by the crowd near the entrance, where Jacob caught up to him.

"What's with all the black?" he asked.

Winthrop shrugged. "It's New York."

"Want a drink?" asked Jacob, and Winthrop nodded slightly, maybe to Jacob, and maybe just to nod.

Jacob went to get that drink anyway, not knowing how it might mix with the drug, hoping it might calm him down. He wasn't feeling too good. He felt like he had made a bad entrance. He was on top of the diving board, looking at the lucid blue pool below, feeling graceful as he jumped, extended his arms, then belly-flopped, smack parallel to the water, skin throbbing pink as he held his breath.

Even the bartender looked at him funny. Not sinister but funny. Like Jacob had just walked into a costume party in a business suit. The bartender offered a drink with just his eyes raised in that snide *didn't you get the memo?* expression.

Jacob turned behind him. No Winthrop.

"Scotch," he said, feeling mature.

The bartender made another face and jabbed his ear at Jacob.

"Scotch," Jacob repeated, dropping his voice deeper, though not louder.

"Yeah, what kind?"

"Oh, Dewar's."

The thin, effeminate bartender with his product-heavy blond hair quickly slid him a glass with brown liquor settled at the bottom.

"Sorry, can I get some ice in that?"

"You didn't say on the rocks," said the bartender.

"Okay . . . can I get some ice in that?"

He rolled his eyes and complied in half the time it took him to point out that Jacob had never said "on the rocks."

Jesus, thought Jacob. *You'd think I'm the one making drinks for a living.*

He liked where that train of thought was going and went with it.

I'm rubbing shoulders with important people here. Not shoveling ice and cruising for dudes. Big-time people with

*big-time money have recognized my character and so I'm
here. Why? To show them more character. Make contacts
and network like they taught in Columbia. How did the
seminar go?*

*Hello, Jacob Glaser. Great place here. Who are you here
with? How do you know him/her? Really? So you're into
(business specialty). I have some experience with (specialty)
from when I was (a, in, at) (specialty). Then find a polite
way to ask how much money they make.*

Jacob was locked and loaded. He turned to a man at the
bar with red cheeks and a forlorn face.

"Jacob Glaser," he said, extending his hand, which the
man shook without eye contact. "I'm here with Carlyle
Winthrop," Jacob said, thinking he had the order wrong.
He was supposed to ask about the other guy first, but the
man looked at him funny. So he dropped a name. Growing
up in Manhattan, he'd learned to drop names when his cage
was rattled.

So what was next? *Say something about the place.*

"Great place, never been here before. Kind of low-key.
Little bit of a downer, though, don't you think?"

The man's long face held Jacob in a longer look. He
enunciated four sour words that would rot in Jacob's mind
long after.

"This is a wake."

Eva held her elbows, shivering slightly.

"These things aren't as warm as they look," she said.

"What's that, a shawl?"

"It's not a shawl," she said with a smirk. "It's a poncho."

"Oh, okay, my bad. What's the difference?"

"A shawl is like a scarf, you wrap it. This you put on
over your head."

"Either way, I like it."

"Do you?"

"Yeah, it's a good look. Pretty hot, honestly."

She tilted her head to the side, reluctantly pleased. "Thanks," Eva said, looking herself up and down. "And thanks for the clothes, too. I really needed a change."

"That's for sure. I know it's been a hell of a night. Least you got something to show for it."

Eva nodded, looking out her window. A man was on the sidewalk by Columbus Circle carrying a big sign, reading WHO ARE WE? Just above a photograph of a mature-looking fetus. She remembered the other day on the train; a man was walking around with an anti-Bloomberg sign, getting a big head start on November elections.

"What's with all these random protests?" she asked.

"That's how it was back in the day. Every New Yorker had a cause in the eighties. Buttons, rat tails, BO, picket signs with no picket lines. Black people wearing every color at once. Guardian Angels and Latin Kings looking like red beans and yellow rice."

"I liked it back then. I was a little girl. I like the music still. Freestyle. Techno-pop," she said, liking the sound of the words.

She thought about what Izzy was doing in the late eighties. Just say no. Drugs everywhere. Reganomics. Crack, the new ghetto enterprise. Izzy likely got rich.

Izzy was stuck on the fans, sports fans, getting annoyed about it. Idiots. Fans were fucking idiots. Every last one of them. His cheeks felt hot. He gripped the steering wheel, cued into the ball game as Eva zoned out the window. Cute girl. Really blazing, actually, a blazing hot female. Izzy couldn't think about that, though. Only that fans were just idiots and he couldn't believe how fans could be such idiots. And how bad he wanted to smoke just then.

Why, Izzy? said a distant, sensible voice in Izzy's head. *Why are fans such idiots?*

Izzy didn't want to answer. He was angry and it felt good to be angry, and not have to respond to sensible questions.

Izzy thought of men nested in bar stools, heads tilted to the blue flickering wash of TV screens above, images running in their eyes. Drink after drink of trying to repress one instinct, and replace it with a drunker one; yelling back and forth in incestuous banter like it meant something; seeing a hit and thinking they did it. *You didn't hit shit. If you want to hit something so bad, then go hit something.*

Sensible again. *Why do they make you angry?*

They don't mean anything.

"Something wrong?" Eva asked.

"Nah," replied Izzy. That was it, nice and smooth. Easy. *Keep talking like that and you'll believe it too. Maybe you'll want to hit something. The longer you don't want to hit something, the madder you'll get, the more you'll feel like hitting something.*

Izzy turned to Eva, hoping she had said something over the low commercials rumbling from the radio, but she hadn't. She zoned out and she was gone. The minute she shut her mouth she was miles away. Looking so good right next to him like she might look so good on a TV he was watching; slick black heels, snug jeans, holding herself beneath her poncho like she was cold or scared. Maybe scared of him. She did not understand that he had stumbled onto this unsavory path because he was alone, and there wasn't any more to it. You make a blind, wide turn, wind up on it, try to read the road signs and keep your tank full. Eva wasn't really there with him. Even if she was his passenger.

Mal examined the red and bone chips on the wall, amazed at how the woman's head had opened up like a spray can.

Break your goddamn selves, niggas! The kid is bizzzzack!

Huna didn't like it, but Mal felt big as Shaq. Alive, god-damn it. Alive. He looked at the slumped, bloody carcass. *What more proof do you need than that?*

"Crazy fucking monkey. I thought you were the one using your head."

Mal looked down at his gun, wondering why he had to take all this "monkey" bullshit. He never took that non-sense before in his life.

"You better cool it with this 'monkey' business. Fucking pea-brained dinosaur."

Huna didn't like that, either, giving Mal that hard, side-ways eagle look, all brow. Mal could take it, though. He was good now. His gat was right there, the line was well crossed. Do one, what's two? Fuck a Teflon vest. No miss-ing that big Albanian head.

"How we going to find him now?" asked Huna, his face still hard.

"We don't need her anyway. She got to have his number somewhere."

Blood still racing, Mal went into the next room, some kind of office, with a glass-top desk and messy piles of paper. He didn't bother with those. Beside a laptop was a Palm Pilot, standing straight up in its mount. Mal picked it up. He had seen them before but couldn't work one for shit. He brought it out to Huna.

"You know how to work these?"

Huna took it, though he looked less competent than Mal had been. He pushed the screen with his meaty fingers, giv-ing the machine that same hard look like he might scare the info out of it. Mal sat.

She was sending her son his bills. Big envelope ad-dressed to him with his bills. *When do you mail bills to your son?*

"When do you mail bills to your son?" he asked Huna.

Huna didn't respond, wrestling with that tiny device, and by the looks of it, losing.

Mal went over to the couch, reached beneath Gail to the phone line, and reconnected it. He picked up the phone, wiping blood from the receiver, and pressed REDIAL.

"You mail bills to your son when he reminds you to."

Chapter 14

The W Hotel. Izzy and Eva rode the elevator up to the seventh-floor lounge without speaking, Isley Brothers singing for the swift ride, "Footsteps in the Dark." The doors opened to a bright, white marble floor that stretched far on both sides. They stepped in, the elevator doors closed, and Ronald Isley was still singing, tall ceilings nowhere in sight. "I keep hearing footsteps, baby," over a silky, mournful guitar riff. *Why?* To their right was the lounge, just as austere as the front desk to their left.

"They left their high beams on," said Izzy, having to squint in the brightness that was everywhere, reflecting up from the buffed white floors.

They waited in the roped-off line for a teller. Nothing separated the lounge from the concierge. You could have put the liquor behind the desk and computers at the bar and it wouldn't have made much difference. The lounge itself stretched far back to small VIP rooms, sectioned off by cream linen curtains. Most of the people wore black, like mingling rain clouds in a white sky, ranging from big shots to well-dressed posers, women from gold diggers to straight-up escorts. The white all around suggested the wired cocaine smiles, the mover-shaker laughs, the crazed, hungry eyes, and the glistening, self-satisfied jewelry.

Izzy felt fine in his baby-blue hoody, worn jeans, and low-tops. The more you dressed down in a scene like this, the less you had to lose. The less you had to lose, the bigger you looked. Onlookers might mistake Izzy for a tragically casual backpack rapper, or a fresh-from-Hollywood actor.

The teller punched in their request and read from her computer screen.

"I have no rooms with two beds available," she said, face glowing with the computer screen. "King-size bed okay?"

Before Izzy could get a word, Eva jumped in. "How about two singles?"

The teller typed in some more. "I do have two rooms that are connected."

"Perfect," said Eva.

Izzy wanted to know the rate. Eva had been quick to speak, but she didn't know how much money they had. She was right, though. They had plenty.

"You clearly don't know what white people really think of Oprah," the Puerto Rican girl informed Jacob.

About a half hour earlier, Jacob had been all set to implode, consumed with a soul-crushing anxiety, hating life and terrified of death all at once. He was at a wake. His suspect point man had set him up, likely for kicks.

Jacob saw it then. The black and conciliatory gestures; the low, incomprehensible talking all around, not a single word making sense; smirking mouths betraying the voices; all the eyes looking at him, even those on the faces that looked away. Along the bar a panorama of red eyes from disjointed, smirking faces—the bartender whispering to a guest and laughing. The provocative burgundy curtains ghoulishly curled around opaque windows. The gold, pompous chandelier swayed in the shadows on the ceiling. Jacob saw them now, too; sinister shadows rippling across the ceiling into hungry walls.

Then a soft, consoling hand touched his wrist.

"I'm so sorry," said a female voice. "You must have been very close to Mr. Heller."

Jacob pulled his head from his narcissistic spiral and saw a soft, pretty, elfish face. He could only nod, still too rattled to explain himself, and not sure that would be such a good idea anyway.

Anna was Puerto Rican, but Jacob wouldn't know it to look at her face. He would have guessed Italian. She was around Jacob's age and a poet, dragged to the lounge by a girlfriend. She looked damn good, outright heavenly, which Jacob observed with a rare clarity. She made him want to write about it. Every line of her face, down to her thin jaw to the elegant tendons in her long neck, was a map (*jeez, I'm tripping*) of loveliness. As though the picture of every other female in Jacob's memory was in grainy, aged VHS, and this one was crystal HD, DVD Progressive Scan. When Jacob heard she wrote, he got excited, telling her about his literary aspirations.

"Why do you want to write about violence?" she had asked him. "So played out."

"I don't know. I'm a hip-hop kid, you know?"

She looked him up and down, and brushed his shoulder pad. "Yeah. I noticed."

"My day job."

"Right. Clark Kent."

"I just figure that guy, that ruthless gangster deserves to be thrown into a more literary story. People would like to read that, I think."

"I guess," she said. "But who?"

"I just graduated from college. You know how many well-read, average white kids can recite Jay-Z songs front to back? Half of 'em got no clue what they're even saying. Maybe they're curious."

"I don't know. I figure they want to read a book so they

can feel different from Jay-Z. They only want to be Jay-Z when they go out and party."

"Maybe I'll start with the hood, you know? Get word of mouth. Then get it to Oprah. Let her pull the rest of the U.S. in."

That's when Anna told Jacob he clearly didn't know what white people really thought of Oprah. Anna proceeded to let him know.

"They think she's a joke. That she's contaminating *their* books. They'd rather their superior literature die with the last two people who truly understand it, than let the unwashed masses pretend to get Steinbeck."

"Well, how do you explain her popularity?"

"Popularity? Martha Stewart is popular. But she doesn't tell people what to read. She stays in her place—in the kitchen, in minimum security, in the garden, stuffing taxidermy and manipulating the stock market." She took a drink. "Sorry, I like to rant."

"That's okay. I like rants."

"Can I tell you something else?"

"Sure."

"Don't take this the wrong way, but the hood likely won't read your book either."

"No?"

"Go to Barnes and Noble. They have a shelf now called Black Literature. Wright? Ellison? Baldwin? No. K'Won. Triple Crown. Ghetto Lit. Most of the time don't even use real words. You use real words when you write?"

"Sure, I guess."

"Then you won't get on that shelf. That's the hip-hop Lit. Ghetto anyway. Like book-long R. Kelly songs. Only sure things are death and alimony. Don't even bother."

"Well, maybe I could separate hip-hop from the ghetto."

"That's an idea. But it'll likely lose its soul."

"Jeez," said Jacob. "Then what do you suggest I do?"

"Keep your day job. Make some money, be happy. Wear your suit. You look good in it anyway."

Finally, some positive news. He looked good in his suit. He suspected he might. Just then, he felt his Razor phone vibrate in his pocket. It was his mother.

"Excuse me," he told Anna with a smile.

It wasn't his mother. Sounded like a black guy.

"Mr. Glaser? Listen to me for a moment. Your mother is quite sick and we're going to have to take her to the hospital, once the ambulance comes. You might want to get home as soon as possible."

The elevator opened, leaving Izzy and Eva looking at a sign. Their rooms were to the left. A convention center was to the right. The mixture of classic and neo soul that had been playing throughout the elevator, lobby, and lounge finally shut off. Instead the frenetic bounce of booming southern hip-hop rattled through the hall. Izzy and Eva exchanged glances, and curiously approached the convention center.

The double doors opened on a riot of primary colors and pastels. Once their squinting eyes adjusted to the shock and awe, they began to make out just what they were looking at. Men posed like peacocks, in pink hats, perms, shiny furs, canes, capes, rocks for teeth, and costume jewelry. Women in skintight leathers and pleathers, with peekaboo asses, studs, two-inch eyelashes, dangling boas, clear and ridiculous heels. A sign by the door read PLAYERS BALL CONVENTION.

"Don't look directly at it. You'll burn your retinas," Izzy told Eva. She quickly shut the door and followed him down the opposite hallway.

The room was as sterile as the rest of the hotel, but darker, with a grainy gray carpet and chrome dresser, desk and lamps, handles sloping like small horns. Just to the left was a door, and Eva tried her key and opened it, looking right at Izzy, also opening his door. She walked into his room, too restless to even sit down. She went to his window and watched the rooftops and wild, animated billboards and cluttered streets below. Times Square resembled just what futuristic eighties movies like *Blade Runner* had suggested. It bothered Eva that people could be so predictable.

Though most of her life was a struggle to maintain predictability, she perpetually wound up in unpredictable situations. There was nothing predictable about her job, her profession. There was nothing at all predictable about that night. Yet she felt oddly calm, like it was the fourth, fifth time she had been through it, and like Izzy had been there with her before too. She had to ask herself, how serious was she about wanting predictability?

Izzy had been acting funny since she got her new clothes, like he was trying not to look at her. She wanted him to. Somebody should appreciate her tonight. A bright, blue square lit up just above her reflection in the window. She heard the hushed roar and aimless muttering of a baseball game.

Izzy was sitting on the edge of the bed, leaning back on his elbows with the remote in one hand, bandages on the other. Eva walked across him to the minibar, crouched down, and looked for her old friend. Jack was as sure to be there as a Bible by the bed.

After a few long-legged strides back to the window, sipping from the fifth, she allowed her mind to amble.

"What about the money?" she said. Just put it out there. See if Izzy reacted.

The bright blue square reflected in the window disappeared.

"He had to have left with it, right?"

Izzy took off his sweatshirt, leaving him in just a simple, white V-neck T-shirt. Simple and damn sexy on a guy with the right build.

"How much was it?" she asked him directly.

"Between three and four."

"Grand?"

He got up off the bed, looking at her, distracting her. He took the bottle and sipped it. "Between three and four hundred grand."

"Wow."

"Mal had to've stashed it somewhere. He wouldn't have brought it home, even if he had time. He wouldn't bring it anywhere I know about."

"So?"

"He must have improvised. Could be anywhere, really. Within the last couple of hours, where has he been? He would have stashed it before he met the Albanians."

"Maybe in his taxi?"

"I doubt it. The windows are shot. Anyone could get in there."

"Not with that wild cowboy inside," said Eva, thinking. "The windows got shot after he met the Albanians anyway, right? I mean, just think about that money, Izzy."

His brow crinkled.

"No, I don't want it," she said. "Think about it for you. You could work with that. Four hundred grand? That's a down payment. You could start a new life with that."

Izzy put his good thumb in a belt loop and tilted his head. Her words lingered in the room. When did he ever say he wanted a new life? Since when did she care? Maybe it was force of professional habit, always wanting people to clean themselves up.

There was an undeniable what-if? underscoring their time together, ranging from what if Eva was a killer to what if Izzy had a law-abiding life. Izzy's silent response noted the first verbalized what-if? Eva also noted that she was the first to suggest it.

"Here, give me back my Jack."

Izzy handed it over. Another silence.

Izzy broke it this time. "You want to know how I got that other money?"

"I don't know, Izzy, do I?"

He turned to the window, mulling over how me might confront her. She looked so good he didn't want to look anymore. That urge to grab her and kiss her was about as strong as he ever had, and he wanted to smoke his blunt again, so maybe he could look at her smooth face and not care.

"Maybe you should know," he told her. The problem with how bad he wanted to kiss her was that she might let him. It was throwing him off. She had to know she shouldn't let him. If she didn't know, who would stop them?

"Only if you want to tell me."

"I robbed a spot. A prostitution spot. We—I needed money. The guys who run it are after us, or me."

"It's your life, Izzy."

She wasn't running or screaming. She wasn't exactly happy, and maybe she wouldn't let him kiss her now. Tough to be sure. As well as she lived, she wasn't exactly a stranger to the darker side of life. So maybe he should tell her more. How he shot an innocent man in the leg. How he killed another. How he almost killed that young girl. How when he got bored, he tended to shoot people. That was the point, right? That was why he had brought all this up, so she could understand what an apathetic, rude son of a bitch she was riding with.

"So? What happened?"

She was making eye contact, calmly listening, sitting on the windowsill with one leg over her knee, and her elbow on that leg, her chin in her palm, almost smiling. Her long lashes blinked twice.

Izzy rarely lied to women. There were too many who wanted him for who he was to worry about those who wanted a lie. "Nothing. I got us some money, is all."

Eva held another long, condescending blink. "It's your life, Izzy."

Izzy smiled. When he was really young, and he used to tell dumb lies, he used to smile. He felt so transparent lying to his mother that he would smile almost to apologize. He had long since trained himself out of the habit, but he did it when he was with Gail, and now he was doing it again. He was sure Eva knew he was lying, but maybe she would go along as well. They were in a small, cozy hotel room. It was easy to nurture romance. Izzy's conciliatory smile morphed into a bedroom one.

"Why are you smiling?" she asked him, a little defensive.

"I like how you say my name."

"Why do you like it?"

Because I know you're here, talking to me. "You hit the 'I' hard. I can hear the Caribbean."

Eva raised her eyebrows. Izzy sat on the windowsill beside her. Eva straightened up.

"And because I like you."

She unfolded and refolded her legs, taking a swig. "Why do you like me, Izzy?"

"Aside from the obvious?"

"Of course."

"You're easy to talk to. You're different. You're . . . a good person."

"Would you like me if you didn't think that was also true about you?"

Izzy inched a bit closer. She lost her smile, looking nervous.

"Do you think it's true about me?" he asked her, softly.

She fidgeted, hesitating, and raised the bottle again.

Izzy stopped her, holding the hand that held the bottle. "No more Jack."

With her hand, he gently pulled her to him. They kissed.

Chapter 15

On another night, Jacob might be more upset about hearing his mother was sick in such a strange way. But the triumph of getting Anna's number and the morbid fear about his mother seemed disconnected. When he thought about one, he couldn't seem to recall the other.

His cab stopped at a red light, his driver finding a friend in another cab in the next lane.

"Khalid! How are you?"

"Good, good, Dris. How's your car?"

Dris pulled up in his lane a bit before he could answer.

Anna. Damn, that chick was his type; fine, funny, fuckable; with that bohemian Rican thing, the curly hair, beaded necklaces, and cluster of bracelets. Plus she was smart. Sharp. Clearly she knew more about books than he did. Not shy about it, either. He liked a woman who could take charge, teach him things, like . . .

Mom. Mom took charge and taught him things. Taught him how to overanalyze enough to ruin anything, including the boost of getting a pretty girl's number.

The two cabs met again.

"Car's good, good. New model. Eats up all the gas. How's yours?"

"Ah. I got no shocks."

Mom. Sick? What the hell was that guy talking about? Didn't make sense but Jacob just wanted to see her. If the guy was helping, wouldn't he just take her to the hospital? And they would call Jacob? Unless she couldn't be moved, he guessed. He just wanted to get home.

"They going to fix them?"

"They never fix nothing. They wait for me to crash it and give me new one."

Felt bad, real bad about Mom. Had to feel bad, or else she would be mad. Felt resentment because he had to feel bad. Mom was sick, and Jacob resented her. What a son. Jacob felt guilt for resenting his mom for making him feel bad or else she'd be mad; because she was sick, therefore he must feel bad. Adequately bad. So Jacob resented her and now she was sick so Jacob wanted her sick. Even though she was sick before, Jacob felt guilt for wanting her sick because now she was sick.

He liked Anna because when she talked he could stop thinking. Sometimes, Jacob hated thinking.

Eva's eyes were shut as she felt the kissing. Damn good kissing; soft, honest kissing. She didn't want to open them at all. Not when he got closer and their bodies pressed against each other. Not when they left the cool, chrome windowsill and tumbled to the warm duvet cover on the bed. Not when his good hand wrapped around her back, her torso cupped by his long arm, and she felt safe. Not just turned on but safe. She stopped shaking. She barely even knew she had been shaking all along. She thought she had been cool about things, calm as could be expected. But really she had been shaking and now she really wasn't. So she didn't want to open her eyes because she might start to shake again.

It was Theresa who made her open them; right when physical comfort took that erotic turn, and instead of not shaking she felt hot. She just wanted a kiss, damn it, was that okay?

To Theresa it wasn't, who had the nerve to appear just as she had a few hours ago, blood and puke on her mouth, looking away—a relative waiting out some rude offense. Eva saw the knife and the blood clearly, and that was it. Her eyes snapped open and she pushed Izzy away, holding him at arm's length.

When the kid saw his mom, he crumbled quicker than Mal had expected. He knew the kid would fall apart, that was the idea, but the kid looked like a wreck when he opened the door. Big, dilated eyes, looking bruised. Likely he didn't buy Mal's story, and was suspicious from the get. Still, he showed up as expected and fit right in. However you looked at it, a corpse and a crying kid kind of set things back in their proper order. Mal was the killer again. Sometimes it took victims to remind him.

Before the crying got too annoying, Huna hit the kid in his eye so hard the kid's feet picked up off the floor. Kid's head hit the door on the way down and he was out for a bit, leaving some silence again, like when they had been waiting.

"So. What now?" asked Huna, seemingly taking cues from Mal again.

"Call his bitch ass. He'll come running."

"Okay. So. Go ahead, then."

"You want him to come here? This place 'bout to be hotter than July in Jamaica."

"So we take him to your place."

"My place? Hell no. I'm in a residential neighborhood. This dude's coming heavy. You want to blow up Striver's fuckin' Row?"

"Oh, you want to blow up my spot, then, nigga?"

"You tell me, H. Since you got all the answers. Since he

killed your people, I don't know. Seems to me like you got a debt to collect, some peoples to impress. Show them how the niggers of Europe get down."

Huna nodded. He didn't like agreeing with Mal in any way, but he nodded.

"Wait, this is just too intense right now," said Eva, her hand on Izzy's chest, sucking in heavy breaths.

Izzy nodded, catching his own breath, calming down. Yes, she was right. It was intense. Synapses were firing off like AK-47s. Izzy had no idea what his pulse was at, likely high as all night. He fell backward on the bed, heaving, staring at the crystal chandelier.

"That image just popped in my head," said Eva. "My cousin, Theresa. Ruining yet another pleasure."

Izzy thought he should console her, but he didn't know how. He went to put his arm around her but stopped. Anything physical might get more of the same reaction. That's what set her off to begin with. He didn't know what to say. He never did. Like with Tess, when he (allegedly) cooked sausages when she told him she was pregnant. Stayed there cooking in his private way. Tess was likely right in her accusation. Izzy couldn't remember, but the way she had described him was the way he felt just then. Not that he liked when women were upset. He hated it. Watching a woman cry was like watching a glass of red wine spill on a white linen suit in slow motion. That was how it made Izzy feel, helpless. He liked problems he could fix, questions that had answers. What was there to say?

Eva continued. "Nothing inside her, you know? Just that dead look. Eyes like the windows of a gutted house, just empty. Staring at nothing. Tiny, little pupils. Like specs."

"Wait, pinpoint pupils?"

"I guess you could say."

Izzy had an answer. "Then you definitely didn't kill her. Pupils pinpoint when people die of overdose."

"Really?"

They held eye contact again. An ambivalent relief washed over Eva's face. She wanted to smile but restrained herself. "Makes sense. Still. I kinda feel like a born-again virgin."

The clouds parted from Jacob's sleep so his waking nightmare could lightning through. He barely took his first breath before the wind was knocked clean out of him. He coughed and caught glimpses of these two demons, and the gruesome, bloody flesh of his mother. He wasn't thinking. He couldn't even look, it was too unreal. Her bloody body illuminated just how precious she was. He screamed. He wanted to run, to fly out the window, to tear his own flesh off. The demons held him still. One with a giant white head, in a long white outfit like a mock angel; the other black and small, with a rodent's smile and mischief, laughing. Laughing at his mother, him, all of it. Jacob could feel the heat coming from them, could see their breath rising like steam in his mother's house. Their shadows moved and spoke in contradiction to their hosts. Jacob then realized that hell couldn't be some distant, strange, and fiery place. Hell was home, unimaginably perverted. He was there.

"Eva, there is something I guess I should tell you," said Izzy, head propped up by the headboard, with Eva's lying on his chest.

"Yeah?" she said, barely audible, toward his stomach.

He wasn't sure why he wanted to tell her. "When I robbed those Albanians, it didn't go so smooth. I almost killed a young girl."

Silence. When she didn't speak, it seemed like she was gone again.

"This guy was using her as a human shield. You believe that?" he asked, wanting a response.

"Yeah," she said, deadpan. "And you shot him?"

"Yeah."

"As he was holding the girl."

Izzy shrugged. "I was feeling accurate." He hadn't shrugged in a while. He realized that he always shrugged when he was full of shit. "Don't know why I even told you." He had to be honest with her, if it was worth anything at all. He knew, after that night, he might never have the chance.

"Why did you save me, back in Queens? I mean, you been jumping people how long? You knew the risks."

"I froze."

"After that. You had to know it was either me or Mal."

"Still . . ."

Izzy knew she was dead-on about something, but still, he didn't want to think about it. Still, it was a damn good question. Still, if he wasn't ready to do what he'd come to do, how had he allowed that situation to begin with?

"Really it seems to me the problem was that I was there at all."

"How is that, then?"

"Eva, it's been so long since I ever cared either way. Not caring was my strongest survival skill. Life's been downhill, and you build up so much momentum after a while, you'd rather get to where you're going than scrape your hands to stop and think about it."

"Well, your hand is scraped up now," she said.

"Yeah." Izzy looked at his bandaged hand, the small, dark circle of blood in the center of the layered white tape. He looked up at her face. "You know," he said, finding a smirk. "I remember talking about getting together one time."

Eva smiled. "The aquarium . . ."

"Then a nice cold shellfish sampler. It sounded good to me. Did it sound good to you?" he asked.

Eva's thick lips twitched in a half smile as she looked away.

Izzy's phone rang, MAL flashing in LCD.

"Yo! Papa was a rolling stone! Guess who we got!" Mal called into the phone like a gleeful preacher, awaiting his congregation's unanimous response.

None came.

The kid was lying on the floor, head propped up by the wall, looking very uncomfortable. Mal crouched by his swollen face, putting the phone up to him.

"Scream, bitch," he told him.

Hovering above, Huna kicked him in the ribs hard, like he was trying to break through.

The kid cried out, sounding pathetic enough. He kept crying, chewing on his words. "They killed . . . killed her . . . they . . . killed Ma, Ma, Ma . . ."

Jesus, crying like a damn baby. Mal reared his head back, sneering in disgust.

"Not for nothing, Izzy, but your kid's a fucking bitch," Mal said into the phone. "I can't believe you never told me about him. I woulda got you a *ci*-gar."

Nothing on the line again. This whole process was getting old and Mal was over it. It was time to get it poppin', no sleepy Albanians for Izzy to murk this time. Still, the line was silent, like he wasn't even there. Had to be, though. Izzy wasn't that cold, for sure. No way he would give up his kid. If he was able to keep it secret so long, it had to mean something to him. Not that this whimpering little cunt had any of Izzy in him, aside from maybe his eyes and jawline. Kid had a good, bougie life, wasn't packing or nothing. Born victim.

"Where?" creaked his old friend's voice from the phone. Finally.

"The Alban's spot. You know, the basement."

Izzy hung up the phone and thought about weed. Would a little hurt him? Just to soften things a bit, let him focus on what he had to do. As it was, it was too hard. He had fucked up real bad, getting Jacob involved. Now Gail? Twenty-plus years out of her life and Izzy reached back and took it. Not Izzy himself but Izzy's situation, out of control. No one was safe. Time to man up. Hit back.

He stared at the phone, thinking of the next step, and unable to move.

First, he had to stop hating himself.

"What's happened now?" asked Eva.

"He's got Jacob. He . . ." Izzy said, and shut his eyes, as a flood of the forgotten slowly submerged him. Gail's measured stare, how she laughed when eating popcorn, how greens invariably stuck in awkward corners of her teeth, that tuff of hair that always seemed to stand up. Memories he was unaware of, bracing himself for Eva. Her cutting disapproval was inevitable.

Something broke. He was motionless. He couldn't tell Eva and face her scolding, couldn't open his eyes, and leave the images he saw: Gail's tiny apartment, all those years ago, cluttered with books and liberal politics, candles and constant reassessing; the insular quiet of lying on her bed, barely hearing the faint Midtown traffic. Then the rejection; Izzy again out in the streets, exposed in the wide open spaces of Upper Manhattan's abandoned periphery; suffering absolute boredom, waiting for the inevitable, random terror and violence.

Izzy was alone again. Eyes closed at the W, but a kid alone in the grocery store again; sleeping bodies all around, frozen like he froze in Queens; a child waiting to die. The pitch was thrown. The bat flew from the shoulder. And nothing. It was all stuck just then; no hit, no miss. No foul ball, no strike three, just a blink at the wrong moment and his eyes still hadn't opened. The rest had all been the in-between. It still was the in-between. That lunatic had made a promise to Izzy that day he had yet to fulfill. Izzy had spent the last thirty years waiting for that bullet to find its mark.

Back in the grocery store, the body propped up against the counter like he really wasn't alone. Making fun of him. Maybe he had tried talking to it. Maybe that was in a dream afterward, if his memory wasn't such a joke he might know. Maybe the propped-up body had said something through its gaping neck. Talking to him like his mother's creaking bed behind her closed door; like Knuckles muttering to his cronies while Izzy played wallpaper; like his screaming sergeant over the beating helicopter; like Mal's perpetual complaining; like the solitary sound of his soft beating pulse, when he closed his eyes and there wasn't anything else at all.

He thought of the corpses he'd seen. He thought of Won and Theresa and Arben and the Albanians. Then he saw Gail's face on them. He wondered how Mal had done it and felt sick.

He couldn't tell Eva. As long as she was near him, she could be next. Izzy's eyes had swollen closed. Welling up now—Izzy fighting out of instinct. The glass was full, rocking. Couldn't let it spill.

He felt Eva's hand fold over his good one, her soft fingers caressing his terse palm.

The glass spilled.

Izzy opened his eyes, and through a sticky cobweb blur, saw Eva gently looking. Her other hand rose to his face, touching him above his cheeks.

Izzy began to calm down. Eva's face grew clearer. He

blinked and blinked, until he saw her perfectly again. She held something and brought it to his hand.

It was the rubber grip. The heavy .45.

She spoke firmly, nodding. "Go. Finish him."

Mal was grateful Gail lived in a building without a doorman. No passersby, no one to notice Huna in the lobby behind him, manhandling the kid, whose sock was duct-taped inside his mouth, wrists taped behind his back. Huna gripped his arm, as he had gripped Mal's not too long ago, pulling the resisting kid so hard his feet picked up off the granite. Huna's gaudy Benzo, double parked outside without the courtesy of hazard lights, beeped to life once the Albanian reached the stoop. Mal, still keeping lookout, spotted only a few dog walkers meandering in the distance by Riverside Park. He opened the Benzo door and Huna grabbed the kid by the back of his neck, lowered his head just a bit, and threw him in the car, Lil' Izzy's knee banging the side on the way. Jesus, Huna was a strong dude. Especially when he was all yipped up like that. Must have had a session when Mal was uptown. That toss was all arms, sent a grown young man airborne for a second. Kid had to weigh at least 185, no shoes.

"Get in," growled Huna.

"I got my ride. I'll follow."

"You having memory problems? You don't leave my sight."

Just then the door on the other side of the street opened up. The kid was trying to squirm out, feet first. Must have opened the door that way. Had a little heart after all.

By the time his feet hit the pavement, Huna was on him. Hit him so hard his head did a clean 180-degree turn, dislocated jaw looking at Mal through the window. Another moment and the kid was back in, a bit calmer now.

"Get in the fucking car," Huna said to Mal across the slanted trunk.

"I'm good. I'll meet you." Mal wasn't about to give in. He needed separate transportation, the ability to leave the party at his discretion.

Huna began to walk around the car, toward Mal.

"What? What am I going to do? I'm with you, Huna, c'mon. I want Izzy right now. I want that girl that's with him. Nigga stabbed me in the back, H, took my damn paper. That bitch saw me do like three niggas." Was it three?

Huna stopped, turned, and eyed Mal's wreck of a taxi-cab, thinking for a belabored moment. He slowly nodded, his furrowed eagle's brow unchanged, as though he'd figured something out, some reason not to hurt Mal just then. Maybe he thought Mal might get pulled over in that junk heap ahead of time, cutting him out of the money Izzy didn't have.

Chapter 16

The ball game came on the car radio. It was still tied deep into extra innings; bull pens were being emptied, a favorite scenario full of intrigue and strategy. Izzy didn't care. Not the way he usually didn't care. He was too distracted, worrying that having a conscience might ruin him.

Izzy's accuracy with a handgun was an emotional phenomenon. His hand was steady because he didn't care too much, holding the grip so tight it shook, or too little, falling asleep as he aimed. Izzy had mastered his loose hands, the way a great pitcher lets the ball fly at the perfect moment from his extending fingers. Like with any contest, if you slept, or pressed, you lost. Izzy was pressing. He could feel it. In how the firm rubber steering wheel left imprints in his palms; in the heavy block in his throat, as though trying to swallow a plumb pit; in the random curses that flew from his mouth. Cursing at dumb drivers like Mal would.

Mal.

Fucking piece of shit.

"My father, one time, owed a man money," Huna announced, loud and authoritative as a judge's gavel. He let the words hang in the spacious Benz interior, face to the side, blinking three consecutive times with his finger pointed at nothing in particular. "Another Albanian man. For some reason, my father did not want to pay this man. Now, I was young at this time. I had maybe been to the pool hall, gambling spot three, four times. I didn't know what my father was about, but I heard things. Being a kid in that type of place, around the skeezie motherfuckers and scumbags, you hear things. Now, I believe he owed this man money for a long time, and this man was nobody to play with. One night, my father watched the window all night. Then he grabbed me. We walked outside, and there was a black Caddy, and one man, who was just getting out of the driver's seat, in an overcoat, and something in his hand. This nigga had a gat in his hand, and my father had me.

"'You want to kill me?' my father said to him in Albanian. 'You kill me, motherfucker. But you better kill my son too. Because he will come for you, and your whole fucking family.' And that nigga drove the fuck off, I kid you not. Took his ass, and his gat, back in that Caddy and drove the fuck off."

Jacob, barely listening in the backseat, was speechless.

"That man understood what I know. If you want to kill a man, you must be ready to kill his whole family."

Huna pulled the Benz over and parked it, glancing over his shoulder to check on Jacob. Kid didn't seem to hear a thing. Fine by Huna. That explanation was beyond any obligation. Apparently, the kid didn't care why he was about to die.

Huna dialed Louon and told him to come outside. His young cousin quickly bounced from the restaurant, his face red from drinking. Remaining in the front seat, Huna waved him over.

"What up, cuz?" said Louon.

"Everything's taken care of. You can marry whoever the

fuck you want. There is just one last thing, I gotta murk this motherfucker Izzy, need you to keep an eye out here. You strapped?"

Louon grinned across his face.

Below Benny's Steakhouse was the storage they used for dry food, garbage bags, liquor, and Huna's locked gun case. Five cages were lined up against the wall with combination locks, filled with bottles. Behind those cages was a heavily reinforced door, to another staircase, leading farther down, where cooks, waiters, bartenders, and busboys weren't allowed. Not that they had to be told. Benny's wasn't an environment that promoted inquisitiveness.

That staircase led to the bottom basement, two connected rooms with soundproof ceilings. One room was bigger, directly to the left of the staircase, which you could see as you descended the stairs. The other room was to the right, and blocked by a wall alongside the steps. In the center of the floors in both rooms was a pile of large sheets of plastic, perfect for rolling up bodies. Seated in the middle of one of those sheets was Jacob, taped to a chair, with a pillowcase over his head. Mal spoke fast. Huna was trying to keep up.

"I'm telling you now, don't trust this slippery nigga. He gives any trickery dickery, take his ass out. Forget the cash. He handled three of your Albans like some doorknobs. Matter of fact, I'll be in the other room, back there. He does anything sick, and I pop him from behind. He's dead and we can still find that paper, don't sweat it. We got his boy here, he can call that bitch Iz been running with and straighten it out. He been with her all night, she got to know where's the loot."

"That's fine," said Huna, like he had to interrupt Mal. "I want to be alone with him. But he'll wonder where you are."

"Tell him you killed me, he'll believe that shit."

* * *

Izzy pulled up in front of Benny's, right to where he was an hour or so ago. He sat still for a moment, noticing his bandage was loose. The roll of tape was on the dash, and Izzy, glancing over the artillery in the armrest, unwrapped the tape on his wrist.

He got out of the truck, locking it with the remote. The same crew from hours ago was still making noise in front, smoking cigars and monopolizing the sidewalk. Izzy went to the side, where a gate lay on the ground. A big Albanian in a tight Lacoste shirt stood, looking different than the well-dressed group to his left, in sneakers, designer jeans, and sunglasses in the dead of night. He wasn't listening to the conversation or laughing with the rest. When Izzy approached, he seemed to notice, just barely turning his head. He puckered his wiry lips and blew a kiss to Izzy, then grew a joker's smile, laughing with an accent.

Izzy crouched and opened the gate, climbing down the dark stairs without paying that punk any mind. The storage room smelled like grain, and toward the back there was a thin line of light below a large, open door.

Mal, alone in the smaller room, took off his sweatshirt, and began to remove the white medical tape from his shoulder. He lay down on the plastic, and faced the dim basement light and stucco ceiling. *Good Lord,* he thought. *This is going to hurt.*

Mal punched himself in the shoulder, hard. He closed his eyes, bit his lip, and held in a groan. Jesus, yes, that hurt. He felt the blood ooze from his shoulder, slow. Too slow, so he reared back and hit himself again, right where his chest met his shoulder, trying to force the blood out his back, drawing tears. Motherfucker. That coughed up a good glob, and a puddle began to fill in the plastic.

Mal grew woozy. May have needed that blood. He dug his thumb into his shoulder now, biting his lip so hard he thought he might draw blood there too. His eyes shut again, this time without effort, as he hovered near the edge of consciousness. Not time for that, he thought. Not yet.

Mal picked himself up and forced his eyes open, assessing the blood pool, dripping a bit from lower down the back of his white tee. Head wobbling back and forth, he wrapped his bandage back around his wound and put his sweatshirt back on. He then positioned himself so his head was in the pool and closed his eyes again, gradually calming his breathing.

Izzy's .45 was already drawn when he saw Huna from above. He wasn't even on the third step yet, aiming down over the railing at his big-headed target. Next to Huna was Jacob, in the same clothes he had worn earlier, with a pillowcase over his head, and the barrel of Huna's gun buried in that pillowcase.

"Put down your gun, cocksucker," Huna instructed.

Izzy lowered his barrel, creeping slowly down the moaning wooden stairs. As he reached the bottom, he took his finger from the trigger and flattened it along the barrel. "Where's Mal?"

"Dead. Where's the money?"

"I don't know. Mal took it."

"Liar. Drop the fucking gun before I empty your kid's brains."

Izzy crouched, holding the gun along the floor, watching the giant man's scaly suit gleaming in the soft basement light. Jacob's frame hunched over, his face formless inside the draping linen.

"Jake, you okay?"

Jacob twitched, and then shook his head, unsure. Izzy

sort of made out which direction he faced. He then shifted to Huna's head—that wide, inviting target, looking so easy, so hittable. Just lift up and squeeze, make that gun clap and end all this. Lefty or no. Izzy could hit that mountainous head with his eyes closed, empty out his clip and never miss. He thought of that slug, head side by side with the girl's, an even tougher shot Izzy had made easy. So easy.

Izzy held the gun, pointed nowhere, parallel to the floor, lowering it, contemplating the six or seven muscle movements required to aim it and shoot. Huna's wide forearm tensed as he read Izzy's pondering eyes. Huna was quick. He wasn't some sloppy slug, he was ready to handle himself. Still, it would be so easy.

Righty, maybe. But not lefty. Not now.

Izzy placed the heavy metal on the stiff basement floor, clanging in the cavernous hall, as Huna's hungry eyes widened. He turned his gun to Izzy, briskly walking toward him.

Huna smacked him. A big, meaty smack. Didn't hurt so much as burned, insulted.

"Four of my countrymen dead." Huna came to within a kiss of Izzy's face. "This is *unforgivable*."

"Just leave the kid out of it," offered Izzy with a bored tone, knowing his words were futile.

Huna's heavy hand held Izzy beneath his jaw, fat fingers along his cheek and up to his temple, thumb jabbing his jugular. Huna tilted Izzy's neck so they made eye contact.

"The kid?" he said, intimately. "Him? You killed four of mine. Say you have three more like him, then, maybe, I let you live." Huna moved Izzy's head around in circles, maintaining eye contact, as though getting gooey with a girl. "But then only so you could suffer in their loss."

"Make me suffer, then," said Izzy. "Kiss me already."

Izzy's head was way back, the pressure of Huna's thumb

choking him, when the gun handle dropped like a succinct hammer. Izzy fell hard.

The cold concrete floor pressed against his cheek as the blow reverberated from his head, through his jaw, to his ears. Dumb fuck hit hard. He could still hear the hit, over Huna's purposeless banter.

"In Albania, we have a code. From our book of law, when we formed the first Mafia."

Huna took two steps into a penalty kick to Izzy's ribs. He rolled over a few times, the force throwing him against the wall.

"Sicily took their laws from *us*. The most important is the code of revenge."

Izzy rolled himself one last time so his chest hovered where the wall met the floor.

"If you kill my brother, I don't kill you. Not right away. You kill my brother and I murder *your* fucking brother. So you feel my pain, cocksucker."

Huna gave Izzy one more shot in the back of the ribs with the toe of his Jordan. Thank God the man never wore shoes. With his back to Huna, Izzy fidgeted with the tape on his right hand.

"Arben was like my son," said Huna, backing away from Izzy now. "You killed my son. . . ."

Huna pulled the slide back, making two clean metallic clicks, and moved his .380 to the boy. Jacob squirmed.

Izzy got the last piece of tape off in time, and he felt it, the steel hammer to the old slug's small revolver, pressed against the inside of his wrist. He drew and fired.

The shot came off low and hit Huna in the chest, and he staggered back against the wall. He didn't fall, or come close. He even held on to his automatic, chrome barrel now rising at Izzy.

Izzy's damaged, aching back was now propped against

the wall in a painful recline. The revolver wavered in his left hand. Lefty was tougher than he'd thought. He tensed his arm, making small circles as he tried to aim. *C'mon, one more good one, let me hit that sweet spot again. Just one more.*

Huna had a similar moment of staggered focus, reeling from the bad bruise in his chest, not wanting to miss. They were two hopeless drunks in a race to throw a dart.

No matter how Izzy tried, he couldn't keep his hand straight. Then, catching a rhythm to the circling chrome site, he realized the movement was reliable. He waited until a moment before that tiny rotation saw the eye of his target, and squeezed. The gun clap buzzed through his wrist. Deadeye. Before Huna could get himself right, he took one above his eagle's brow, throwing his head backward against the wall. His body wanted to stand but it had lost its guide. He slumped straight down to his knees, and then fell flat on his uncomprehending face.

Eva took another big swallow and looked around the hotel room, feeling alone. The door to Izzy's room was open. Or her room. They hadn't yet decided who would sleep where. If they hadn't been interrupted, it might not have mattered.

Regardless, the open door leading to that dark room made her feel alone, and she wasn't in the mood. Not any-more. A few hours ago, and she would have offered her health insurance benefits for some alone time. Careful what you wish for, and all that. Her blood was still hot. Jack wasn't helping. Something inside her was awake, wide awake. Maybe because of Izzy. Maybe Theresa, maybe not. She wanted to talk, relate. She was thirsty, not for more to drink, but for something more out of that evening, and she couldn't stop pacing, incurably restless.

She paused at the sight of a gun, looking naked and ex-posed on the dresser. Izzy had left it; likely on purpose. Izzy was convinced of her instinct, but when she had her chance, holding Mal's long gun in her two hands, she choked. Now, staring at the nickel-plated piece on the dresser; there was something so compact and efficient about it; graceful like a high-end luxury car. Amazing how it had reduced the mechanics of killing to pulling a trigger. Eva thought of how brutal killing was in her youth; her mother killing the chickens from the backyard pen, twisting their necks around her forearm and snapping, then letting the cleaver fall, like any simple prep cut. The body and head jumping, bleeding; the cleaver stuck in the stained tree stump. Eva remembered her pet bunny, Onella, who disappeared the same day as her mother served a mysterious stew. Eva knew what her mother had done, impatient with finding shit and piss all over the house. For years Eva recalled that cleaver, sticking at a stiff angle from the stump, her stomach in a tight guilty knot, long after the stew had passed through.

She had never shared that memory. She picked up the hotel phone and began to dial Gail's number with the vain hope of hearing her voice. It was the guilt, she wanted to tell her. *I could never be tough with Theresa because I'm of better, stronger stuff and we both know it. That's why she fed off me; we blamed me. That's why I was willing to admit murdering her.* But there was no one to tell now. The line rang until her voice mail picked up. Eva knew it was too late at night to call.

Eva played how that day would have gone in a session with Gail. First was the discovery of her client's corpse. If there were a session after that, Gail would have heard an indignant rant; what a miserable, pathetic lowlife her client's PCP-smoking boyfriend was, how much better Eva was than her job. Gail would have patiently, economically made Eva aware of her less sanctimonious emotions. Then not much later, the mysterious circumstances of Theresa's death; that would have led to the session of all sessions.

Gail would have been quick to pry Eva from her own condemnation, much like Izzy was. Gail would have kept her
grounded in fact, restrained her assumptions. Maybe they
would have gotten to Eva's guilt, and her belief that Theresa
was still a measure of some unrealized acceptance. Maybe
Eva would have finally cried in a session, making use of the
untouched box of tissues on Gail's coffee table. Maybe it
would have made Gail proud, who had worked so long to
penetrate her hard Caribbean heart, to see those stoic de-
fenses fall.

Pacing, Eva chased the thoughts away. Now she was past
guilt, past doubting, past regretting, or missing. Eva was
hungry, and there wasn't anything wrong with that. She had
seen bodies today. She had held guns and dealt with true-to-
life killers. She was tired of reliving her night in that lonely
room. She was going to do as she damn well pleased.

Easy, Eva. Check the tube.

On the TV was a grainy Erik Estrada, once again.

Aw, fuck this.

Eva made sure she had her hotel card key and that gun in
her purse, letting the door close behind her.

The pillowcase whipped off Jacob, and Izzy emerged
from behind red ink blotches. He was fast, the heavy red
ink trailing him, leaving prints of his movements. He pulled
the sock from Jacob's mouth, who sucked in a huge breath,
unaware how deprived he had been. Izzy used five hands to
cut the tape on Jacob's wrists. Jacob was ambivalent about
the whole rescue.

If he had to choose whether or not he would die just
then, he would have chosen . . . It would have been a tough
decision. He would have hemmed and hawed, not answered
right away. It was all just too much. If seeing his mother like
that were a blow, he had only begun to fall. He wanted that

pain to end so bad, dying seemed as good a solution as any. The only distraction he got was when that monster beat him. That was a relief. He didn't think about it anymore when he was in pain. He didn't relive the shock, see the image. He just felt that good, simple pain, and now that was gone, along with most of the white giant's head.

That felt good, though. Big gorilla on the floor, legs carelessly split like a broken chair, head with a slow leak, dark like oil draining from a tank. Seeing that almost made it worth it. Made him less mad at his father.

Izzy swiped a metal piece up off the floor, bright, shiny chrome streaking through the air like a shark through water. Jacob stayed put, as Izzy checked the room next door.

A thump sounded from upstairs. They heard footsteps.

Izzy paused to see his old partner, faceup, head soaking in a pool like those Mal himself had spilled.

Then the staircase door flew open, and without checking first, Izzy opened fire, four, maybe five times, echoing flat in Jacob's head. An Albanian with big shoulders, hair jelled up in a fin, who never got a shot off himself, slumped to his knees against the door frame, small streams running from different parts of his body.

Mal knew he didn't have much time after the shots were through. Some loud fucking shots, sure to attract attention, and Mal wasn't going to play dead for another moment. Izzy was sure to be in such a hurry, if Mal had ever been out of that man's mind, it was now.

Mal got to his feet, reeling from a heavy head rush, and took a few drunken steps left and right. He grabbed the wooden banister for support and pulled himself up, taking two steps at a time, checking Izzy's job on Huna on the way. Got that dinosaur good like the rest. Huna underestimated Izzy, like everyone except Mal.

When Mal reached the sidewalk, it was chaos. Izzy had apparently charged through the gentlemen out front, already driving away. Must have not minded his manners; a couple of them were reaching for their weapons. Mal was behind them, and luckily, the cab was around the corner. Mal slinked off away from the commotion, and was on the road soon enough to see the Navigator, halted at a red light.

Chapter 17

Eva wondered what she had wanted to happen, staring at the sterile, monotonous white lounge, and greasy, almost laminated people in black. As ice melted in her favorite rust-colored soup, an unfamiliar voice from behind made Eva a proposition.

"Damn, girl, I'd like to suck you like a neck bone."

Rolling her eyes, Eva figured, why not this now? Kind of thing that happens when you don't know what you want to happen. She turned, and to her surprise, that voice belonged to a woman.

Clearly astray from the players club, but without a sexed-up ho-fit, or flashy pimp-fit, the woman was dressed like any young boy slinging on any ghetto corner. Do-rag, fitted Falcons cap, a Michael Vic jersey, baggy jeans, and custom Adidas shoes with red and black camouflage. All that separated her from a man was a single long braid coming from under the do-rag. On either side of her were two trashy but sexy hookers, one in white, one in pink, showing teeth.

"Excuse me?" said Eva, in response to all of it.

"Miss. Miss Diva, or D, Pimp D, if you like."

"The 'D' stands for 'diva,' then?" Eva asked, dubious.

"Among other things," said Pimp D, licking her lips with

a short tongue. "Check what I said. I want to suck you like a *smoked* neck bone."

"That is just nasty." Eva was half offended, half amused.

"So, what's really good? Come roll with Pimp D and I'll take good, good care of you, girl."

The rap on some of these hood lifers never ceased to amaze Eva. Thought they could talk their way into anything, no matter how improbable. Why would she speak to a mature, classy woman like Eva as though she were sixteen and on welfare?

Eva leaned in close, to which Pimp D smiled a row of bright laced fronts.

"I'm not a whore," Eva said in a conspiratorial whisper.

"Are none of us perfect," said D, unfazed. "But come on down, get with it, baby. Barbecue or mildew. Ho up and blow up."

As Eva laughed, she glanced over D's shoulder to where a familiar shifty frame skulked close to the white walls, looking exposed.

The elevator ride was quiet. There was no talking to Jacob. He trailed behind Izzy, face tortured and shocked, as they walked through the lounge, passing pink and white hookers with that short dude on the way to the other elevators. Izzy wondered what happened to the music that was everywhere before. Now the ride was just quiet, underscoring their estrangement. Izzy wanted to apologize for Gail. He was sorry as all hell. But speaking it seemed ridiculous, especially then, in that elevator. It wasn't a wrong you could apologize for.

He was trapped, no variation, no freedom, just the simple truth that he was one thing and at the time, not much else. One sorry murdering motherfucker.

*   *   *

Eva breezed by the valets, immediately seeing what she was looking for—that junk heap of a yellow taxi parked illegally on the curb. No point sticking around Mal's radius. Might as well check her hunch about the taxi. She began to look around it, frightened for a moment.

"That your car?"

It was the valet, a squat young black man with acne in a red blazer. Eva shook her head.

"I was about to have it towed," he said.

"You have a cell phone?" she asked sweetly.

The awkward kid smiled and offered her a thin Nokia. Eva dug in her pocket and pulled out Izzy's number, calling him. Straight to voice mail. The electronic voice. "You have reached . . ." *Shit.*

"Izzy, Mal's in the hotel, where are you?"

She hung up, looking around for some unlikely, simple answer, and gave the valet back his phone.

"Can you give me one minute with this thing?" she requested, gesturing to the car.

With a shy smile, the valet shrugged and nodded.

Eva rummaged around the dank backseat, put her hands in the dirt under the front seats, and popped the glove compartment. Nothing but two empty fifths of rum, a couple of earrings that didn't match, and plenty of loose change. Hand in grime, she felt nasty. Maybe she wasn't up to anticipating Mal. Discouraged, she reached to the driver's side and popped the trunk.

"*Coño!*" called a voice from outside.

Eva hurried out of the car to the trunk. A Latin man popped up like a puppy from a kennel, suspiciously looking around, with a goatee, open shirt, and heavy gold around his neck.

Bright as a diamond in this bitch. Didn't it say LOUNGE on the elevator button? Weren't lounges dark? Mal had nowhere to hide, head under his black hoody to cover up the blood spot, looking too hood for this place. Although there was another kid over by the bar even more G'd up. Had a couple of fine-ass chicks with him too.

Mal had one objective: to figure out where in the tele was Izzy's girl. He'd better make his move; one of these clerks would hit him with a "Can I help you?" soon. He figured the best bet was a bellhop; at least one of them must not give two shits about his job.

Mal crept over to a black guy, standing stiff at attention, arms holding his elbows behind his back. Before Mal could open his mouth, the guy jumped hop-to, grabbing someone's luggage, all teeth. Fucking coon-ass nigga.

That left a white kid with bleached blond hair, hunched back, squinted eyes, and a familiar chip on his shoulder.

The Dominican, she was sure Dominican, with that thick, slurring accent and aggressive voice, shot rapid-fire Spanglish at Eva, not all of it making sense.

". . . and this *loco puto maricon diablo* put me in *mí* own trunk. I swear I call the *policia* right now, swear on my mother. Crazy motherfucker, this guy, *pop, pop, pop,* I hear, crashing, motherfucker going to pay. He make me bury body for him, sick, loco motherfucker."

"Wait, what was that? You buried what for him?"

"*Seguro, algo* something, I don't know *pero,* I dig him a hole."

"What was your name again?"

The Dominican straightened up at the personal attention, mustering all the suave he had after spending the evening in a trunk. "Felipe."

"Felipe. Where did you dig a hole?"

"*Pero, yo no se.* He give me blindfold, señorita."

Oh, right. Especially on a day like this, nothing was free.

Eva dug in her purse, coming up with two hundred-dollar bills. "Two hundred if you take me there."

He nodded. "*Pero*, I did happen to look, *claro*."

No Eva. Two quiet, dark hotel rooms, no life signs. Shouldn't have been a surprise, but it was. Maybe she was getting ice, having a drink somewhere.

Whatever. The woman was gone. The two bedrooms seemed vastly empty. Izzy's lonely stomach sank, isolated by Eva's departure and Jacob's silence. Maybe he deserved it, all of it, and he would just have to accept it.

Jacob lay down on the bed, all fucked up, without the energy to cry anymore. Izzy kept his distance, as though respecting an invisible five-foot circle around the boy, never stepping inside. He could almost see the line on the floor. Before he could fixate, he checked on Jacob. The lights were so dim it was difficult to make out shadow from bruise. The busy Times Square lights from the window traced Jacob's silhouette, and he rolled over, as though to shun it. Izzy didn't know if his eyes were open or closed, but it didn't matter. Might as well go for it.

Izzy crossed the invisible barrier, sat on the bed, and made eye contact. Jacob looked vacant, the way a corpse faces you, looking miles beyond.

"Jacob." He made sure he said his name, using all of his voice. "I'm sorry."

The words sounded empty as Jacob rolled all the way over, head in the bed. At the very least, thought Izzy, it might mean something, somewhere down the line.

After a brisk straight shot up the West Side Highway, Eva and Felipe got out of the taxi by the disturbed bed of grass. The bridge was well lit, with a towering archway covered by an enormous white tarp, for work being done. A blue-gray fog blanketed New Jersey's low skyline, one with the murky water below.

A protruding mound of dirt was by Eva's feet, surrounded by grass, neatly patted down. She wondered how deep it went. Felipe came up beside her, stretching out.

"Another fifty if you dig it up for me."

He nodded, raising his thick, expressive eyebrows and holding up a shovel.

When he got the message, Izzy was less surprised that Mal was alive than that Eva had called. "Mal is in the hotel. Where are you?" she had said, concerned. She was still riding with him, at least in spirit.

Izzy wasn't eager to deal with Mal, but that scene back on the East Side didn't make sense. Mal would've been brain dead to let Huna do him in the Alban's own basement, on his own plastic. The minute you walk down those steps, you knew someone was not walking back up, barring any silly Albanian initiation. Mal would have been too alert for that, too quick. If Huna had any sense he would've had twice the men around, instead of being lured this way and that by a shifty little prick. Mal did have a little game to him, Izzy had to give him that. All along it seemed it would come down to the two of them anyway.

"Jacob," Izzy said to the unresponsive body. "This business isn't over yet. I'm going to need you to be extra quiet for a while. I'm going to shut all these lights, and it's going to be like nobody's home, okay?"

Jacob lay there without moving. He was extra quiet. The lights were basically off. Nobody was home.

Dirty duffel on the seat beside her, she promised Felipe another fifty to get out of there, and he was happy enough, like his night wasn't such a loss after all.

Eva just didn't know which way to go. Across town, to

the Harlem River Drive, over the Triborough, and back to
Queens with a few hundred grand? Or back to Times
Square, where Izzy might or might not be? Where Mal certainly was? Where, if Izzy were there, was about to be like
an Old West saloon after someone got caught cheating at
poker?

"*Dondé, senorita,* where to?"

The white bellhop little shit got Mal up to seventy-five
before he even admitted that Izzy was on the sixteenth floor.
It took another fifty to get him to knock on the doors and
check who was in each room.

"Just making sure everything is okay with your stay, sir,"
the kid lazily spun when someone irate answered.

The floor was mainly full, except for a few scattered
doors where no one answered, and two right next to each
other, 1609 and 1611.

"What are those rooms over there?" asked Mal, pointing
to the even-numbered side.

"Those is doubles, king-size beds."

"And the odd numbers?"

"Singles."

"These two, 1609 and 1611, they're singles?"

"Yeah. Connected."

More than likely, faggot-ass Izzy hadn't worked fast
enough to get that uptight chick into a king-size bed.

"All right, thanks, playboy, now get the fuck outta here,"
said Mal, considering stiffing the kid on the hundred two
five, then reconsidering, not wanting a snitch on his hands.
He hit the kid off, who scurried to the elevator.

When Mal turned, he saw the door to Room 1611 crack
open, and stay that way.

All the lights were out, the shades drawn, as Izzy sat on
his chair inside Room 1609, facing the open doorway lead-

ing to Room 1611. His .45 on his lap, and his cell in his good hand, he cradled the light of his open phone with his right arm. He pushed the side button on the phone all the way down, until the ringer was off, and slid the phone in his pocket. The cracked door in the next room was all the light in either room, a thin line slicing across the carpet, getting wider as it met the far window shades.

The open door threw Mal. Had to be a trap. No question. Or just an invite. Like Mal had wanted all night long, come on in, let's do this, get it on and poppin'. Izzy was maybe faster than Mal at full strength, but nigga had a hole through his shooting hand. The night was Mal's in every way; he had Huna off his back, Izzy gone AWOL and all the loot tucked away for himself. Might as well ride it out, get Izzy, then the girl, and be done with it.

Mal flattened his back against the wall, reached his palm over, and pushed the door all the way open, quickly reaching for his piece. He waited for the shots from inside, looking at the hallway across, as a cop might. Nothing. He waited a bit longer. Still, nothing.

Barrel first, he stepped into the open doorway, hyper-alert. A seemingly empty room. Spying the open door to his right, connecting to the next single, Mal heard another door open.

Izzy hustled Jacob out into the hallway, his gat by his ear, keeping his eyes on Mal's two options. He could either step out into the hallway after Jacob, giving Izzy an easy shot, or step into the light inside the room; another easy shot. Jacob's footsteps raced down the hall. Izzy could see Mal's room, lit up bright by the open door with Mal's long shadow. Instead, door 1611 closed, the light disappeared, and Izzy immediately shut his door, squinting in the sudden darkness.

No Mal yet, but he was inside now. Izzy reached for the back of his chair, slowly sitting down and laying his gun on his lap. He had set up the chair facing the doorway leading to Room 1611. He reached for his cell phone, knowing Mal was somewhere in front of him.

"Give her up, Izzy," his old partner's voice called from the other room, breaking the silence. "You don't have the heart for this."

Dumb ass thought Eva was here. Izzy's dumb ass had thought she would be too.

"What you got on that?" asked Izzy.

"What I got on that? We placing bets? Okay, I got whatever I take off your corpse, nigga." Then that chilling, irritating cackle, which, one way or another, Izzy was glad he would never hear again. "Difference between me and you," Mal continued, "I die today, I'm happy how my life turned out."

"Okay, then," Izzy announced into the dark room, "You're about to be a happy man."

Izzy pressed the SEND button on his phone and tossed it softly on the bed. He then stood, heart racing, holding the gun, and creeping closer to Mal's room. He realized, before the basement with Huna, and all that time he'd had sitting there, he had never taken his pulse.

Maybe hearing the creaking chair, Mal was in front of the door when his phone rang, bright green light shining through the pocket of his sweats, illuminating his waistline.

Izzy fired, aiming just above the green light. The rooms flashed white twice, like successive lightning. Two loud shots and a body thudded on the floor.

When the elevator doors opened, Eva was sick of neo soul. It all sounded alike anyway, Angie Stone, Jill Scott, Erykah Badu, dressing crazy, trying too hard to be different and sounding safe and nice as can be.

She strolled through the sixteenth-floor corridor with a little attitude, imagining a runway, until a sound stopped her.

She heard sobbing, coming from the opposite direction of the room. Eva turned around and followed the sound, the sincerity of the crying giving her a chill. It was the kind of sobbing she might hear from her window late at night, waking her up and making her want to call the police, though she saw no source of the sound, no direction. When she turned the corner toward it she was in the ice room, the sound coming from behind the large, humming ice machine. Jacob was curled on the floor biting his trembling lip, releasing terrified sobs and sucking them back in, eyes bright red and swollen.

Eva kneeled to him and touched his arm. "My God, what's the matter, sweetie?"

Ice tumbled and crashed inside the machine as Jacob's wet mouth spoke.

"What?"

She barely recalled his words, so overcome by the flood that followed them. Her stomach twisted as though to revolt against their weight; maybe there was some part of her still cold enough to deny what the boy had said. Not that it wouldn't be true, but only in the way that awful things are true but irrelevant, the way life was awful in Trinidad but she had floated away, like some crash dummy had retained the scars of her abusive childhood while the real Eva remained pristine and unharmed; not hard and invulnerable like a diamond but a weightless specter who didn't have to repel attacks because they went right through.

Eva wished for that face now, the same one her aunt wore on trips back to the village of her humbled roots; that private, self-contained grin like the heat, dirt, toughness, and poverty went right through, like she could float from Darien to Arima and no weight could ground her. Eva practiced that face when she went back South, carrying bags of gifts for her myriad little cousins, seeing their twisted, toothless smiles and knowing their young jealousy, using their smiles as an inverted mirror to practice her own. She had to practice. She knew she had to, because she was a fraud. She felt things. She could only float for so long before she was grounded with exhaustion, like now, when through Jacob's anguished siren cries he managed, They killed Ma, Ma, in a revolution like he had said them so much they became a mantra, and unconscious repetition so overwhelming Eva wasn't sure he had even recognized her. At first she was okay. They killed Ma, his ma, until she realized who his ma was, and plain lost it.

She wasn't sure how she made it to the hallway, what gesture or words got her away from Jacob, but she knew she was walking. She didn't feel the stiff awkwardness of her heels anymore, only heard the air breeze by as she marched toward the room, when the sound of two gunshots stopped her cold.

Izzy had missed. Not altogether, but enough, thought Mal. Got him somewhere in the stomach. If he could make it, he could make it. Mal had fallen for effect. Let Izzy get comfortable, turn on the lights, and *bang*. Mal held his stomach where he oozed with his bad hand and adjusted his grip on the .22 with his other. He lay flat on his back, waiting. The door clicked.

When he saw Izzy, it wasn't from the room light. It was the hallway light from the door that just opened. Mal rose anyway.

Eva was glad she had drawn the gun from her purse, and pulled the slide back, which she now knew to do, in the hallway before she opened the door. So when she saw Mal raising his arm on the floor, and Izzy standing exposed, she didn't have to think at all, just point and squeeze, simple muscle movements.

After the bang, the flash, the echo, the kick, and the vibration, she looked. She'd gotten him good. The man was bleeding from his stomach, and his head, where a pool stretched in an even circle in the carpet, a black-red sun filling a gray sky.

Now she couldn't fucking believe it.

For a stunned moment, Izzy took the scene in; Mal was done, blood filling a hotel room floor in the echo of some very conspicuous gunshots. Then Eva, frozen, wobbly, and amazed, a baby who just took her first steps.

Izzy dropped his gun and grabbed her by the arms, looking right at her eyes for a moment, wanting to wake her up, hoping he would wake up. He shook her for a second.

"We—we've got to get out of here!" he said, and then realized he had to do a few things first.

He snatched the gun from Eva's hand and wiped off the handle and barrel with the stomach of his shirt, then dropped it. Then he picked his up from the floor, doing the same thing. "Jacob! Time to go!"

Izzy thought the elevator moved in slow motion. It was Angie Stone now "I Wish I Didn't Miss You." That old seventies downbeat, and steel guitar strings, funky yet remorseful, and that voluptuous chorus, surrounding "*I wish I didn't miss you anymore.*"

The seventh-floor lounge/front desk was in panic, security marching to the up elevators, muttering into radios, patrons frantically rushing, their glistening cool looking more like sweat. No one noticed those three, with their dirty duffel bag, curling in a line behind Izzy to the staircase. No one was looking for them. Everyone likely thought it was the pimps. The staircase was as sterile as the lounge, the song now really echoing, "*I wish I didn't . . .*"

The valet was swamped and Izzy hailed a cab. After he told the cabby the Morningside Heights address, not another word was spoken. The bright, sporadic city lights flashed through the windows with passing shadows. Bumps jolted their heads about in unison. Izzy only heard the cab radio announcer, doing the game recap.

". . . and Mariano Rivera, who wasn't supposed to even pitch today, brought in in the fourteenth inning on short rest, gives up a game-winning bloop single to Jose Reyes, surrendering the victory to the Mets . . ."

My man, thought Izzy, *the indomitable Mo.*

The lights in Jacob's apartment came on and went off almost as quickly, as Eva fell on the couch, and Jacob went into his room. Izzy settled onto the floor, his back hurt, staring up at darkness in his compromised stretch. He pulled his knees to his chest; wrists on his shins, feeling his lower back flatten and crack against the floor.

Eva rustled on the couch, turning over.

"Thank you," he said up to her.

No answer.

These "thank yous" and "I'm sorrys" were getting redundant.

The bright light hit Izzy's face from the open window. It felt like years since he had seen the sunshine. He rose, his back creaking, into a groggy, standing stretch. He went to the window and looked out at the new morning hitting Morningside. Students shuffled into breakfast shops and Starbucks, with heavy book bags, portable coffee, dragging dark shadows. Light blazed from the chrome and glass of passing cars. The sunshine felt so good he could taste it.

When Izzy turned, there was no one to share it with. He relished that warm morning, but felt a sharp chill when he looked at the couch. Eva was gone, in her place the dirty duffel, with a scribbled yellow note.

Your down payment.

Izzy remembered the mashed-up cigarette pack in his jean pocket, and removed the lone rolled blunt inside— short, brown, and curved like a bow. Izzy grabbed the lighter from on top of Jacob's TV and sparked it up. The smoke filled his lungs as he looked back out the window, meditating on the chemical bliss.

Chapter 18

The heavy detective reluctantly set down Eva's third coffee. She wouldn't need so many if they'd give her a decent-sized cup, she thought. They offered coffee, like she should now take them into her confidence. She told her story, over and over, asking for a new cup each time.

The thinner cop, another white guy, had slanted, almost Asian eyes, as though he'd squinted at perps so much his face got stuck. "Sounds like an ordeal," he observed, likely biding his time until he thought of a better question.

She didn't respond to the sarcastic ordeal comment. She waited for them to ask her a real question. She was ready. After everything last night, this part should be the least difficult. Eva settled back in the uncomfortable chair, in her comfortable college sweats she had put on this morning, after having to climb up her downstairs neighbor's fire escape to get into her apartment. She knew they were watching her from outside on a monitor. The room was small and the detectives big, making her claustrophobic.

"Tell me again about this Ezekiel Levin. I understand he rescued you, took you to the hotel, but how was he even involved?"

Keep asking. When in doubt, recycle a question; let the girl screw herself up.

"Izzy is a friend. He and I were having drinks at the bar when I got the call about my cousin."

The fat man started in. "You know what my problem is? You say this guy, this Malik Dumont, killed, what was it, five bodies in Queens—"

"I never said that. Some of them shot each other. Mal— Mr. Dumont killed three, the three who were there to begin with."

"Okay, then three in Harlem—"

"I wasn't there."

"Anyway, nine bodies, nine. With five murder weapons. Who kills nine people with five guns?"

"Someone who wasn't going to stop until he was stopped," said Eva, mustering some gravity in her voice. "So that's what I did. I stopped him. I told you that in the beginning. I mean, do I need a lawyer? Are you going to charge me?"

Detectives Bert and Ernie, as Eva had nicknamed them to herself, glanced at each other, as though realizing the thin ice they stood on had just cracked.

Gail's apartment was cluttered with friends and family, mostly Jews huddled in black, paying respects to another fallen chosen person. In the apartment, the bullet hole had been plastered but not yet painted, as well as the dent in the hallway, and all the mirrors were covered by dark drapes. The low muttering of Upper West Siders barely reached Jacob, sitting below its orbit, on a milk crate. He adjusted the *yarmulke* on his head, and shook the hand of another acquaintance, ignoring another well-said, appropriate condolence.

No one said much of anything to Izzy, sitting beside Jacob on another milk crate, wearing an identical *yarmulke*. Jacob hadn't spoke much to him, or anyone, but he clearly wanted Izzy there, and Izzy was happy to sit on a milk crate, not just to respect Judaism, and Gail, but to be there with Jacob, and do what he did.

The room quieted, people forgot Jacob, and his tears had dried into faint dirt tracks on his cheeks.

"Likely she died protecting me," he said.

Izzy nodded. "No doubt about it."

Outside, the fall weather worsened. Their company shouldered into dark overcoats, huddling out together. The window light faded on Jacob and Izzy, sitting as they had all day.

The doorbell rang. The door was unlocked for people to come and go as they pleased. Whoever it was would either open the door or go away. It rang again, then eventually creaked open, followed by heels on hardwood.

Eva wore a long elegant overcoat, hands in its pockets, shoulders damp, black scarf wrapped a few times around her neck. Jacob smiled faintly. Izzy didn't move.

Her smile was calm. She gave Jacob a sincere hug, and Izzy a similar one, though a bit more restrained. Jacob didn't want to talk, so she let him be, gradually drifting around the apartment, of which for eight years she had only seen one room. She stopped at a small fish tank, watching their tropical colors and dull eyes pass about.

Eva had been trying to make sense of that night, and she was wishing she had Gail there to process it with her. It wasn't that she needed her there for support; after eight years of work, she knew what Gail would say without having to hear it. Now, more than wanting Gail to know her, which she was sure her shrink already did, she wanted to know Gail. If Eva was guarded, the role of therapist had doubly guarded Gail, perched impassive in her chair; inquisitive, knowing, and inexplicable. Eva fantasized about social time, having coffee with her; thinking of the rare moments when their sessions strayed into talk of their profession, when they felt like colleagues. In that way, she was thankful for knowing Izzy, as he was a window into her unlikely past. That made her wonder about both of them, and how such a woman could be so cruelly taken, just as she was getting interesting.

A shadow came over the fish tank, and the glass revealed Izzy's face, looking very Jewish in the *yarmulke*.

"You good?" he asked.

"Yeah. Great," she said in a low voice.

"You arrange your cousin's funeral?"

She nodded.

"How'd it go?"

"Hardly anyone there."

"How you holding up?"

Eva began to shake her head. "That night!" she replied. "Jesus Christ, that night."

"It wasn't exactly routine for me, either."

"Yeah . . ." Eva said, the word doubtfully trailing off. "You think about what's next for you?" she asked.

"Well, yeah, but you're going to laugh."

"No, tell me," she demanded.

"It's just an idea."

"Tell me."

"I want to buy a big warehouse, maybe in the Bronx," he said, smiling.

"A warehouse?"

"Yeah. Then I'm going to gut it. Then build a big set, like from some Bond movie, with different levels and corridors. Then I'll rent paintball guns to businessmen and let them run around, shooting each other."

Eva laughed.

"I told you you would laugh."

"No, it's good, it's good. I like it."

"God, what would I be?"

Eva thought. "Paintball Stadium Owner."

"Paintball Stadium Owner. Can't *get* more respectable than that."

"Jesus, Izzy, what am I going to do with you?"

Pondering something, Eva's long stare drifted past the fish tank. The brilliant freshwater colors each wore a face of suspended human expression, moving with a steady, sinister creep like a drive-by. They reminded him of how faces of dead men would stay in his mind, final expressions never changing, drifting in and out of sight without reason. Izzy adjusted his focus from the water to Eva's reflection, and like the opaque eyes of the fish, he could not read her. She had stiffened.

Throughout the last few days, watching people deal with his mess, he had been overwhelmed by his responsibility, and he paid his indenture like a sentinel, waiting for permission from others to talk and breathe at ease.

"That night," Izzy said softly. "Do you blame me?"

"No," she answered immediately, like she expected it. "Yes and no," she continued. "You saved me, I know you did. But I'll never be the same."

"Neither will I. But who else could understand? We learned a lot. Right?"

She nodded, looking away from Izzy, but definitely hearing him. "Some things," she said softly, "I'd just as well not know."

Izzy turned, and saw the caterer carrying a bowl of shrimp cocktail from the kitchen. Izzy waved his hands and went over to him, as the Latino peeled the cellophane cover back from the dish.

"My friend," Izzy began, picking the shrimp up off the spread. "No, no." Izzy carried the bowl back into the kitchen.

"What is it?" asked the caterer behind him.

"This is a *shiva,* a Jewish wake. I don't know how reformed these people are, but let's play it safe and hold off on the shellfish."

"Nobody tell me kosher," the caterer said with a shrug, and went to the counter for another dish.

Izzy looked down at the bright orange and white fish, wanting to taste one. He reached and took one by the stiff tail, dipped it in the cocktail sauce and ate it. By the time he went for his third, Eva was next to him, holding a shrimp between her fingers as though she had not yet decided what to do with it. Izzy looked in her eyes as she paused, never realizing how dark they were; pupils a vibrant, consuming black. He thought of the tropical fish and how it was hard to tell by their eyes if they were alive or not. He wondered if there actually was any difference, and watched Eva dip the curling meat into the red sauce and take a bite.